Praise for *Slow Recoil*

"An excellent sequel … a solid plot and excellent use of
Toronto's famed ethnic diversity."
— *Globe and Mail*

"Brimming with explosive twists and fired by superior writing."
— *Hamilton Spectator*

"*Slow Recoil* hits the mark …"
— *Kanata Kourier-Standard*

Praise for *The Weight of Stones*

"… an introspective, reflective and literate work that will
resonate with readers."
— *Sherbrooke Record*

"… eloquent and precise … a good piece of crime fiction."
— *London Free Press*

"I couldn't put it down. It's a must-read …"
— *Hamilton Spectator*

C. B. FORREST

The Devil's Dust

a Charlie McKelvey

mystery

DUNDURN
TORONTO

Editor: Allison Hirst
Design: Courtney Horner
Printer: Webcom

Library and Archives Canada Cataloguing in Publication

Forrest, C. B.
The devil's dust : a Charlie McKelvey mystery / C.B. Forrest.

Issued also in electronic formats.
ISBN 978-1-4597-0192-2

     I. Title.

PS8611.O77D48 2012   C813'.6   C2011-906007-8

1   2   3   4   5   16   15   14   13   12

We acknowledge the support of the **Canada Council for the Arts** and the **Ontario Arts Council** for our publishing program. We also acknowledge the financial support of the **Government of Canada** through the **Canada Book Fund** and **Livres Canada Books**, and the **Government of Ontario** through the **Ontario Book Publishing Tax Credit** and the **Ontario Media Development Corporation**.

Names, characters, businesses, organizations, places, and events are fictitious. Any resemblance to actual persons, living or dead, events, or locales is entirely coincidental.

Care has been taken to trace the ownership of copyright material used in this book. The author and the publisher welcome any information enabling them to rectify any references or credits in subsequent editions.

J. Kirk Howard, President

Printed and bound in Canada.
www.dundurn.com

Dundurn
3 Church Street, Suite 500
Toronto, Ontario, Canada
M5E 1M2

Gazelle Book Services Limited
White Cross Mills
High Town, Lancaster, England
LA1 4XS

Dundurn
2250 Military Road
Tonawanda, NY
U.S.A. 14150

For Mom and Dad –
Thanks for the first typewriter.

In the end you don't even know yourself
only the hill you must climb;
but not even the hill; a bump on it, one hump of grass
a flint, a blade thin in the wind as you climb
each step, each breath taken in a dissimilar time.

— John Newlove

Prologue

He is neither a chemist nor a pharmacist, but he finds that by working slowly, methodically, following the instructions which he has printed out in neat block letters, he makes surprisingly good progress on his first try.

By the time he is onto the third batch, his hands move with the confidence of experience. It is as easy as he has come to understand from reading the news articles about what is taking place in the sheds and basements and trailers of small towns in the rural United States. It is labour-intensive but simple, and the ingredients are so readily available it is disturbing.

Easy, yes, but not without risk and danger. The slightest miscalculation or sloppiness in the combining of at least two of the main ingredients required for the cooking — lithium and anhydrous ammonia — can lead to disaster. The ammonia alone is sufficiently caustic to utterly dissolve flesh. He can smell and hear and watch the chemical reactions taking place in the large stainless steel container that is intended for agricultural or industrial purposes. The fizzing, boiling froth, the stench that makes him wrap an old T-shirt around his mouth and nose.

He feels like a kid conducting a science experiment. And he is, for this is precisely an experiment: to introduce a new element to a town which has carved its survival from the mining of another element. But this new element holds the power to destroy, or conversely offers the chance for redemption. The choice exists between darkness and light, good and evil.

The baker measures the three batches out into equal portions. He grinds the crystals to a powder as the reports and instructions have set out. He uses a spoon to measure roughly equal portions onto squares of foil, which he wraps and creases tightly. He weighs the packets on a mini scale and marks the gram weight on each in black felt marker.

When he is finished, he sits back and looks upon his work. The packets are set in rows, three high and eight across. Twenty-four lots. They are each marked in sequence with a number in black felt marker in the bottom right corner. He marvels at the simplicity of the production. There is something straightforward and methodical in the work that appeals to him. Orderly. This is the result of weeks of research, weeks of sourcing the raw materials, three days of production. In the end, he must trust that he has followed the recipe to the letter, for he has no appetite or even curiosity to sample his handiwork. His interest lies in what happens next. What happens when this element is introduced to a town already short on luck — will it be the breath to blow out the final light?

He gathers the packets into a canvas satchel and swings the bag over his shoulder. Outside the night is cool and smells of composting leaves, the rich and fecund earth of late fall. The ground, the air, everything is readying itself to accept the cold and the dark and the death that winter brings. He gets in the big black vehicle and sets the canvas bag on the passenger seat.

As he turns the engine, he considers once again the simplicity of the operation from concept to completion. It is no surprise that methamphetamine is destroying rural towns all over the United States, eating them from the inside out like a cancer. At least this is what he has read and come to understand. Now he will see for himself, firsthand. The choices to be had, the choices to be made.

He puts the black vehicle in motion.

One

S te. Bernadette
January, 2003

On this Sunday morning sunshine glints off the hard-packed snow like blinding beams shot from a mirror. The azure sky is clean of clouds, as though swept by a painter's hand with a trowel. Constable Ed Nolan is parked and idling behind the hockey arena, just starting into his second doughnut of the day when the call about a disturbance at the Lacey household comes over the radio.

"Eighteen Murray Street. Neighbours called in, something about their son going wild," says Shirley Murdoch, who works the dispatch from her home. Calls get routed to her via the main line, and for some reason Ed Nolan often wonders what the woman is wearing as she dispatches official police business. It is conceivable that she could be in a nightgown or perhaps even naked, though the thought gives him a shiver. Shirley Murdoch is not the sort of woman you want to picture naked as she talks to you over the two-way police radio.

"Ten-four. On my way," Nolan says. "Over and out."

He drops the cruller that tastes like cigarette smoke from sitting out at the Coffee Time, and he swings the cruiser around. The Ste. Bernadette force is small, with two full-time cops and a chief; but at least they get to drive nice wheels — Nissan Pathfinders — thanks to the fact the mayor's brother runs the only dealership within a fifty-kilometre radius. The cruisers are painted midnight black with the Saint B town crest emblazoned in white on each door. When he slides behind the wheel each morning, smells the leather, and looks at the dashboard and the two-way radio controls, Ed Nolan feels that he might be a real cop after all.

Now Nolan hits the lights, but he doesn't bother with the siren. In fact, he can't recall the last time he employed the sirens on his way to a call. The cops of Saint B deal in accidents out on the highway, drunken arguments at the Station Hotel tavern on a Friday night, tussles between lovers the day after the welfare cheques have arrived, teenagers wrecking town property out of boredom. Most of the time the local cops drive around in their cruisers or they sit at the little station on Main, reading magazines and drinking coffee and trying to rationalize the boredom against the fact they draw decent and steady pay with the promise of a municipal pension at the end of the long row of uneventful days.

Nolan is a local, or what the locals call a "townie," was raised here but left in his late teens for a decade, a short stint in the armed forces, a failed year living in Edmonton with a wife in a turbulent marriage that was ruled a youthful mistake by both parties. He believes he returned home not because he couldn't make it in the greater world, but because this is the place where he wants and needs to be. He tries to remind himself that this is his choice — the highway leading south waits out there at the town limits; he can take it any time he wants. He is a rookie himself, but Pete Younger, the other full-time cop on the force, is the greenest at just twenty-three years old. The oldest of four strapping boys, Younger took the Law and Security program down at the community college in Sudbury, and was hired before he had even graduated. His father, a town councillor, put forth a motion to effectively double the size of the force from one to two full-time officers — his rationale being that the further decline of the Carver Company mining operations would necessitate a reinvestment in the town, the attraction of new industry, and these men of business would want assurances they weren't dealing with some frontier backwoods. The notion of "conflict of interest" was never so much as broached. It made Ed Nolan smile sometimes to think how things weren't really so different in small towns and big cities. They were just easier to see in small towns. People didn't use fancy terms like "influence peddling" or "corruption." He was quite sure the always-smiling mayor, Danny Marko, couldn't spell *nepotism* if he had a gun to his head.

"Unit two to base." Nolan speaks into the radio as he pulls into the driveway at the Lacey house on Murray Street. The home is a three-bedroom bungalow with a stand-alone garage. He parks behind a GMC minivan with a blue and white Toronto Maple Leafs sticker pasted on the back window. He thinks perhaps this alone could be grounds for arrest. "Just heading in," he says. "Over."

"Have fun," Shirley responds. "It's a full moon night, sweetie. Over and out."

Nolan hooks the receiver back on its cradle on the dash. He knows Bob and Margaret Lacey by name and to see them around town, but this is his first interaction with them as the law. They have a son and a daughter, he knows, but he believes they are good students or at least never in trouble. The list of diehard troublemakers, those kids born to the toughest families and seemingly hell-bent on a path to the penitentiary, runs about a dozen in a town this size. He steps out of the cruiser and walks up to the front door. He adjusts the wool toque coiled on his head, fixes his belt that holds the handheld radio, sidearm holster, cuffs and flashlight, and knocks loudly on the door. He hears hollering from inside, muffled voices. Furniture being moved about. A loud crash.

Come on, Eddie, he thinks. *Put your game on now.*

"Police," he says in a voice deeper than his own — his cop's voice.

The front door swings open. Bob Lacey stands there, wild-eyed, his nose bloodied, the blood half-dried and dark around his nostrils, spatters of red across his light blue dress shirt. The buttons have been popped, exposing his grey, hairy chest and white belly paunch. Three large suitcases sit in the hallway. Nolan looks past Bob Lacey's shoulder and sees a tall teenage boy grappling with a woman in the dining room, hands wrapped around the woman's throat, bending her backward over the table.

Nolan pushes past the father, crosses the room in a few long strides. He gets behind the boy and locks an arm around his neck, a leg set against the teen's hip, and he pulls and twists at the same time, getting the boy's weight off balance. Travis is off his feet, sideways on the carpet, screaming in an otherworldly voice. Nolan can't make anything out. It's like squelch cracking across the radio. What he's got here is an MDP — *mentally disturbed person*. This is a first in his young career.

"Relax," he commands, and uses his knee to hold the teen in his place.

The mother is crying and shaking, and Bob Lacey moves to comfort her, an arm around her shoulders.

"Are you all right, ma'am? Do you need medical assistance?" Nolan asks.

She rubs at her throat. Shakes her head. She is in shock, confused.

"Take her in the other room," Nolan says to Bob Lacey.

"What's going to happen to Travis?" she says as her husband ushers her toward the hall. "You're not going to hurt him, are you? We just came home from a vacation down in Florida for the week. Our first vacation in eighteen years."

"Who else is in the house?" Nolan asks.

"He said he's got a friend down there in the basement," Bob Lacey says. "They must be on drugs. Jesus Christ, he's out of his mind. We just came in the door and he went wild at us."

"You have a daughter," Nolan says. "Where is she?"

"She went to stay with my sister," the mother says. "Travis was supposed to be old enough to stay by himself. He lost our dog, too — my little Jenny."

Travis Lacey jolts alive as though he has received a current of electricity straight from a transformer. He bucks and twists, and with a strength that belies his lanky hundred-and-thirty-pound frame, manages to throw the officer like a wild bronco bucking its rider. Travis scrambles free, hands clutching and swinging, clawing like a rabid animal. Nolan regains his footing and corners the teen behind the dining-room table.

"You made this happen!" Travis shouts and points a wavering finger. His eyes are bloodshot, huge and blank. He topples a chair in an attempt to form a barricade. "You don't even know what you're doing here; you're a tool for these guys. You're a spaceman with a laser for an eye. Don't even touch me with your light, dude!"

"Easy now," Nolan says, and he thinks for an instant of calling for backup. Pete Younger is sleeping this morning, but he is on call. Shirley would rouse him from his slumber and have him here in, what, fifteen minutes? He decides it's not worth the effort, and certainly not worth the ribbing he will endure when the Chief hears that he has called for backup to handle a skinny teenager. There is, however, the matter of the unknown equation in the basement.

"Travis," Nolan says, looking the teen in the eye, attempting here to connect and drive home some sense. Drugs or mental illness, he can't say which, though he knows for certain the boy is not of right mind. He read an article in *Psychology Today* just a few weeks back about teenage schizophrenia, how the onset can literally occur overnight as though a switch has been thrown. It can sneak in and destroy a family like an insidious fog. "You need to calm down, buddy. I want you to come and have a talk with me. Okay?"

Travis stops. The machine has ground to a sudden halt. Emptied of gas.

"I'm hungry," Travis says in a monotone, as though he is reporting on the day's weather.

"All right," Nolan says, hoping to capitalize on the opportunity. "We'll go for a drive and stop and get some doughnuts. But first we need to find out who you have downstairs, Travis."

Travis nods and smiles, and suddenly the madness seems to be gone from his body as though evils spirits have simply tired and sought alternative hosts. He shrugs and puts his hands through his shaggy brown hair. He is dressed in jeans and a black T-shirt that says NICKELBACK with a silkscreen image of an electric guitar. He looks like any sixteen-year-old.

"What are those ones with the cream inside?" Travis asks, coming around the table. Nolan watches him, ready for sudden movement.

"Boston cream," Nolan says. "Listen, Travis, who have you got downstairs?"

Travis only laughs. Nolan places a hand on the boy's shoulder. They walk together to the stairs leading to the basement. Nolan instantly smells the stale smoke, a choking residue that burns his eyes and settles on his tongue like a taste of metal and iodine. This is not the stink of marijuana's earthy funk; it is the result of chemistry. The stairway is dark. Nolan finds the switch on the wall but it does not work. He pauses at the top.

"Come on up," Nolan calls down the stairs. "Party's over."

"Just starting," Travis says. "Never ended. Always is."

Nolan gets his Maglite out and illuminates the stairs in a band of yellow candle-glow. He turns to Travis.

"Don't move. Stay right here," he says, and then descends the stairs one at a time.

He feels like an explorer entering a cave, or perhaps this is what it is like to work in the mines. He has always wondered about that. The world revealed in increments by a narrow band of light, your steps tentative, toes searching for purchase or the end of the world. At the bottom of the stairs he turns and shines the light to the top, making sure Travis is still standing there. The spotlight paints Travis in a ghastly glow.

"Don't move," Nolan repeats.

There is a door to the right. Nolan nudges it open with the fingers of his left hand. His light shines against a washer and dryer, clothes folded or piled on the floor, a shelving unit stacked with cans of apple juice, jars of jam, preserved vegetables. He turns and moves down the hall which opens up to a family room. There are two couches set out in an *L*-shape; a large TV sits in a corner. The floor is littered with pop cans, bowls of Cheezies and chips, candy wrappers, pil-

lows and clothing, a few sleeping bags knotted and twisted. He spots a coffee table and steps closer with the light
trained. The table is covered in squares of burnt foil, ink
pens that have had their stylus removed in order to be used
as pipes. Nolan reaches out and picks one up, turns it in his
hand. *So this is how they do it.* The emptied pen is scorched
at one end from the constant flame. He raises it to his nose,
curious, and flinches at the strength of the caustic residue.
He tries to conjure an image of Travis Lacey sitting in the
darkness, smoking drugs around the clock; his parents in
Florida, oblivious.

What makes a kid in a decent family do this, he wonders.
The cause and effect of this fascinates him, truly. Is it the availability of drugs that make them desirable? Is it the forbidden
fruit that tempts us? In the absence of evil and danger, what is
it we shall seek for thrills?

Nolan sets the pen on the table and straightens up. He
wipes the light across the rest of the room. His breath stops,
his knees go weak. He hears himself emit a sound. There, in
the far corner, hanging from an electrical cord, is what remains of a small dog. It appears to have been skinned. And
on the wall behind the dead animal words and strange sym-
bols are scrawled in what can only be blood. Circles and tri-
angles, crosses and arrows. Nolan feels sick to his stomach,
out of place in the semi-darkness, this strange basement. It
is as though in this instant he forgets he is a cop, why he is
here, witness to something that seems so private and closed.
He squints in an attempt to decipher the writing as though
he is truly an explorer who has discovered hieroglyphics on
a cave wall. His mind floods with ideas of what he must do
next. *Take the boy into custody, radio the Chief and Younger,
get a psychological consult from Dr. Nichols up at the medical
clinic …*

So there is no friend in the basement after all. Travis has conjured an illusion with his drug-addled mind. Images, incantations, whispers in the darkness. Nolan hears footfalls and he swivels with the light, startled by Travis's sudden appearance — as though he simply appears from vapour. Nolan attempts to reconcile the youth standing before him with the hideous acts committed in this basement.

"You found Jenny," Travis says in wonderment, and he points.

"Back up," Nolan says, but his voice sounds unsure even to himself.

Travis turns a twisted-lip smile and he is gone up the stairs. Nolan's body surges with endorphins, fear and excitement, panic and exhilaration. He takes the stairs three at a time, the flashlight heavy in his hand like a sidearm. There is only time to think this focused thought: *I am in a police foot chase ...*

"Travis!" Bob Lacey yells from the hallway.

The teen pushes through the front door, Nolan at his heels. The sunshine hits Nolan's eyes and he squints hard. A world of whiteness, the snow reflects the light and makes his eyes water. Travis is in sock feet but this does not slow his sprint across the front yard, the snow reaching to just below his knees, this wild animal sprung from a trap. Travis careens to the left, disappears around the side of the garage. Nolan's boots provide better traction and he gains his footing now. He catches a glimpse of the teen's dark shirt around the side of the garage and he hears the boy's mother crying from the front step. Nolan negotiates the corner of the building at the same moment the clearest thought enters his mind: *never come around the corner of a building unless you know for certain what is waiting for you ... approach with caution, approach low and slow ...*

In the void of recalled training there is now a looping arc of blurred motion as Travis swings a snow shovel like a home-run hitter. Nolan does the only thing he can do in the short time he has to react, which is to raise a forearm to protect his face. It is the last thing Ed Nolan does just before the concussive connection, sounds of disembodied voices, his seemingly weightless body falling, falling.

The cold burn of snow on his face.

And then blackness.

Two

That first night off the Greyhound he takes a room at the Station Hotel, the only real hotel in town. The old guy behind the desk is watching a hockey game on one of those black and white TVs that also has a built-in radio. The arrival of a guest seems to catch him by surprise, and he looks up from the little TV with his mouth open. A quick scan of the room keys hanging behind the desk indicates the hotel has full vacancy.

"Looking for a room, are you?" the old man asks.

The disembodied sports commentator talks excitedly through the TV's mono speaker. You can hear the threshing crowd, this rising sea of voices joined in passion. Players are in a corner, fighting for control of the puck. Someone is winning and someone is losing.

"As long as it's got a bed," the visitor says, and sets his heavy duffle bag on the hardwood floor, straightens his back.

The old man reaches behind for a room key. He places the key on the desk, licks his thumb, and flips a yellow invoice pad to a new page, looks around for a pen.

"Forty-eight, tax in."

The guest pays the night clerk with the last of his American money, having come north in a meandering way through Michigan for no other reason than boredom and the availability of time.

"You want a coffee or anything? I could brew a pot," the clerk offers. His eyes tell the guest that he would welcome the company to pass the long hours.

"It's been a long day, thanks," the guest replies, and then hefts his duffle and walks over to the broad staircase with its thick wood banister.

The clerk nods. "You're probably tired, don't feel like talking tonight."

A wayfarer's hotel, the hardwood of the Station is gouged and well worn from the heavy boots and hard lifestyle of its nightly occupants over the long decades, mostly miners coming in or going out, hydro workers following the power lines ever northward, and once in a while a platoon of soft-faced geologists or engineers from the head offices down in Toronto. The four-storey hotel sits across the street from the old train station. The train comes through town just twice a week now, Tuesdays and Saturdays, but at one time, back in the 1970s, it arrived like clockwork each morning.

The only thing keeping the hotel in business these days is the one-room tavern located off the west wing of its main floor. A pool table sits out front near the big window with the faded neon sign advertising Labatt 50, four round tables and six stools at the bar, a dartboard in a dark corner. The felt on the pool table is bald and torn, and the urinal in the men's room often clogs and overflows, sending a slow cascade of piss trickling down the hall. The place is only ever a third full at best if there is a good hockey game on, but the business is regular and can be counted on. The draft beer is cheap, and

Terry, the owner and bartender and janitor, isn't averse to letting a regular's tab grow beyond what might be considered prudent in these tough economic times.

Room 27 is small, spare and simple. A twin bed with a handmade afghan folded over the bottom half, a desk in front of the window looking out on Main. The street at this hour is bathed in the false yellow of street lamps, still and empty. Nothing to do in Ste. Bernadette on a Friday, let alone a Sunday night. Dead of January. Dead, period. The guest sets the duffle by the foot of the bed and closes the faded curtains to mute the street lamps and the silver glow from a nearly full moon.

There is an old calendar from a tool company tacked to the wall near the bathroom, stale-dated by four months. Someone has circled October 15 and scrawled the words *Out of Ste. Bernadette!* It is underlined not once but twice. He figures he knows how the author must have felt in this town, in this little room: the walls closing in, the town itself shifting inward, smothering, growing smaller by the hour. It plays tricks with a man's head.

He unties and kicks off his boots then goes and takes a long piss. The flow is uneven, and at one point he clenches his eyes to the effort. The low-watt bulb makes the stained porcelain sink, toilet, and tub appear older than they are, chipped and badly used, like his reflection in the square of mirror. Fifty-nine or a hundred and six, it's a coin toss. He splashes water on his face and sees that he needs a shave and a haircut. Nothing that can't wait another day, another week. There is no one to impress.

He pulls off his clothes and showers in the lukewarm water to wash away the sweat and smells from the Greyhound. Long hours of highway from Toronto, then pushing back up across the border to the Sault, the whole time sitting next to a great-grandmother who smelled of sharp cheese and eye-watering lavender. And she had wanted to talk to him about everything that was going on with her and her children, the demise of the modern family, the shame of the country as a whole, his lost generation. Pretending to sleep, eyes closed to keep the old woman at bay, his mind had fluttered with dark thoughts, the tangled briar patch of fear or anxiety that seemed to be part of coming home after a long time gone. Or it was the illness, his being sick, and the game of pretending it was not the truth.

In boxer shorts and sports socks he stands at the sink and rummages through his shaving kit for the pain pills. *What are they for again?* A gunshot wound or a strained oblique muscle, a broken heart, a hang nail — it hardly matters anymore. He has long since passed the destination where pain is possible to pin down with any accuracy or honesty; it is now as much a part of his biological chemistry as carbon, oxygen. He gobbles three capsules and washes them down with a mouthful of tap water. The water tastes of sulphur and smells of moist, fecund earth. The taste of Ste. Bernadette; the taste of home.

And so Charlie McKelvey crawls beneath the sheets, pulls the quilt up to his chest, and waits there in the darkness for sleep to show him a little mercy.

Three

The oblong capsules wrap the occupant of Room 27 in a cocoon of gauzy, tongue-thick sleep until just after ten the next morning. Eventually and inevitably, the aches and pains located indecipherably throughout McKelvey's body begin to stir, shaking off chemical slumber. First the hip, then the knees, the back, the shoulders. The wind chill and the dampness in their air up here give a cruel twist to the first signs of arthritis that sit like rust in the cracks of old broken bones, abused joints. He swings his feet to the floor, teeth already clenched to start the day. Groggy from the pills, head stuffed with cotton, he licks his lips and rubs his puffy eyes with the heels of his palms. Yawns and stretches and looks around the room, wondering yet again what in the hell he thought he was doing by coming back here, what sort of loop he was looking to close. Maybe there was no loop after all. Life, in all of its purported mystery, wasn't so mysterious after all. Things as they are and always will be.

He moves to the duffle bag that sits on the floor and digs through the jumble of clothes for a clean pair of underwear and socks. His hand finds the cellular phone he so loathes and he sets this on the bed. It is not the implement or even the strange cordless technology he despises — though there must be witchcraft involved in a telephone that has no cord leading anywhere — it is the fact they are making them so small, his thick fingers struggle to enter correct numbers. There is also the matter of how tiny the digital display is, and he has not and will never admit to needing glasses.

He fishes a hand in the bag again and this time pulls out a stack of pamphlets. An array of informational pieces graphically designed in soothing colours, featuring photographs of salt-and-pepper-haired men smiling and playing touch football with ruddy-cheeked, smiling grandchildren, with reassuring titles like *Prostate Cancer: A Survivor's Guide*. He tosses them on the bed. His gaze alternates between the pamphlets and the phone. The red light that indicates a missed call flashes on the phone like a poke in the eye. The calls — for he knows they are in the multiple — are from any number of people who have taken umbrage with his sudden pulling of stakes. As though it is somehow shocking that a man who finds himself poked, prodded, goaded, cajoled, and generally fucked with should one day decide he has reached the limit of his tolerance. It happened just like that: one morning he simply woke, threw clothes in the duffle, and walked up to the bus terminal on Bay Street at Dundas. Scanned the list of destinations on the board, paid for the ticket in cash like some deadbeat on the lam, and was off.

Now he steps into the bathroom. He turns on the shower and waits for the initial explosion of rusty water to subside, these barks of brackish brown-red, and then he is in and under the flow, hands to the tile, head bowed. This may be as close as he comes to absolution this day, and he'll take it.

*   *   *

They are waiting for him down at the front desk as he knew they would be. It is the night manager and two other old-timers. They are all in their late seventies or early eighties, with white hair and yellowed, rheumy eyes. They are drinking coffee from white Styrofoam cups. They stop talking when McKelvey comes down the stairs. There is just no getting around it. This is life in a small town so far removed from the cities that any visitor is considered an aberration until all facts are investigated, sorted, and filed. He could just as well be Tom Selleck in town to film a Sunday night movie.

"Sleep okay there, buddy?" the manager asks, trying to show his friends in some way that he has already formed a relationship with the guest.

"Not bad. You wouldn't have an extra cup of that coffee."

"Endless cup," the manager says, and goes to the pot sitting on a stand by the reception desk. "Comes with the room. Just one of the many perks of the Station."

The men chuckle and the manager hands McKelvey a cup. The steam rises in tendrils and McKelvey can already taste the stale brew, feel his guts cramping. It smells like burnt leaves and mud. One of the men is eyeing McKelvey as though he knows him, or thinks he does, trying to place the facial features against the family names of the town roster. McKelvey thinks he might recognize the old man right back, one of the old Finnish miners. The old guy is wearing a navy wool toque rolled tightly on top of his head.

"You wouldn't be Grey McKelvey's boy, would you?" the man finally asks.

And here it is. Forty years gone, save for a few short visits during his father's final illness, and still they know the face and the surname, the history attached to it like a set of roots planted in this stubborn soil.

"Yes, sir. Charlie McKelvey."

"Nick Jalonen," the man says, and then nods to the man at his side. "And this here is George Fergus. 'Course you already met Duncan last night, Dunc Stewart. Hope you had a good trip in. What brings you back this way?"

McKelvey can see in the men's eyes that they are sewing together memories, perhaps of his father in certain situations, or all of them together as young men, hard-bodied and full of life. How time slips away.

"Grey McKelvey, Jesus Murphy," George Fergus says. "We had some times, didn't we? Your dad was the toughest SOB ever ran the union."

This stops McKelvey's mind, for he recalls the late-night arguments in the kitchen below his bedroom as his mother and father debated the merits of union leadership and an impending strike. In the end, McKelvey believes his father turned down the nomination. He seems to recall that his father was somehow philosophically opposed to the notion of co-operatives and unions, believing each man was responsible for his own representation in this life.

"I always thought my dad shied away from the political stuff."

This makes the trio of old-timers laugh. They eye one another in conspiracy.

"I never said he was president, or even on the executive," Fergus says, "but make no mistake, your dad was the go-to guy. He was the balls behind the whole operation, that wildcat strike in '54."

The information hits McKelvey like a punch to the stomach, and for a moment he thinks he should sit down. He hasn't eaten in eighteen hours, save for half a wilted ham sandwich bought at a gas station outside Sudbury, and this coffee has gone straight to his head. The inference that his father may have been involved, or more to the point, a leader in the strike and the ensuing violence of that historic year, it is akin to discovering the man had a second family holed up somewhere. McKelvey knows a scab was killed at the height of the strike. He knows, too, that no one was ever charged in the killing. The scab was a Native from the nearby reserve, just some guy looking to support his family. It was the 1950s and it was the North and times were different.

"He never talked about it," McKelvey says. "I remember that year. A supply shed got blown up. A scab was killed."

The men seem to lose themselves in private and collective memories. They look down at the floor and nod their heads. There are no smiles now, no laughter.

"Was a hard time in those days," Duncan says. "They was goin' to put us out of work, the way the management was running things, talk of that merger with INCO. We had families to think about. Your old man had been over in Korea, and let me tell you, his training came in handy. That scab was in the wrong place at the wrong time."

McKelvey doesn't want to hear or learn anymore, not now, not standing here in the lobby of a one-star hotel less than twelve hours after arriving back in his home town. He drains the cup against his better judgment, tosses it in a wastebasket.

"I need a place to stay for a while," he says. "Is there anybody in town that rents apartments or houses?"

The men shoot one another quick looks, and then Duncan smiles and moves to the desk. He opens a black address book and writes a number down on a piece of paper.

"How about your old homestead?" he says with a grin. "Carl Levesque bought up most of the Carver Company houses, including yours. He's got some plan to tear them down and build a goddamned casino, if you can believe that. But I bet he'd take a few dollars in rent while you're up here."

George Fergus laughs. "The guy'd charge rent to his grandmother."

"Welcome home," Duncan says, and hands McKelvey the slip of paper.

Four

Carl Levesque answers on the third ring with some rehearsed tagline about business coming back to Ste. Bernadette, blowing in on a northern tailwind. He appears eager to meet McKelvey and discuss rental opportunities. He asks McKelvey to meet him at the Coffee Time on Main Street, three blocks down from the Station Hotel. McKelvey walks with the collar turned high on his too-thin trench coat, for the day is bone-chilling and he has forgotten how the cold works so quickly, how your back hurts from the strain of your body's attempt to fold into itself. More than half of the storefronts are boarded up, and McKelvey finds himself slowing down, trying to remember the various incarnations of these places so long ago.

Murray's Five and Dime, where he bought comic books and jawbreakers, the place always smelling of sawdust and those bricks of bright yellow soap that Murray kept stacked in pyramids on tables — so that McKelvey as a boy imagined they were gold bricks, probably dug from the mine where his father worked. And there had been Poulson Mercantile and

Sundry, where you could buy rough underwear that had been manufactured by people whose primary goal was to punish small children, or sit at the small lunch counter in back and order a creamy malted milkshake if your mother was in a generous mood. McKelvey smiles now at the memory of asking his mother repeatedly what exactly "sundry" was supposed to mean. And how she tried unsuccessfully to explain the strange notion of dry goods and paper products and envelopes and, well, everything in the place that didn't happen to be something you could wear.

He bought a package of Club chewing tobacco in there when he was sixteen. Kept a wad in his mouth for exactly fourteen seconds before spitting out the glistening tar-black gob behind his house. He had been aiming for toughness, these miners he saw with their cheeks full of the stuff like chipmunks storing food for winter.

He stops in front of a boarded-up unit with a sign that says VIDEO AND GAME SHACK, and steps into the alcove to read the paper posted to the inside of the glass door: a foreclosure for failure to pay rent. Almost eighteen months ago now. He catches the name Carl Levesque within the legal mumbo-jumbo. This place was, at one time, perhaps fifty years ago now, a barbershop called Bud's. He closes his eyes and he can actually smell the inside of the barbershop …

He can see the multi-coloured bottles of aftershave and hair tonic, the neon blue disinfectant for the black combs, the lather creams, the strong, manly scent of sandalwood and alcohol, tobacco smoke, and sweat. How old Bud would set a board across the chair, heft him up, wrap a red apron around his neck, push his head forward, and begin to work with the scissors. The sound of stainless steel parts working in concert. McKelvey keeps his eyes closed, pretending not to follow the conversation between his father and Bud and the other men assembled in the barbershop, this sanctuary of all things male. They speak in loose code about local women, about their physical attributes, then on to hunting, drinking. When the haircut is done, Bud takes a hard-bristled brush and whisks away the hair trimmings from the back of his neck, and the brush hurts, but he doesn't say anything, not ever. Bud with his big boxer's face that reminds McKelvey of an old bulldog with sad, bloodshot eyes. Bud always gives him a lollipop from an old coffee tin he keeps under the cash.

McKelvey opens his eyes, stamps his feet against the cold, and moves on down the sidewalk, filled with a sense of loss for something that is gone both for himself and the rest of the world, all of the generations to come. And he thinks it might be something called innocence or perhaps the unspoiled pleasures of simplicity and gratitude for the small gestures in life.

*   *   *

Carl Levesque is leaning over the counter chatting with the middle-aged clerk, a woman who looks as though she believes despite overwhelming odds in the promise of meagre satisfaction from this life. She is attractive despite a world-weary weight to her eyes and her face, though McKelvey can tell she was likely a knockout in her youth, black hair tied back. There are two old men seated at individual tables near the window, each of them quietly sipping coffee and reading newspapers, likely enjoying the time away from their wives. The swivel stools that run along the counter are empty.

"Well, that must be Mr. McKelvey," Levesque says as he turns upon hearing the jingle of bells tied to the door.

McKelvey nods and holds out his hand as he approaches the real-estate-agent-cum-small-town-entrepreneur.

"What'll you have, Charlie? Do you mind if I call you Charlie?"

"It's my name," McKelvey says. And he smiles at the woman now as he squints to read the nametag pinned to her ugly beige uniform blouse: *Peggy*.

"Anything you want," Levesque says with a sweep of his hand across the vista of stale doughnuts, a half-empty fountain well of lemonade, and two pots of coffee. Levesque smiles, pleased with himself at this generous offering. McKelvey sees instantly that this man is a salesman, has likely sold a little of everything in his life — toilet brushes and cars with bad radiators — and he would get on your nerves if you spent too much time with him.

"I'll take a small coffee, black," McKelvey says. He no longer cares about the regimen imposed in the aftermath of his gastrointestinal hemorrhage, which was partly, though only partly, responsible for his early exit from the force. No more plain Balkan-style yogourt, no more celery snagged in his teeth for him, no sir, not since Dr. Shannon delivered The News. *So, fuck it. Black coffee, please.* And suddenly his entire body thrums with desire for a cigarette, even though it's been a miraculous three months since he gave up on trying to ration himself or otherwise control the uncontrollable, which is to say he quit cold turkey.

"No cherry stick?" Levesque asks, and pokes McKelvey in the belly. It's a move that instantly provokes a reptilian response within McKelvey — he clenches his teeth and swallows the urge to snap the man's finger. *Don't touch me*, he could say. *Not ever.* "I gotta tell you, they're goddamned dynamite," Levesque continues. "I eat, what, two or three a week?"

He says this to Peggy, who has already poured McKelvey's coffee.

"A day, more like it," Peggy says.

Levesque laughs, and it sounds like gravel pouring through a tin culvert, forced and over-loud. At the tail end of the laugh there is a wheeze in the man's lungs, this constricted exhalation. McKelvey imagines the man chain-smoking two packs a day. Sitting behind a cheap metal desk in some trailer on a used car lot, watching the door, willing it to open, asking everyone about the weather, how about that rain, how about that goddamned heat. McKelvey is already finding it hard to like this man.

"Thanks, Peggy," McKelvey says, and nods. "I'm Charlie."

"You're welcome, 'I'm Charlie,'" she says, and then turns to busy herself with straightening things on the counter behind her.

Seated at a table, Levesque proceeds to pour half a pound of sugar into his own coffee, stirring and stirring. McKelvey is reminded of someone mixing cement. He takes a pull on his coffee and is relieved to discover it is not as bad as the bowel-blitzing sludge the old-timers are swilling down at the Station. It's a wonder they're still alive, though he supposes what hasn't killed them has in fact made them stronger.

Levesque noisily slurps a taste of his coffee and, satisfied with his chemistry, he sits back and clasps his hands. McKelvey notices a Mason's ring. Levesque says, "So then, friend, what brings you to the whirling metropolis of Ste. Bernadette?"

Levesque is a squat man, shaped like a block, and he is unable to accept the fact of his balding. The long strands of brown-grey hair that remain have been swirled in a loop in the centre of his head, likely held there by a combination of sheer determination and hairspray. McKelvey notices everything — clothes, posture, eyes, gestures — the smallest indicators that for years were his stock and trade as a cop on the beat in Toronto, in fraud investigations, and finally on the Hold-Up Squad. He sees Levesque now, sitting across from him with a wide grin, his sports coat too tight and the bad comb-over, and he is reminded of a case he once worked when he was on the Fraud Squad. A pyramid scheme of sorts, worth about a million all told, and it turned out the mastermind behind the whole operation was an unemployed shoe salesman — and Levesque reminds him of everything about the perp.

"It's been a long time since I was back home," McKelvey says. He glances over at the counter and he catches Peggy's eye. He gives a small smile.

"You were born and raised here? I didn't know that. Well, welcome home, Charlie. I bet the place has changed a lot."

"You could say that."

"Sure as hell has changed in the four years since I moved here. Came through town on my way out east from Kenora. I was running a business up there, had the rights to a process whereby you remove this substance from pulp, you know, from the mills, this substance with a name I can't even pronounce — *placto-u-nameen something* — about fourteen consonants in it and sixteen chemistry elements. Anyway, it's used in the production of industrial-grade adhesives. We never got off the ground because of the goddamned banks and the assbackward government in this country, but ..."

McKelvey watches the man and notices the exact spot where he loses himself, his words simply evaporate before him. Rather than jump in to pull Levesque from the strange tangent, he sips his coffee and waits. He has nowhere to be, no plans.

"Anyhoo," Levesque says, drawing back. "Stopped for a few days in Ste. Bernadette and bingo, four years later I own half the town."

"Duncan at the hotel was mentioning something about that. You want to open a casino resort?"

Levesque laughs again, and again it is too loud in the small coffee shop. Like someone trying too hard at a party to laugh at all of the host's jokes.

"Oh, I've got plans, you could say that. Yes, sir, I've got plans. But we'll have time for all of that, my friend. Right now let's talk about how I can help you. You're looking for a short-term rental, is that right? Something maybe semi-furnished?"

McKelvey sits back and exhales a long breath. What he is looking for he can't quite say. Short-term, long-term, a parade, a trip to the moon, a little peace and quiet. His eyes move to the front window, the view of Main Street. A few cars roll slowly by. No pedestrian traffic. He misses Front Street with its shops and restaurants, the grocery store open twenty-four hours, the swirl and smells of the St. Lawrence Market with its hanging meats and strange slippery seafood. He misses Garrity's Pub just below his condo, the way his whole mood would change when he crossed the threshold. He is suddenly overwhelmed with the sense that he has been foolish, both for coming all the way up here with no real purpose, but also for trusting this used car salesman to look after his primary need at this point in time, which happens to be shelter.

"Duncan mentioned my old house might be available," McKelvey says.

"Where did you live?"

"20 King Street."

Levesque's eyes brighten, and McKelvey can practically see the dollar signs turning like lemons and crowns rolling on a slot machine.

"It's your lucky day, Charlie," Levesque says. And he smiles.

*   *   *

Levesque's car is a 1995 black Cadillac sedan, something with a lot of miles on it, but McKelvey figures that looking out at the hood ornament makes the man feel as though he has somehow arrived. They slip inside the vehicle and Levesque turns the key. It takes a moment to catch, the teeth in the starter grinding against bone, and then the car fills with a booming voice from some self-help tape.

"*True leaders wake up every day and they ask themselves this one question —*"

Levesque reaches out and switches the volume off. He flips the sun visor, grabs a package of cigarettes, and pops one in his mouth.

"Don't mind if I smoke there, Charlie?"

"It's your car," McKelvey says. "I smoked on and off for forty years."

And it is hard to believe, hearing himself admit this out loud. For close to four decades he stuck cylinders of nicotine and tobacco into his yap. This would be twice as long as his son lived on this planet. Life is not fair. *Gavin would be twenty-two this year. Probably finishing college.* And here he is, old and skinny, sitting in a pimp's car beside some shoe salesman sucking on a goddamned cigarette. He wants a pain pill. Something to close around him like a glove.

"What was the longest you stayed off them?" Levesque hits the button to roll his window down a few inches.

"Six, seven years one time," McKelvey says. "When my son was born, both my wife and I quit. I guess I quit with her just to be in solidarity. She stayed off them. But you know, eventually you start sneaking your way back."

"I can't quit them. I've accepted my failings in that area, you know. I'm going to smoke. I'm a smoker. Probably kill me one day, but ..."

Levesque sucks at the cigarette. It is a Player's Light Regular. McKelvey's old brand. The sailor on the cover with his stoic face ...

"I'd take one, actually," McKelvey hears himself say. And he senses within himself this mechanism at play — if it had a sound, it would be a *click*. Something he attempted but failed to properly convey to his therapist, the one to whom he was referred by his family doctor. Dr. Shannon saying he should see a therapist a couple of times a week, keep a journal of his "feelings" — *anything and everything, just to write it out*. The "mental stuff," Shannon explained, being just as important as the "medical stuff" during cancer treatment. The thing is, McKelvey wants to know why he should care. As though keeping a journal or discussing his fears — or sparing himself from the ravages of tobacco, for that matter — will be the tipping point in his so-called "breakthrough." There is no trick to this; it is simply one foot in front of the other. Whatever waits for him up ahead has been waiting there all the days of his life.

"Oh, I don't know, friend." Levesque laughs, and this time it comes across as sincere, a chuckle between friends. "I don't want to be aiding and abetting a recovered addict. But you're a grown man, I suppose. Fire away."

He hands the pack over. McKelvey lights one. His first in ninety days. The nicotine rushes to his head and he feels nauseous, dizzy. Stoned, perhaps? Yes, that's it. The power of this drug is revealed in its true light when you have spent some time away from it. He enjoys the rush, the buzz. As always, it simply feels good to feel different. And then, like an alarm sounding his guilt, the cellphone he has shoved in his jacket pocket goes off. He fumbles, gets it free, and looks at it while it continues to ring.

"I think you have to flip that thing there and say hello."

McKelvey gives Levesque a dead-eye glance, flips the phone open, and moves it to his ear and mouth.

"McKelvey," he says reluctantly.

"Charlie. *My god*. Do you know how many messages I've left?"

"Good morning, Caroline."

"It's not even morning out here yet. You've had me worried sick. Jessie has been calling me, too. Where *are* you?"

McKelvey looks out the window at the passing bleakness of a small northern town at the apex of winter.

"Back home," he says.

There is a moment of silence. Levesque is listening but trying to look busy, adjusting the car's temperature controls.

"Is everything okay, Charlie?" she asks. "That's a stupid question, I know. You were supposed to go for counselling after the incident by the waterfront, but I don't think you ever followed through. Why would I expect you to if you couldn't even stick with counselling when Gavin was killed. And you're drinking. You know you called me a few times in the middle of the night. You didn't sound well, the messages you left. Do you remember that?"

McKelvey takes a long drag on the cigarette, blows smoke out the window, then rolls it down farther and flicks the butt outside. His brain warbles now, he is a bobble-head character. The succubus nicotine whispers *again, again, again.*

"I needed a change of scenery," he says. "And I'm not drinking. Anyway, you don't need to worry about me, Caroline. You don't have that burden anymore."

"Fuck off, Charlie." The vulgarity takes him by surprise. He sits back as though he has been slapped across the face by his mother. "You're such an asshole sometimes. You need to pull your head out of that place you keep it and look around. You've got a granddaughter. You've got Jessie. They need you. Grownups don't just run away and hide, Charlie. Is that what you're doing, running away?"

He can no longer sustain the conversation. He is being pulled away and muffled by an invisible hand. The phone must have turned on by accident, perhaps bumped or jostled. He will be more careful in the future. Not knowing about missed calls, not seeing the flashing red light won't bother him nearly as much.

"It wasn't an *incident*, by the way," he says. "A good cop got killed that day."

"Oh, Charlie … I wish you could see what I see. What everybody else sees …"

"I'll call you when I have better reception," he says. "You're breaking up."

"Sure. Whatever you say —"

McKelvey hangs up and ensures the phone is off. He slips it back inside his coat and turns to Levesque, who he imagines has conjured all sorts of visions.

"My wife," McKelvey says, and leaves it at that. There is nothing more he needs to say. Levesque nods once and they drive through the town, out from the small and dying business section to the grid pattern of two- and three-bedroom simple bungalows the Carver Company built decades ago to house its employees and their families. The homes are, for the most part, all the same, appearing much like the PMQs on a military base.

"All these company houses, I scooped them up just under two years ago," Levesque says. "Cheap as hell. I got a consortium of developers from Toronto backing me up on the deal."

"How many are still occupied?"

"About a third. Carver executives tell me the mine is in its last year and a half, but that's confidential. They've got a skeleton crew mucking the bottom, ready to do the cleanup and shut the lights off on the way out. Of course the mine has been hobbling toward this for a long time, but still. You know, as long as there are even a few jobs down there, people feel we've still got a beating heart."

"My father told me a long time ago what this day would be like. How it was coming and, more important, how the town should prepare for it."

"Our mayor, Danny Marko, has this big plan. He calls it his twenty-year vision. There's serious talk about a new transmission line being built up here, bringing power line jobs and construction dollars through town for a five-year period. Then there's our chief of police. He wants to truck Detroit's shitty diapers up here, maybe use the mine as a big hole to fill up. Meantime, the dropout rate in Saint B is into the double digits. Kids are taking off for the oil fields in Fort McMurray or the diamond mine up in Yellowknife. Hard to keep a kid in school when he can go to Alberta and make twenty bucks an hour just sweeping the floors, no experience required. Some days I think maybe I should follow them on out there."

Levesque rolls the window down all the way to flick his cigarette butt. A blast of cold air rolls in and wakes McKelvey from his nicotine stupor. The air, at least, is fresh and clean and smells of a coming snowfall. It is strange not to smell Lake Ontario, the stale subway air wafting from sidewalk grates, the chromium and coal ash.

"And that's it for today's depressing small-town news," Levesque says, and laughs like a dog barking. His chest wheezes. He catches his breath and adds, "Welcome home, Charlie. Welcome home."

Five

The boy who always has some marijuana now has something else. He stands in the centre of the boredom of this dying place and it offers the promise of amusement, an antidote to the tedium. At the same time, he offers himself the gift of small-town popularity. He will never want for friends as long as he always has a few grams of weed in his backpack. And now this, the magic powder.

At first he thought the yellow-white substance in the foil was cocaine. He got it at the arcade, the same place where he got his pot, but had no idea what he was looking for, what cocaine or any other hard drug smelled or looked like. He rubbed some of the powder on his gums, as he had seen narcos do in the movies, and it gave him the edge of a tiny buzz. He sprinkled it on a pinch of tobacco and rolled a joint. In this way he discovered the pathway to the waterfall. And now, standing here in his parents' garage, he shows the others how to smoke it using a ballpoint pen with the ink cylinder removed. Heat the foil with a lighter, inhale the chemical reaction. Instant payback. No waiting required. Flick the switch and you are perfect.

"Hey, Scott," one of the girls says, "I heard you gave Travis Lacey some shit that made him go crazy. Is that true? He's at a mental hospital in Sudbury 'cause he tried to take that cop Nolan's head off with an axe."

Two of the six teens have smoked. They have instantly found and occupied their own private wavelength. They are standing in this cold garage with their breath visible, boxes of empty beer bottles stacked in a corner, four summer tires awaiting the retreat of snow, tools hanging on a pegboard, and everywhere the smell of two-stroke oil and gasoline. The square of foil is passed to the girl and she holds it, her face stricken in this moment of choice. Her hand shakes, fluttering the foil like a leaf on an autumn tree.

"You think weed is amazing, Casey, this stuff is insane," Scott says.

He smiles. His eyes are lit up like LED lights. They are vacuums that suck her into his private world. He owns a confidence she can't quite understand.

"What about Travis?" Casey says. "He tried to kill his mom, I heard."

"Travis did too much," Scott says. "You got to be smart. Hold the lighter there just for a minute and you'll see. You don't have to sit in your basement for two days and smoke it all to yourself."

"Anyway, Travis was always a little crazy," someone says, and they all laugh.

The teens who have smoked start giggling, lost in a shared joke. The girl hesitates, but she looks over at Scott, this boy with the killer smile, and she doesn't want to disappoint him. She holds the hollow Bic pen between her teeth and sparks the lighter with a flick of her thumb. The little yellow flame heats the foil. Grey-white smoke lifts and curls in a wispy tendril, and she draws it away with the makeshift pipe.

She stands there in the dim garage. The roof pulls back like the screen on a convertible sports car, and sunshine pours in like golden summer-day warmth, and she feels so good, so light and happy, like Christmas morning and your birthday, too, and the boy with the killer smile is right there with her.

*   *   *

A brassy light streams through the window and fills the small kitchen of the bungalow where Constable Ed Nolan stands fixing a cup of tea. The hand stirring sugar in the steaming cup freezes there while he gets lost in memory, tripped or snagged. He seems to be doing this a lot lately, simply getting stuck in mid-thought or mid-stride, sitting there with a forkful of potatoes or a coffee cup hovering three inches from his lips. How long he stands here with the spoon in the cup, he has no idea — thirty seconds or six minutes, it is all the same. And then, as though released from the binds of a magical spell, his hand begins to work again. This condition is not the result of the recent concussion, he knows, for it dates back more than a year, to those long days when he straddled his job and tended to a mother dying in a hospital a hundred kilometres down the highway, all while watching his father slide into the void of dementia. The concussion, in addition to this newfound worry for the fate of his town, has likely only piled onto the tail end of a bad year. Ed Nolan knows that he needs a vacation, a break away from this place. If he is honest, he knows he must leave altogether one day, or face a life of loneliness and slow suffocation. The truth is, he can't leave. Not while the kids in town are in danger from this new, dark stranger called methamphetamine.

Nolan stands now with his back against the counter and surveys the room — his mother's needlepoint designs of deer and flowers in country fields, the framed religious verses, the dozens of spice and herb jars organized in alphabetical order. He brings the cup of tea and walks through the living room. Once cluttered with bric-a-brac of all varieties, clunky furniture picked up by his bargain-hunting father at yard sales and church fundraisers, awful oil paintings created by the wife of a mining friend, the room is now as sparse as a monastery. He is slowly, tediously working his way through the house one room at a time, a machine that cleans and clears. The walls are blank, the shag carpet has been rolled away. His father has no memory of these rooms, or this house even, except the odd and seemingly random blurting out of a snapshot, something shared here or there one Christmas, a Sunday in June of 1983. Nolan wonders now if the fog that has settled on his brain like a rag dosed in chloroform is similar to what happened to his father in those early months. The days when he sat across from this once seemingly omnipotent man with the tight biceps, the neck muscles taut and corded, and had to remind him what a knife and fork were for.

He taps softly three times at the bedroom, a habit and societal ritual that overrides the reality that his father likely can't comprehend the notion of privacy. He slips inside the room and the stale air mugs him like a hand over his mouth and nose. The floor is planted with clumps of dirty clothes, old bedding, and he feels guilty and ashamed. The day is quickly approaching when he will need to make the call and have his father taken to a nursing home in Timmins or Sudbury, perhaps somewhere even farther away.

"I have your tea, Dad," he says, and steps over some clothes to the night table.

Nolan can hardly breath, the air is so ripe. He moves to the window and opens it a few inches. He will take the risk of letting sub-zero air into the room, despite the fact his father now lies in bed and is at constant risk of developing pneumonia. A slice of cold winter air does in fact immediately change the temperature. He closes the window and turns back to his father.

"I have to go to work, Dad," Nolan says. "We have problems … new problems here in Ste. Bernadette. If I told you, you wouldn't believe me. The whole world has changed."

His father doesn't respond, and makes no move for the tea. Nolan listens for a moment, believing he may have heard his father make a sound, but there is nothing. The son can't recall the last time the father spoke his name, or any word for that matter. Nolan nods, as though he is once again accepting that it is simply the right thing for a son to do, to make that call. Breaking the promise his father made him make when Nolan's mother was sick — that he would never, under any circumstances, surrender him to a nursing home, that he would be afforded the simple luxury of passing away in his own bed — this is something Nolan will have to live with.

Six

Ste. Bernadette — or *Saint B* as she is known by the locals —
is nestled in the thickest of the wild country of the Cambrian
Shield, due north of Timmins and just west of the Quebec
border. Unpolished, with the ragged and torn-open beauty
that only the North can produce — a beauty born of adversity
and stubbornness, this place where trees jut impossibly from
grey sheer rock walls, wildflowers surviving in barely a dusting
of soil. Ste. Bernadette for two generations has straddled a
vein of gold — her luck and her curse. The community centre
that thirty years ago rocked with Saturday night dances now
rots in its place, leaning to one side, the whitewash faded,
cracked, and peeling. The once-prosperous shops along Main
Street now own boarded windows, except for those few whose
owners refuse to let go.

A little more than twelve hundred people live there now,
but at the height of the Carver Company mining operations
located just outside the town, Ste. Bernadette was home to
more than double that number. Ste. Bernadette never really

figured in the mining news, not when stacked against the big players — Sudbury, Thunder Bay, Timmins, Red Lake, even Cobalt in its gravy days. Ste. Bernadette was that rare secret; a small operation, yes, but it was prosperous and stable. Most of the locals didn't mind that outsiders never mentioned the place when they thought of mining; it was just as well to keep their ambitions away. Many worried aloud that a small boom would both invigorate and eventually destroy the town. Paranoia of the south and the cities down there was simply a part of the embedded culture in a remote northern town where sharing gossip and passing judgment were a part of daily life.

Unlike the Hollinger Gold Mine of Timmins, which was at one time the richest gold producer in the western hemisphere — or even the mines of Rouyn, which operate still — the vein deep beneath Ste. Bernadette was seemingly *not* infinite. Like many remote towns in northern Ontario — or northern Quebec or Manitoba or Saskatchewan — there was a Native reserve nearby, in this case half an hour northeast of Ste. Bernadette. A short trip up the two-lane highway, followed by a ten-minute drive down a gravel road would deliver you to a new universe: the Big Water First Nation.

It is surreal: McKelvey stands in the kitchen of the home where he was raised. It is silent. Sun streams through the window and warms the side of his face. He remembers standing just like this on cold winter mornings, eyes closed to the warmth, feet cold on the linoleum floor. Later, as he unpacks, the medical brochures once again poke him in the eye. He stands at the dresser and regards them like a fan of cards, the worst royal flush he's ever drawn, and then he opens a drawer and tosses them in. He adds to the drawer the journal he has been keeping with no sense of regular dedication. Some of the entries simply record the date and a line or two about having nothing to say, dispatches from the front lines of mortality: *Rain today. Fuck it.*

Now McKelvey stands at the bathroom sink, the porcelain cold against his stomach, and he swallows the tablets with a backward snap of his head. He closes his eyes and imagines the chemical molecules dissolving, entering his bloodstream on their mission of salvation. This bathroom, this small place. Remembered smells, voices from down the hall. He forms a grainy vision of his father standing at this very sink, shaving cream slathered on his big handsome face, a cigarette propped between thin lips. In the vignette his father turns, notices him standing in the hallway with a foot stuck between the banister posts; and Grey McKelvey smiles and winks. It's a good memory of a man who rarely let you know where you stood within his silence.

The warmth of the sun through the window feels good now, in the dead of winter, but at the height of summer the top floor of the old house will be stifling. McKelvey wipes his mouth with the back of his hand and puts the pill bottle in the medicine chest above the sink. His razor is in there, too, untouched for the third day now. The stubble is beginning to itch, especially at night with his face pressed against the pillow, but laziness wins out over discomfort. Seems to be a theme in his life these days. But it wasn't always this way; for once he had a purpose, and drive. He can't help but admit the waning of his energy, the slowing of that internal propeller. Is this getting old, he wonders, or is it giving up?

It is as though a parallel universe opened up the day he left the force, stumbling inside an upside-down place where time no longer had meaning. He had given himself a period of holiday from total responsibility after so many years of increasing stress on the streets of the city. The murder of his son at the hands of bikers and a crooked Drug Squad cop, Raj Balani. The shootout with the Montreal biker, Pierre Duguay. The kidnapping of his friend Tim Fielding. And within it all, through those darkest of days, his wife gave up on them and moved to the west coast. He discovered he was a grandfather. And he also discovered he had cancer. Some people clawed their way through a tough year; McKelvey felt as though he had eaten the shit of an entire decade. It was just getting too hard to swallow.

He often wakes in the early morning from a dream of the shootings in the old Canada Malting Company factory on the shore of Lake Ontario. The echo of the gunshots, the sounds of wounded and dying men. He shivers in the darkness, alone and confused. This weight, this guilt he carries. McKelvey came through the investigations without drawing any formal charges. There was talk of obstruction of justice, but he kept his mouth shut and there was little to go on. He knew the truth, and those who knew it with him were dead. While McKelvey accepted his role in the conclusion of events, he did not feel responsible for Detective Leyden's death per se. That trigger had been pulled by someone else, a madman, and McKelvey had done his best to keep everyone — Hattie included — out of the line of fire. In the end, Tim Fielding had been found, he had been saved. Whether it was worth the cost was a question beyond McKelvey's salary grade. What was done was done.

In those days and weeks following the kidnapping and all that it brought to his life, McKelvey came to understand and appreciate the depth of his losses. His wife, Caroline, was still living in Vancouver, and her plans to return to Ontario seemed now to be on hold in light of the violent events of that day at the Toronto harbourfront. She admitted in one of their long and rambling telephone conversations that his actions seemed *desperate*, though she stopped short of deeming them either homicidal or suicidal. And perhaps, McKelvey believed, she was only now accepting the truth of this man she had loved and the things of which he was capable — the violence that rested there just beneath the stillness. Jessie, his son's former girlfriend and the mother of his grandchild, had taken the little girl back to Manitoulin Island, where Jessie was right now opening a hair and beauty salon in the quaint harbour town of Little Current. Detective Mary-Ann Hattie was entirely through with him, having passed her exams to make Homicide on the country's largest and busiest municipal police force. Tim Fielding was sleeping on the floor of a hut in some remote northern Chinese village, teaching English to farm kids and sending irregular emails that said little in their brevity, though he claimed to be at peace, finally at peace. Exactly as expected, perhaps even precisely as planned, McKelvey was finally and completely alone. He had lost everything and everyone in his life. There was a strange sense of relief in knowing that his swirling vortex could no longer harm the ones he loved. He had only himself to drive crazy.

It was in the midst of this newfound solitude that The Diagnosis arrived. He had expected it, and yet it was still a surprise. A sucker punch you were sort of waiting for as you stepped into a darkened room — it was coming, you just didn't know when or from where. He read the brochures he was handed, and he sat on the couch in his condo and thought about things he had never hoped to think about. His mind got caught on the notion of religion, and what those people were getting that he wasn't. Hope or blind stupidity, he couldn't tell which. And he thought, too, of taking matters into his own hands, to switch the tables here and gain a modicum of control. He understood himself sufficiently to know that he lacked any sort of grace required to surrender, to lie down and wait out the last hours on a regimen of hospital rice pudding and visitors lying to your face about your prospects. He wanted to go quietly, but he was too loud, always had been. Crashing and banging, kicking and fighting. And he realized the fundamental truth of the equation: *you walk ten miles into the woods, you've got to walk ten miles out.*

McKelvey spent the first two months following the shootings in and out of the police headquarters on College Street, the offices of the Crown attorney, the Special Investigations Unit, answering and not answering questions for hours on end. He grudgingly spent a small fortune on a lawyer who helped him navigate the minefield. He drew rudimentary diagrams of the plant, where they had entered, where they had been ambushed, where the bodies had fallen. It was during this time that McKelvey's drinking took on a new and darker nature. It was the sort of drinking that had somewhere and somehow edged across a line, something to be reckoned with. It was the sort of drinking that felt more like *need* than *want*, and he found himself drinking more and more at home, sitting on his couch or at the desk by the window overlooking the alleyway, trying to write things down in this journal, figure out what had happened to his boy and his own life. Those hours of total solitude wherein the drinking became measured, steady, like medicine dripping from an IV into a patient's arm. He was rarely drunk, or perhaps he was almost always drunk, at least to some degree, and he finally understood the concept of *alcoholic tolerance*. He found that he could drink a six-pack of beer and half a mickey of Jameson between eleven and three, and then pull on his sports coat and head downstairs to Garrity's Pub in time for happy hour. He could slip inside the stream of after-work drinkers buzzing within the glow of their first drink, and he could carry on as though he'd perhaps only had a beer or two on his way over. He rarely changed, in terms of demeanour or mood, and the bartenders and waitresses called him a "good drinker," as though it were a profession in which one could proudly excel or perhaps receive certification. When the alcohol lost its ability to extract him from himself completely — the way a dentist made your tooth numb before drilling — it was then that he turned back to the pills and their promise of disconnection.

He was no professional, and in the end it was mixing the two potions that got him into trouble. He quit drinking on a Tuesday night in late December, having found himself earlier that morning sprawled on the bathroom floor, drool gluing his cheek to the tiles, one arm frozen asleep from being tucked at an awkward angle behind his back. Fully dressed, one shoe on and missing a sock, the light burning above the sink. He sat up and felt his face, his teeth, his pockets for his wallet. There was no cash left, but his credit cards and ID were all there. And he pulled out a mess of folded receipts and attempted to comprehend how it was that he ended up spending over a hundred dollars at Filmores on Dundas Street East at quarter after one. The strip joint was a twenty-minute walk from Garrity's. It reminded him of the days of his police work, piecing together the movements of a suspect or a victim through their purchases and the corresponding time stamps. In terms of memory there was nothing to go on, simply blackness. It was terrifying to think he had been walking about like some automaton. It was a recipe for disaster.

He clenched his teeth through a week of withdrawal, hardly venturing outside, and he felt empowered, newly born to the world. But always he had the pills. He lined up his doctor's appointments with the fastidiousness of a hypochondriac.

"You've had a rough ride the last few years," the always sympathetic Dr. Shannon assured him. And it was true, after all. His boy Gavin was dead, his wife was gone, he'd been shot, for God's sake, and what was a man to do but seek some solace? "Take some time off the sauce and see how things go. I wouldn't worry about you being a drunk though. Being Irish, I've seen my share, Charlie. There's a fine line between heavy drinking and full-blown alcoholism. But watch out for those pills, they can kick you in the arse …"

Then one evening for no apparent reason he overshot the mark with too many pills, found himself stoned to the point of blunt incomprehension, fingers tripping on numbers as he attempted to dial everyone and anyone in his address book, leaving messages and perhaps on occasion babbling or crying into the mouthpiece. Hattie called back as he sat in a stupor on the couch, CNN cycling eerie night-vision footage of the bombing of Baghdad.

"What the hell are you doing, Charlie?"

"Some baking," he managed, still capable of making her laugh.

"You've got to pull your shit together. You're a *grandfather*. Don't you ever think of that? You've got people who depend on you, Charlie, people who care about you." She sighed. And then, softer, she said, "Listen, I'm not going to call you again. And I don't want you to call me. Okay? I mean it this time. You know how I feel about you. But I can't do this anymore. Jesus H., I'm working seventy hours a week these days. We've got two kids shot in the head up at Jane and Finch and nobody's talking. I put in for a transfer, too ..."

This last piece of information was thrown in quickly, like pulling a bandage from the flesh. His addled mind clicked and groaned, attempting to decipher the meaning.

"Transfer. To where?"

"Back to Halifax." It was almost a whisper.

I love you so much, he thought. But he could only sit there and listen to the dial tone.

Dut-dut-dut-dut-dut-dut.

Seven

Constable Ed Nolan is back at work three days after being released from the hospital in Timmins. He has suffered a concussion — or MTBI (mild traumatic brain injury), as his file states — and his lacerated scalp is closed with eighteen staple stitches. He lies when the doctor asks if he feels dizzy upon standing, if he experiences double vision, a general feeling of being "out of it." Of course his head spins when he stands — he was hit with a shovel, for God's sake — but he holds his ground. He remembers those days he stood for early morning parade back when he was a soldier in basic training. Out all night with the boys in the platoon, having literally crawled back to barracks as the sun was rising, it was a monumental achievement to stand at attention and try not to breathe as the platoon sergeant screamed into your face.

Nolan wears his toque all day now, even as he sits at his desk in the station, because it hides the bandages wrapped about his skull like a mummy. The Chief has ordered him to a week of administrative duty, which means he can't attend calls.

Administrative duty on a force this small, with so few calls and reports, may as well mean a week of staring at the coffee pot. He tries to read the various magazines to which he subscribes in his attempt to remain connected to the greater world — *The Economist, Newsweek, Maclean's, Atlantic Monthly* — but the lines jump and his head begins to pound from behind his eyes.

His first concern upon his return to the station is obtaining a status update on Travis Lacey. He pulls the report and scans it, squinting, taking long breaks to close his eyes in a vain attempt to clear his vision. The report, filed by both the Chief and Pete Younger, pieces together the moments which are lost to Ed Nolan's memory.

At 9:48 a.m. dispatch received a call from Bob Lacey reporting Officer Nolan had been assaulted by Travis Lacey. Constable Younger is dispatched. An ambulance is also dispatched from the small medical clinic in town — there is one ambulance which runs between Saint B and Big Water First Nation. At 10:06, Constable Younger arrives at the scene and reports "Officer Down" to dispatch. The report lays out the facts: "Constable Nolan is lying sideways on the snow, unresponsive but with vital signs, blood pooling at his head." Younger asks the Laceys to gather blankets to keep Nolan warm until the ambulance arrives. The scene secured, Constable Younger's attention immediately turns to the search for Travis Lacey.

Younger does not need to look far. Younger reports that as he makes his way down the laneway, Travis appears "around the right side of the garage, holding a snow shovel in a threatening manner." Constable Younger pulls his weapon. Here Nolan stops, conjuring the image in his mind's eye, knowing it is the first time the young cop has removed his weapon from its holster — not insignificant in a policing career. But the chaotic arrival into the scene of the boy's mother, her shouts and pleas, must reach through the trance. Travis Lacey sets the shovel aside and starts to laugh as though it all must be some sort of joke.

Nolan scans through the report, his headache pulsating with each heartbeat. Travis was arrested at the scene, booked into the single Saint B holding cell. The Chief was called down to the station and it was decided to lay a charge of attempted murder. The boy was transferred to Monteith Correctional Centre outside Timmins to await a first appearance on the serious charge.

"Jesus," Nolan says as he sits there in the quiet of the station. He tries to imagine how terrified Travis Lacey must be right now, sitting on a jail range with a bunch of reprobates and hardened cons. Or the worry his mother must be experiencing. He needs to help here, to do what he can. Whatever has been started here, this youthful experimentation with drugs, must be made right again.

He sets the folder of paperwork aside. He sits there for a long time, trying to form clear thoughts against the white noise of his headache. He picks up the phone and calls the Chief, who works from home for the most part these days, at least when he's not out informally campaigning for mayor.

"Gallagher."

"It's me, Chief."

"Nolan, how's the noggin'?"

"Not too bad," he says, eyes clenched. "Listen, I was just catching up on the report on Travis Lacey. I'm trying to get my head wrapped around an attempt murder charge for this kid. Maybe we should suggest a downgrade to assault. He obviously needs help."

"I hear you, Eddie, I do. But listen, we can't have people swinging shovels at our heads without any consequences. You see what I mean? He hit you in the goddamned head with a shovel, Ed. Could've killed you sure as shit. You're lucky he didn't. I was scared to hell when I got the call about you. We work up here in the north all alone, takes the OPP an hour to make it up here. If we don't set an example, the drunks and moonshiners will have their way with us. Anyway, I already talked to the new circuit Assistant Crown, Amanda Jason. She's a real tough cookie."

Nolan eases forward, rests an elbow on the desk and his head on his free hand. He says, "This tough on crime line doesn't have anything to do with running for mayor, does it?"

Chief Gallagher laughs. It's a laugh Ed Nolan has come to interpret as Gallagher offering a polite applause or perhaps an easy way out of a bad joke, the politician in him.

"Eddie, you need to get some rest. Go lay down, will you? Let Younger hold the fort. You don't owe this Lacey kid anything. The courts can get him set up with counselling once he's in the system."

They hang up. Nolan sits back in the chair and looks around the small office. Three desks, a coffee pot, a cork board with notices for a potluck at the church and a charity car wash for the high-school hockey team, a few old posters about drunk driving and seatbelt laws. More than big city cops, he and Younger and the Chief are in a position to truly serve and protect this small community. They know the people, they are of the people. He can't shake the image of Travis Lacey out of his mind, the teen's eyes wild and zoned, his hands around his mother's neck. He wishes someone had spent a little more time with him when he himself was a teen, that corrosive adolescent poison coursing through the veins of his brain. He learned a lot of things, or perhaps most things, the hard way.

Constable Ed Nolan stands and steadies himself. The floor pitches a little as though he is on the deck of a boat. He grabs his jacket from the back of the chair, zips up, and takes the keys to the second cruiser from the lockbox on the wall. He scrawls a note on the chalkboard by the door, a board which they use without any regularity to track their ins and outs.

Gone to Monteith — Ed, he writes.

*   *   *

Dear Journal,

Fuck you.
Cold, tired, sore. Almost out of pills.
Back home. Strange days. Strange feelings.
Did I really come from here?
Where have I been … where am I going?

Love, Charlie

Eight

Peggy has begun to put more effort than usual into her appearance. The fact is not lost on McKelvey, who stops by each morning at the same time for a coffee. He makes sure to comment on her hair. She brings a hand to her head and touches the new curls. She smiles. The smile is small but genuine, and McKelvey gets the sense it is a gesture this woman does not offer every customer.

"Usual?" she asks, already pouring coffee into a take-away cup.

"I'll take one of those cherry sticks I've heard so much about."

"It's all hype," she says as she puts one of the doughnuts in a small brown paper bag.

"You're cornering in on my market," he says. He takes a sip of the coffee and winces from the combination of scalding temperature and bitter taste. He does not come for the coffee, for it does not compare to the high-end and over-priced brew he grew accustomed to in Toronto. A Starbucks on every corner. And if not a Starbucks, then a Second Cup or a Timothy's. Sometimes it seemed to McKelvey that Toronto was not so much a city as it was a series of restaurants, bars, and coffee shops. Every window you passed belonged either to a cafe or some fake British-style pub with a ridiculous-sounding name like *The Syphilitic Toad* — as though the corner of Yonge and Eglinton in downtown Toronto was supposed to feel like seventeenth-century London for a few hours after work every Thursday.

"And what market is that, Charlie?"

"Cynicism," he says. "You know, courting the general belief that things can and will get worse."

"Or maybe it's realism based on experience."

"You win," he says.

"Nobody wins." She flashes her second smile of the day. "That's the whole point. Listen, not that I'm not enjoying our philosophical debate — because believe me, mental stimulation is on short supply around here — but I wanted to tell you about Eddie Nolan. He's the town cop. Or the best cop, anyway. Chief Gallagher wants to be mayor, and Pete Younger is just a kid full of high octane piss and vinegar. Eddie was in here yesterday asking about you."

"Asking about me?"

McKelvey shivers, wonders for a moment if the Toronto cops have called up here, sniffing after him. Has the Crown attorney found some new angle on the warehouse shootings? Are they filing charges? This is the life of a man with ghosts trailing him.

"He said he heard from Carl Levesque that you were up here, and that you were a Toronto cop, a detective. He said he'd want to look you up and get your opinion on some things. He got hurt a couple of weeks ago, hit in the head with a shovel, the poor dear. The kid has had a tough year. His mother died about a year and a half ago and his father has that Alzheimer's that comes on so fast. Ed looks after him and holds down his job."

"I heard about that incident," McKelvey says. "Some teenager went off on him."

"Not the first 'incident' around here. They burned down the bleachers at the sports field this fall. Vandalism is something fierce. And the dropout rate. You see kids just hanging around the convenience store, the arcade, Christ, even the laundromat. Drugs are the issue if you ask me."

"Show me a town or a city that doesn't have its share of drugs."

"Didn't used to be like this. Bad combination — drugs and boredom. Life in a northern town. Anyway, Eddie's uncle was friends with your father. He said they worked together."

"Everybody worked with everybody's father around here."

"Touché, Charlie." She gives him a look, just for an instant, and their eyes lock in a way that does something to McKelvey's stomach. It's a feeling he can't quite describe, but he knows one thing: it hasn't changed since he was twelve years old.

*   *   *

Back at the empty house, McKelvey sets out to find something that he is not sure even exists, or if it does, where he will find it. This notion runs through his brain like a mushroom bullet, destroying rational thought. He gets down on his knees and uses a key to unwind the screws on all the heater vents. He snakes his hand around in the empty spaces behind the wall, pulling out cobwebs and dust. He sits there on the floor with his back to the wall, and he closes his eyes. He wants to see himself as a child again, see his father moving around this house, the places he might have considered safe or sacred. What is it he hopes to find? Some clue or remnant from the past, this idea that his father participated in the violence around that infamous strike in the 1950s. The explosion at a storage shed on company property, the death of a scab worker.

It is a far stretch, he decides, that his father penned any sort of
·confession and tucked it behind the wall, a telegraph of truth
from the past.

*   *   *

Late in the afternoon, with the sun high and glowing behind a
hazy film of cloud, a black police SUV ambles up the laneway.
McKelvey watches from the kitchen window. He is dressed in
faded jeans and a black T-shirt with a white logo for Garrity's
Pub, dark denizen where he spent long hours and small mil-
lions, merciful flow of cold beer on tap, sacred amber Irish
whiskey on crackling ice. He has not had a drink in forty days
as of today. He can't remember the last time he went forty con-
secutive days without a drink, but it is likely going back to his
teenage years. *Forty days*. It is biblical, epic in proportions.
Strange how the thought crosses his mind just now with a
fleeting message of promised relief, satisfaction, contentment,
and ease: *go ahead, Charlie, it couldn't hurt …*

McKelvey watches as the tall and broad-shouldered
constable steps from the vehicle. This would be Ed Nolan, as
Peggy forewarned. The man appears to be in his late twenties,
square-faced, strong-jawed. He reaches back into the cruiser
and pulls out a tray with two coffees. He tucks a file folder
under his arm and comes to the door. McKelvey doesn't wait
for the knock. He holds the door open wide, cold air rushing
in, his breath coming back out in a cloud.

"Constable Nolan, I presume?"

Nolan smiles, nods once.

"Can I bother you for a minute, Detective McKelvey?"

"You got a warrant?" McKelvey stares with a straight face.
It stops Nolan in his tracks. Then McKelvey smiles and says,
"Come on in. And it's just Charlie, please."

Nolan sets the coffees down on the kitchen table and pulls off his gloves, unzips his coat.

"I'm Ed Nolan," he says, and they shake hands. "Small force in the middle of nowhere, we do a lot of things without waiting for a warrant from the circuit justice."

"I can imagine. It's all just paperwork anyway." McKelvey motions for Nolan to take a seat. "I made my way into more than a few rooms just by bluffing, holding up a folded piece of paper. I never implicitly said it was a warrant, and they never asked to see the paper, so it was a bit of a grey zone."

"Things are a little more black and white up here," Nolan says, and lets out a long breath. He reaches up and gently removes the black wool toque, revealing a wrap of bandages around his short blond hair that sprouts from the top of the coil.

"I heard about that kid who hurt you," McKelvey says. He reaches out and takes one of the Coffee Time coffees, knowing full well it will taste like shit and kill his stomach, but still he will drink it. It was, he imagines, poured by Peggy.

"That's what I wanted to talk to you about. I heard you were in town. Big-city cop and everything, I could sure use some of your experience right now. This Lacey kid, Travis Lacey, is a solid A student. Or he was. Up until two months ago, anyway. It's as if he changed overnight into this psychopath. Parents say he stays up around the clock playing video games in the basement or he's out with this group of friends, staying out all night."

"Sounds like a teenager," McKelvey says, remembering his own boy, Gavin. But he also remembers how his boy, somewhere and somehow, slipped across an obscure line. Stumbling from normal teenage angst to a world of hardcore drugs and, eventually, street gangs. Bullets, blades, and bullshit.

"For sure. We all goof around a little, blow off the testosterone." Nolan takes the lid off the other coffee and blows across the top. "I know all about that. I left Saint B when I was seventeen, felt like I was suffocating. I found my share of troubles before I got my head on straight."

"I did the same, Ed," McKelvey says. "Train used to run more regular in my day. It was easier to escape."

"I visited Travis down at Monteith. Poor kid is scared out of his mind. And he's coming off this shit, coming off hard. Said he's been smoking meth. I couldn't believe it. Meth in Saint B. How could we not know? I know who deals pot, hash, who has pain pills from time to time, who can get blow in for the shift workers when they want to celebrate something. But *meth*?"

McKelvey takes a sip of the coffee, then pushes it away.

"Would you help with this?" Nolan asks. "I mean, I don't even know what your plans are. If you're here for a visit or …"

"I don't have a plan," McKelvey says. "I got this idea in my head and ended up on a bus. I can tell you, it's strange as hell being back here. This is the house I grew up in. You have no idea how fucked up that is."

Nolan shakes his head and clenches his eyes. McKelvey deduces the man is suffering the inexplicable ripple effects of a hard hit to the head. It can leave you in a fog for days or weeks, this sudden onset of vertigo.

"Travis told me this is a real problem in Saint B. He wouldn't tell me who he got the dope from, but he said we have no idea how many kids are on this shit. I have to be honest here, Charlie. I don't have any experience in this sort of thing."

"I never worked Narcotics, but Hold-Up is the other end of the whole drug chain. Junkies rob gas stations and liquor stores to get the cash to buy their dope," McKelvey says. "The first thing I'd do is go and press hard on the usual suspects, the guys dealing pot by the gram. Start at the centre and work your way back out. Shake enough trees, the monkey eventually falls out."

"I should bring them down to the station maybe, rattle them a little?"

McKelvey shakes his head. "You want to go in easy at first, easy but hard. Do it in private so word doesn't get out. You need to work against the disadvantage of small-town gossip, don't let these assholes get the jump on you. Let them think you guys are a bunch of Keystone Kops."

"And if that doesn't work?" Nolan says.

"Then you go at them where they live and work, right in the middle of their safest environment. In front of as many of their friends and buyers as possible. Maybe rough them up a little, who knows. Whatever you need to do."

Nolan nods slowly, but his eyes are not convinced.

"I've only ever been a cop here," Nolan says. "I doubt I can pull off the bad cop routine with these people. Maybe you should ride shotgun with me for a few days. I can talk to the Chief, see if we have budget left for consultation fees. Who knows, maybe even get you signed on as an auxiliary officer."

McKelvey looks out the window at the winter day. He has yet to read the pamphlets in his dresser drawer. *A Survivor's Checklist.* He has yet to contact his doctor to have the follow-up discussion on treatment options which were outlined in their last visit. It occurs to him that Caroline is right; he has run away from home. He has run away from his life, from The Diagnosis. He should be right now entering treatment in a Toronto hospital for the prostate cancer that killed his father.

"I'm retired," McKelvey says.

"Your experience could really help. This is your home town, Charlie. The people of Saint B need you right now. Why else did you end up back here?"

McKelvey laughs. It is a genuine laugh, and it feels good from the inside out.

"Save the speech," he says. "I don't owe this goddamned place a thing."

"Maybe it owes you." Nolan smiles his boy's smile.

"You've got a chief here, right? He'll have a plan, kid."

"Chief Gallagher wasn't impressed that I drove down to the correctional centre to see this Lacey boy. It's case closed as far as he's concerned. He's gearing up to run for mayor. He has this idea about using the closed sections of the mine as a landfill. Something about trucking Detroit's shitty diapers up here."

"Sounds like typical police brass. More politician than cop."

"He's a good man, but he's in the wrong line of work. He was a sheriff for a long time in a small town somewhere in the U.S. Midwest. Said he was used to running for election every five years. Prides himself on the fact he never used his weapon. He's all about the status quo."

McKelvey stands now and holds out his hand. The meeting is adjourned.

"Thanks for the coffee, but I don't think I can be of any help."

"I'll let you think about it."

McKelvey shakes his head. The kid is stubborn. Standing there in his uniform, smiling through a concussion. For a moment McKelvey sees himself. *Right there. Standing in this very kitchen. Having driven all night to come home to see his sick mother. She turns from the stove and she sees him. He has left the city straight from a midnight shift and he is still wearing his uniform. Her tired eyes light up. She smiles.*

"My policeman," she says.

Nine

Darkness is falling. The lights of Main Street burn with a phosphorous glow. This far north, the aurora borealis appear on the coldest nights, these dancing and twisting snakes of coloured vapour — smeared streaks of green and yellow and sometimes blue. Nolan often pulls the cruiser over to the side of the highway just to sit and watch the spectacle. It reminds him of being a boy, how his father would do the same thing in his pickup truck. And Nolan remembers how the cab was always warm, how it smelled of his father — Old Spice and stale sweat — and how perfect life was as they sat there on the side of the dark highway, the world silent and uncomplicated. His father was a miner, and yet Nolan had always sensed there was something untapped within the man, some unnamed sensibility. Life was good back then, simple and easy to understand.

"Front row centre for one of nature's greatest shows," his father would say.

"What causes them?" Nolan would invariably ask.

"It's magic," his father would say. And later, when he had started the truck and was pulling back onto the road, he'd always offer a variation on this existential observation. "Those dancing lights," he'd say, "prove just how small we really are. A man remembers that, and he's got his place figured out just right."

Nolan is at the wheel of the cruiser, thinking about his father and remembering how the old man had talked about leaving Saint B, moving southwest to Elliot Lake, because his father had seen a brochure about the town. Once a mining centre in its own right, Elliot Lake had reinvented itself as a retirement mecca, offering cheap bungalows and peace and quiet, good hunting and fishing. His father only ever talked about it, and now it was too late. The big man was lying in a bed, withering away to bonelike fruit left on a shelf.

He is on Main now, headed west out of town. As he passes the police station, nestled between the one-room public library and the two-room town hall, he spots a strange vehicle. He slows to a crawl. The vehicle is a black SUV — a loaded Suburban — with Michigan plates. He glances in the rearview, stops, then puts the vehicle in reverse and eases back to the station. He pulls into a spot beside the Chief's Jimmy. The Chief always drives his own vehicle, and charges mileage to the town, something he says is a holdover from his sheriff days.

Nolan enters the station and the small squad room. Chief Gallagher is leaning back in his swivel chair, boots up on his desk, his guest seated across from him with his back to Nolan. Gallagher is ruddy-faced and his eyes are shining. Nolan spots the tumblers of amber booze. The Chief keeps a bottle of scotch locked in his bottom drawer for special occasions, which are rare in Saint B these days. He keeps his only weapon, a pearl-grip .38 revolver, locked in there, too, and Nolan catches a glimpse of the handle. Gallagher is not a heavy or frequent drinker, and the booze always rushes blood to his face. Nolan has witnessed the rapid transformation of the man's demeanour after just a single drink. He smiles too much and his head lolls as though it is too heavy to hold up, his cheeks and nose flushing red.

"Constable Nolan," Gallagher says, and swings his boots to the ground.

The visitor turns around. He is an olive-skinned man of about forty, and when he stands to greet Nolan, the constable sees that the man is dressed in designer blue jeans and a navy sports coat with pinstripes, no tie, an expensive black overcoat draped on the chair. Nolan holds out his hand and they shake.

"Tony Celluci," he says.

"Ed Nolan."

"Chief Gallagher was telling me about your head," Celluci says, patting the side of his own head in illustration. "I know how you're feeling. I had two concussions back when I played college football. It's like you've got the worst hangover in the world and you just can't shake it."

Nolan finally has an analogy that works for his condition. He smiles and nods.

"Want a drink?" the Chief asks as he reaches into the drawer. He stops and looks up, and points to the side of his head. "Are you supposed to drink with your, you know?"

"No, thanks," Nolan says. "I'm on my way out to talk to Wade Garson."

The smile falls from the Chief's face. He straightens up, shakes his head slowly.

"Wade Garson? Why would you be going out to see Wade Garson at this hour, with your head all bandaged up, and you supposed to be on office duties anyway?"

Celluci looks at a poster on the wall that has suddenly attracted his attention.

"We should talk in private," Nolan says.

The Chief nods and closes the drawer, lifts up with a sigh.

"Excuse me just a minute, Tony, but police business calls."

Out in the hallway, Gallagher puts his hand on Nolan's shoulder and gives a gentle squeeze. This close, Nolan can smell the peaty Scotch.

"Who is this guy?" Nolan asks with a nod toward the office.

"He's from Detroit. Works for the city, Department of Waste Management. He's up here on a tour of northern communities. I told you before they've got their eye on Saint B as a potential landfill site."

"Great. I've always wondered what Detroit smells like."

"Easy now, Eddie. It's early days yet. But listen, what are you doing here? Go home to bed, for Christ's sake. You don't need to be going up to Wade Garson's and surprising him in the dark. That paranoid son of a bitch could have guns for all we know, and we know he's got a goddamned dog that's crazier than he is. You know how much he hates the cops, Eddie, especially since we sent his brother away on that weapons charge. Those people aren't right in the head, never have been. Their old man, Dewey Garson, you know he about killed a man with a pool cue one night in the Station Hotel twenty years ago. Over a spilled beer."

"Travis Lacey told me he was on methamphetamine, Chief. *Meth*, right here in Saint B. He wouldn't tell me where he got it, but he said there's a lot of it going around the last couple of months. I talked to this former Toronto detective, Charlie McKelvey, today, and he—"

"Whoa, whoa there, Ed. What are you talking about? You mean that McKelvey who's renting his old house from Carl Levesque? You need to stay away from that character, let me tell you. I made a few calls when I found out he was in town, see. That's my job, to know who we're dealing with in this little fishbowl. Well, let me tell you, son, McKelvey has quite a history. You best just leave him to his walk down memory lane."

Nolan's head begins to pound with such clarity that he swears he can feel and trace the line of each pulsing artery back to its root. It is after seven. The winter night is pure blackness, even blacker out near the trailer where Wade Garson lives and peddles junk car parts and sells dope by the gram. Nolan forms an image of himself once again sprawled in the snow, his head or chest bleeding, Wade Garson standing over him, a dog barking and howling across the empty night. The Chief is right about one thing. It's not the time or the place to come at Wade Garson. He needs to slow down and use his head. And regardless of what Gallagher says, Nolan wants this veteran cop McKelvey at his side. He will need to convince the man to ride along. Or trick him. Either way, the cause is righteous.

"Maybe you're right, Chief. I should get some rest."

Gallagher's hand squeezes Nolan's shoulder and the Chief smiles.

"Now you're talking sense, my boy. We don't need any fireworks in Saint B these days. We've got a chance here to turn things around. It's our job to keep things nice and tidy, okay?"

Nolan nods. The Chief pats him on the back.

"Watch that black ice," Gallagher calls as Nolan opens the door and enters the cold, dark night.

* * *

The Saint B coin laundromat is located at the south end of Main Street in one of the first collection of low-rise buildings on the approach into town. There is a butchery located on one side of the laundromat, long since closed, and a Kwick Kash on the other side, which is closed at this late hour but otherwise still in operation. This is the place where locals cash their unemployment and welfare cheques when they don't want to follow the seemingly inconsistent hours kept by the Royal Bank branch located beside the library. In exchange for cash-in-hand, they are willing to lose up to twenty-eight percent of the cheque's face value. It's a racket Carl Levesque wishes he had thought of years ago; legalized loansharking.

The full glass-front window declares MODERN COIN WASH, but the paint is faded and someone has used the opportunity to substitute an *L* for the *C* in the word *Coin*. Levesque still smirks every time he sees that, slogging in now with his green garbage bag full of dirty clothes. Actually, he thinks, that's not such a bad business idea either. Why nobody ever thought of setting up a massage parlour in this craphole is a crime. Back in its heyday, the place, like most mining towns, had about a four-to-one ratio of men to women. He knows that Saint B has had its share of "known bawdy houses," these nondescript bungalows, the addresses passed around on payday. He sees the unrealized potential in cornering that market. And it's too late now. The town is caught in that in-between place: too many old people, too many kids. It's the middle group that is missing, the consumers with regular paycheques, and they are disappearing from Saint B in droves.

He's shoving his twisted ball of pants and shirts and socks and underwear into an industrial front-load washer. The bells on the door jingle. Three teenagers shuffle in — two boys and a girl, sixteen or seventeen — and a rush of freezing air rolls in after them like a delayed wave. Levesque eyes them, but continues with his task. Four quarters, a shot of powdered soap, and he slams the door and turns and puts his back against the wall of washers, folds his arms across his chest. The teens congregate near the washroom at the back, where the girl has retreated. There is a corkboard on the wall beside the washroom door. It is pasted with months-old notices for bake sales, campers for sale, winter tires for trade, someone's lost dog. One of the teens rips a flyer from the board, crumples it into a ball, aims at a garbage pail in a corner near the emergency exit at the rear. He misses the shot. The crumpled ball of paper hits the rim and bounces off.

"Tool," his friend says. This boy is the taller of the two, about six feet. He is dressed in jeans and untied Kodiak boots, a wool navy pea coat. His hair is long and dyed jet black.

"Hurry up, Casey," the thrower says. He knocks on the door loudly. "You're not taking a dump are you?" and this makes the two boys laugh.

"Dump," the bigger teen repeats as though it is the funniest thing he's heard.

Levesque looks out the window onto Main. There is no traffic. He does not expect to see any. Only half the street lamps are on, a cost-saving measure, and this creates an eerie false dawn. The town is in dire straits thanks to a dwindling tax base. Garbage collection is now every two weeks. It will be monthly before long, and then the rat population will bloom. One of the town's two snowploughs sits idle at the town garage. Cause and effect. He looks back to the kids, who also keep eyeing him while pretending not to notice him. Goddamned Saint B, how has he ended up in this place? Doing laundry at quarter to ten on a Friday night? That he is owed, that some good luck is due his way, goes without saying. Goddamned right. And if the luck won't come, then he'll just do what he's always done, he'll make things happen. He hears the voice of the man from the tapes in his car — *take control of your destiny. Decide what you want from this life, make a plan, and go for it …*

The door of the washroom opens. The girl steps out and gives the tallest boy a shove. She wears a black toque over long blond hair. Levesque sees that her nose is pierced and her eyebrows, too, and her eyes are ringed in black makeup. She has an edge to her, something he likes. He figures in a mere three years this girl will be someone's pregnant wife. Unless she makes a break for it, heads to a city. And even then the odds aren't good, he knows. And it's a shame is all, how these two young studs are too stupid to see what's right in front of them. She is at the apex of her beauty.

"Hey," Levesque says, and the teens look over.

They stare, as though he is doing his laundry in the nude. He remembers well this age, how the very existence or presence of adults seems an insult to the meaning of life. They simply can't accept the fact they, too, will eventually start their day by gathering what remains of their hair into a swirl on top of their balding skulls, they will wear their shirts untucked in a vain attempt to reduce the visual impact of their burgeoning girth, and they will reach out and snatch from life whatever she offers, and they will be grateful for it.

"Fuckin' cold out there, eh?" he says, as he slides a hand into the breast pocket of his jacket. He pulls out a twisted cigarette and a lighter. He licks the end of the joint and pops it in his mouth. He lights it, inhales long and deep, holds the smoke in his lungs a half-minute. He tilts his head toward the ceiling and exhales a funnel like an industrial chimney up at the Carver Company mines. He sighs and smiles.

"Toke?" he says, and holds the joint out to the group — an offering.

His eyes, though, are on the girl.

Ten

There are few places to which a man in a small town can escape once the walls begin to close in and the memories start. There is the tavern at the Station Hotel with its mouldy reek of floorboards made wet from spilled beer, the spattering of garden-variety losers nursing their drinks, playing dollar-a-game pool. So McKelvey sits at the counter of the Coffee Time, sipping a fecund coffee and picking at a stale cherry stick. The place is empty at this hour, half past ten, except for a lone pensioner seated by the windows with a bowl of chili and a dated copy of *The Mining News*. In one of life's sour ironies, gold is on the upswing, and nickel, too, thanks to the requirement of both resources in the manufacture of today's modern accoutrements. Too bad the reserves of both minerals are on the decline, at least in these parts. In Africa they seem to find new veins and deposits with the digging of every new hole in the ground.

It has been strange walking around town, for he has often recognized the traces of youth in a passing face. An old schoolmate, perhaps. How odd to stand on a sidewalk and look into the eyes of someone you have not seen in decades, to squint and morph away the crow's feet and the silver hair, to erase the forty pounds, to understand the fact of your own aging set against this living measuring stick — and within it all, to also understand the shortness of time, the single breath that leaves your lips between the starting point and the finish line. There was Gerry Bines, who used to try and build stink bombs with McKelvey back in Grade 4, retired now from the accounting department at the Carver Company. And there was Clifford Martin, as skinny as ever but now bald as a polished bearing, still stuttering his Ts. And all McKelvey could think about as they stood and tried to catch up on forty years was the time they were playing hockey on the river and Clifford pissed his pants because he got hit so hard in the kidneys.

Now McKelvey watches Peggy moving behind the counter. She owns something he can't quite put his finger on, but he believes it falls between confidence and indifference, a quiet grace here in the midst of decline.

"You weren't born here. So tell me," McKelvey says, "how did you end up in a place like Saint B? There must be a story there."

Peggy leans in and sets her elbows on the counter. Her dark hair is pulled back in a ponytail and she is wearing makeup around her green eyes. McKelvey has never noticed the tiny dark birthmark on the left side of her upper lip. Like the Queen of France. He can't remember the name.

"There's always a story," she says. "Usually boring or cliché."

"Jesus," he says, and laughs. "Let me piece it together then. Let's see." He leans back now on the stool and surveys her as though she is a piece of abstract art that he is trying to understand. "You were born and raised in Maidstone, Saskatchewan. Your parents were missionaries for an

Episcopalian church. No, wait. Baptist. And you lived in a series of small and boring prairie towns. Until you met a guy when you were seventeen at a fall fair. Guy worked a ride, probably that strawberry that turns around in circles. And then you —"

Peggy is smiling now, and McKelvey is smiling and pleased that he has made her smile — for the smile changes her whole face, as though a mask has fallen to the floor and the real Peggy is here for just a moment, a glimpse of what she looked like as a child.

"This is painful," she says. "And you call yourself a detective?"

He shrugs, and says, "I didn't say I was a good one."

"You're right about one thing. I did meet a guy when I was seventeen. He wasn't a carnie, but it was close. He was a miner. I was born and raised in Winnipeg. My dad was a lit prof at the university and my mom was a nurse. Normal childhood, no skeletons, no trauma. I met Davey at a summer barbecue. He was nineteen and working in Sudbury. He was home to visit some friends, and he had a brand new motorcycle. This black Harley-Davidson. God, it sounded like the end of the world when he started that thing up. He always had a roll of cash. He was fun. And dangerous."

"What is it with girls and bad boys? Do you really think you're going to change them? And if you did, if you succeeded, they wouldn't be dangerous anymore. It would defeat the purpose."

"Go ask a psychiatrist that one, Charlie. All I know is that he was handsome and he was independent. We drank together, too. That was our connection, really. We partied a lot in those days. I mean *a lot*."

Peggy straightens up and folds her arms across her chest. She gets lost there in memory. McKelvey knows all about that, and so he sips the coffee in silence and then pushes the mug aside. He isn't about to ask her to finish the story. He has a pretty good idea how and where it ends. It is one of the unfortunate side effects of a lifetime of police work; his curiosity is close to non-existent, for human nature is predictable.

"And you?" she asks. "What's your story?"

McKelvey shrugs. His story. *History*. Everything is now in the past tense. He was a father, a husband, a cop. Now he is simply closer to the end than the middle, perhaps even closer than he himself can appreciate. There are forces at work within his bloodstream, forces whose primary objective is to decode, dismantle, destroy.

"Born and raised here," McKelvey says. "Left at seventeen and joined the force in Toronto when I turned eighteen. Met a girl, got married. We had a boy."

"Where are they now, your wife and son?"

"They're not with me. Or I'm not with them. I can never remember which."

"Sounds like the abbreviated version."

She smiles at him with eyes of compassion or shared understanding. It reminds him of the way the schoolteacher, Tim Fielding, used to look at him all the time, after they met at the men's grief group at the hospital. This look that said, *I know how you're feeling, I really do, even if there are no words that we can use to spell this out.*

"Top-up?" She reaches for a pot of coffee.

He shakes his head. "I have a confession to make."

"I know," she says, and smiles. "The coffee tastes like crap."

The wail of a siren makes Peggy jump, and she almost spills some coffee. McKelvey swivels and looks out the window. A police cruiser races past, lights flashing, strobing bands of blue and white bounce across the walls inside the Coffee Time.

"Must be an accident out on the highway," she says.

Peggy bites her bottom lip, staring out the window as though the darkness out there holds some answer. "I wonder," she says. "I should call Shirley."

"Who's Shirley?"

"Shirley Murdoch. She does dispatch for the cops and the ambulance. Fire, too."

McKelvey shakes his head, marvelling at the simplicity of life in a small town. There is something both refreshing and dangerous about having everything out in the open, about knowing who everybody is, what they do, and how they do it. He listens as Peggy says a few words into the telephone, nods. She hangs up and turns to McKelvey, shaking her head.

"Saint B is going to hell. Some kid just got stabbed in the washroom at the arcade. Pete Younger just called for backup. Drugs, I bet you any money."

Sure enough, in a moment another cruiser drives past the coffee shop, lights flashing, snow flying in its wake.

"That'll be Ed Nolan rushing over even though he should be in bed," Peggy says. "At this rate they're going to need to hire another cop around here."

"I miss the peace and quiet of Toronto," McKelvey says.

Eleven

On the fringe of the town proper, straddling the township limits, there is a mobile home nestled in thick woods set about half a kilometre in from the road. The laneway is gravel and grass, and in winter it is hardly ever ploughed to a flat plain. There are deep tire ruts produced from a three-quarter-ton pickup truck with illegal chains on the tires, the drift between the ruts so high it scrapes the undercarriage of the police cruiser as Nolan negotiates his way. At one point he is forced to stop and alternate between forward and reverse, rocking back and forth in order to clear the hard-packed ridge. It sounds as though the ragged snow and ice could rip the muffler and exhaust system clear off the vehicle.

"I'll just wait in the truck while you go on about your business," McKelvey says. He is turned to the window, trying to fathom this sea of whiteness that threatens to swallow them. "Seeing as how you lied to me and all. 'Just a quick stop on the way to this emergency meeting with the Chief and the mayor.'

I have to admit, that was slick, Constable. Mailbox back there said 'Garson.' I know about this family."

"I'm sorry, Charlie," Nolan says. He turns to McKelvey and tries to smile. His face appears boyishly uncertain; his eyebrows seem always to be in the midst of elevation. "I figured it was the only way to get you out with me on this. First Travis Lacey and now this Mark Watson kid stabbed in the washroom at the arcade. Over drugs. I need your help. And it's not really a lie. It is just a quick stop on the way to the meeting at the mayor's office."

"Like I said, I'll just stay nice and warm in here. You do what you've got to do. Just be sure to leave the keys with me in case this guy gets a crazy idea and blows you away. I don't feel like walking back to town."

McKelvey winks at the young officer, and Nolan's face visibly blanches. The cruiser clears a curve and the mobile home and its overflowing yard is upon them. It is a spectacle to behold. McKelvey whistles. He counts four, five, six junked vehicles of assorted make and model, scattered and snow-covered, a few of them half covered with blue tarps that flutter in the breeze like so many flags. There are stacks of tires eight and nine high, chains hanging from tree branches as rudimentary hoists, old gallon drums upright and on their sides. The trailer itself is missing four sheets of tin from its siding. The roof sags where it meets the porch, which was an obvious afterthought, thrown together with plywood and steadied on cinder blocks without the benefit of a level. Nolan cuts the engine and the cab falls silent. The engine of the cruiser ticks a few times as the heat burns off. Outside the wind howls and the skeleton branches of the trees seem to undulate, sway as though in time with some unheard beat. This is a lonesome place where anything seems possible.

"You better go on up to the door," McKelvey says. "Whoever is in there knows you're out here. I saw the curtain in the window move as we pulled in."

"I'll buy you a case of beer if you come up with me. You know, give me some tips on how best to turn this guy over."

"Don't drink," McKelvey says. "Besides, we all learn by making mistakes."

Nolan unbuckles his seatbelt and sighs heavily. A dog barks. It barks again and then howls, the sound more wolf than dog.

"Ah, Jesus. I forgot about the pit bull. They had two, but one got shot when the provincial police tactical response unit came in here to arrest Wade's brother, Hank. Sounds like they've still got one, which runs against the court order at least."

"Canine possession as probable cause for entry," McKelvey suggests.

Nolan gives McKelvey one last look. He opens the door and the cold air rushes in. He reaches behind the seat and pulls out a Maglite, long and heavy as a baton. Nolan holds the light and taps the torch end against his palm, testing its weight.

"Shotgun is locked in the back safety box," he tells McKelvey. "Just in case. And here's the keys."

He hands them to McKelvey. The utterance of that single word — *shotgun* — sends a chill through McKelvey. His mind flashes with scenes of the abandoned factory where Tim Fielding was held hostage, where the shootings took place, where Leyden got killed; the place where McKelvey picked up Leyden's police-issue shotgun and made his way through the darkness.

Nolan is at the door, knocking, when a dog springs from around the trailer, all snarling yaps and howls. Nolan swivels and sets the flashlight in his grip. *Damned kid needs all the backup he can get*, McKelvey thinks. *Can't just sit here and watch this.* He gets out of the truck. He takes a few steps and spots something sticking from the snow in the ground, kicks at it and reaches to pick it up. The dog is at Nolan's boots when McKelvey lets out a sharp whistle. The dog's ears rotate like a satellite receiver, and the animal pulls up, turns, and then bounds toward this new target. The dog is pure muscle, underfed mean machinery. McKelvey gets a look at its dead eyes, red as hell itself, just as the beast springs from the ground in its rush for his throat. He sets his feet and waits within the calm centre of this calamity for the perfect moment to thrust his hand forward, to jam the palm-sized rock he has found straight into the jaws of the devil. The dog yelps, confused, and drops sideways to the snow, its yap completely occupied by the stone.

"Holy shit," Nolan says from the front step. "Did he get you?"

McKelvey is breathing hard and fast despite his demeanour of calm. He is terrified, for he has never really understood the domain of the animal world, and yet at the same time he is exhilarated. It is that same feeling he gets any time he has gambled and come out on the winning side, this rush of momentary invincibility. *Fuck, it feels great.* The dog is thrashing its head from side to side, digging its snout into the snow. McKelvey raises his gloved hands and sees that, yes, the dog managed to make contact.

"Just a nip."

Nolan knocks loudly on the door with the butt of the flashlight. McKelvey joins him on the stairs. There is movement from within, the sound of drawers or cupboards closing. A grungy curtain tacked to the door parts to reveal the ugly face that must belong to Wade Garson. His brown hair is stringy and hangs to the shoulder. The curtain falls back into place and the door opens a foot, held there by Wade Garson's left knee. Garson stands there in his jeans and bare feet, his skinny torso naked and plastered with homemade tattoos, crosses and skulls, words which are too faded and poorly inked to decipher. The man is tall, about six foot three, but insufficiently nourished to the point that his ribs can be counted. A cigarette burns between the fingers of his left hand, which hangs at his side. The smoke rises and swirls to his thickly stubbled, wind-chafed face. In his right hand, McKelvey notices, the man grips a rather large crescent wrench.

"Nolan, you dipshit, you better not've hurt my fucking dog," Garson yells.

"I've got a few questions there, Wade—"

But Garson steps forward, a king in his own domain, and he raises the wrench. "I got a few questions of my own," he says, with righteous indignation.

McKelvey does not hesitate. He reaches out, grabs the hand with the wrench and pulls, while at the same time slamming the door shut with a hard push. Garson yells in pain as the wrench hits the step. McKelvey pushes the door all the way open as Garson stumbles back, rubbing his wrist.

"Jesus Christ, that's police brutality," Garson says, bent at the waist, still rubbing his hand as though it has just been freed from a set of too-tight handcuffs. "I'm gonna sue the ass off you dipshits. I'll sue the whole fucking *town*."

"Not so much, dickhead. See, Constable Nolan here is the police." McKelvey wags a thumb toward Nolan. "And he hasn't touched you. Yet."

Nolan follows McKelvey inside the porch. The small room is cluttered with rubber boots, fishing rods and scattered tackle, piles of yellowing newspapers, a ringed stack of assorted hubcaps in a corner. There is a black silk flag tacked to a far wall, a gold cannon with **AC⚡DC** silkscreened above it. There is a lingering stink of stale marijuana smoke, and the whole floor of the porch tilts about a dozen degrees southwest.

"Well, who the fuck are you, then?" Garson says, glaring.

"Maybe I'm from some charity coming out to see if you need a food basket or a haircut … maybe a de-lousing," McKelvey says. "And then your dog out there attacked us. Unprovoked."

"Charity? Well you can't just come in here, you know. This is, like, my private property." Garson looks at Nolan. "You got a warrant there, Officer Dipshit?"

"That's just in the movies," McKelvey says. "Look, we're here. You invited us in. Remember?"

"All right, all right, settle down, the two of you," Nolan says, regaining his footing here, likely remembering that he is, after all, the only legal authority in the room. "Listen, I just want to ask you a few questions, Wade. And then we'll get out of your life."

Nolan tucks the flashlight in his armpit and fishes out a notepad. McKelvey and Garson stare at each other. Garson draws from his cigarette and blows a funnel toward McKelvey's face. But McKelvey doesn't take the bait. He simply smiles and lets Nolan run through his questions.

"You still hanging and drying weed out in your back forty, I imagine," Nolan says.

"No, Officer." Garson smiles, revealing a set of dirty, crooked teeth.

"You're still selling it by the gram down at the Station and the arcade, I know that much. But I'm not interested in pot today, Wade. I want to talk about crystal meth."

Garson's eyes narrow. He waits, in the practised way an ex-con learns to pause before speaking. He wants to understand the context, the potential implications, before he offers up some nugget that will be polished off and used to hang him.

"I have good intelligence on this. There's meth moving in Saint B. I can't imagine someone coming in here without you knowing it. You'd never accept that sort of disrespect, would you, Wade?"

McKelvey nods. He likes what he hears coming from the young cop. His natural instinct has told him to focus on pride.

For a bottom feeder like Wade Garson, it's about all he has.

"Bullshit. I don't know nothin' about cooking no meth," Garson says.

"Who said anything about cooking? I'm talking about moving the stuff. Someone is selling it to these kids. Mark Watson got stabbed last night up at the arcade. He's in the hospital in Timmins, and Scotty Cooper is sitting in the holding cells waiting for the Crown attorney to make her way up here. I imagine you heard all about that."

"I heard about it," Garson says. "But what the hell's it got to do with me?"

"Both Mark and Scotty were higher than kites when we got there. Clear out of their heads. Mark didn't even know he had been stabbed, the blood pumping out of his stomach between his fingers. I suggest you think long and hard now, Wade. You know or you've heard through the grapevine. I know you do. Who's bringing meth into Saint B?"

Garson takes a last drag of the cigarette, pinches the ash end, and tosses the butt into an old paint can to join a hundred other dead smokes. He blows the smoke above his head and scratches his scrawny belly. He goes to say something but stops himself and shakes his head.

"I'm not sayin' another word to you two jackoffs until you charge me and get me one of those legal aid lawyers. Are you gonna charge me, Nolan?"

"I told you, Wade, I just wanted to ask you a few questions. Give you a chance to help us and help yourself." Nolan closes the notebook and pockets it. "But I guess the Chief was right. He said you were a lost cause. Just like all the Garsons."

Garson's eyes flare and the veins in his neck spring out like cords as he clenches his jaw. He wants to do something about this, to not let the comment stand, but he glances between the two men and thinks better of it.

"Some other day," he says, "I'll teach you some god-damned manners."

"I look forward to the instruction," Nolan says.

"Only don't bring your dad here," Garson says. "Just you and little old me."

Nolan nods and turns, pushes open the door. McKelvey backs out of the porch, never taking his eyes off Wade Garson, who stares with cold hatred. It is starting to snow now, thick flakes languidly falling, and the formerly ominous woods now appear new and peaceful. It reminds McKelvey of the cover on a Christmas card. There is no sign of the dog, so McKelvey believes the animal has figured out how to dislodge the rock from its yap and has found a place to lick its wounds. Nolan starts the vehicle and does a three-point turn, heads them back out the way they came.

The two men sit on the side of the highway in silence for a time. A single transport truck loaded with lengths of freshly cut timber roars past. And then Nolan sighs and says, "I appreciate your help back there. But listen, Charlie. I want to do this job on the up and up. I cut corners all my life until I came back here, back home. I know it probably sounds pathetic to you, being a big-city cop and everything, but I want to uphold the law here in Saint B. I want to be an example."

"I understand, Ed. You invited me along to this shit show. You wanted to see how I'd turn this guy over, squeeze some information out of him. Well, there you go. You got to see it up close. You also have to understand that I don't have a job to lose. So I might be the best or worst partner you'll ever have. Either way, that's how I would have played it back in the city or here in town. You've got to be in control from the moment that door opens. Let's get going. We don't want to keep the mayor and your boss waiting."

McKelvey is disappointed only as far as he has let this young cop down. Otherwise, he could care less about Wade Garson or his dog, or the trampling of the man's rights as guaranteed by the Constitution. On the streets, there is only one charter of rights, and that is the right to live or die, to shoot or be shot. It has been so long since he included the moral or ethical aspect to any weighting or valuation that he marvels at Nolan's honesty and purity. The kid is not naive, far from it. He is simply the real deal. Ed Nolan is a lawman. *Goddamn*, McKelvey thinks. *This is me twenty years ago …*

* * *

Dear Journal,

I had a dream the other night. I was walking through a huge room crowded with people, this room that never seemed to end. All these people I've known in my life were there. Caroline, Hattie, schoolteachers, cops I worked with over the years, perps I put away were all there patting me on the back as I passed through, Jessie and Emily were there, neighbours from the old street, even the Italian who lives on the first floor of my building back in the city, Huff my bartender at Garrity's. But Gavin wasn't there. I kept waiting. I kept smiling at people and pushing past them. Finally I got to the end of the room, to this wall, and I turned around and started back through the crowd. I kept looking for his face, his dark hair and that cowlick. The more people crowded around me, the harder I had to push through them. And then I saw the back of his head. I knew it was him, and I called his name. But he wouldn't turn around. I kept calling his name. And then I woke up. I felt sick and ripped off. I had this idea running through my head like the lines from a song. I wrote them down and then fell back asleep. When I woke up later, I tried to read the words I had written, but it was all just scribbling. I could have cried.

Twelve

They are assembled in the mayor's office, drinking from Coffee Time cups, a box of doughnuts open on the desk. The office is small and modest, little more than a desk and three chairs, a bookcase filled with titles on municipal law and infrastructure development. There are framed pictures across one wall, shots of the mayor smiling and cutting ribbons or shaking hands with old people. The photos are all old, from a decade ago or more. The mayor, Danny Marko, stands up when Nolan and McKelvey walk in. Chief Gallagher nods, and Carl Levesque smiles his toothy smile. His lips are powdered from the jelly doughnut he is eating.

"Constable Nolan, Mr. McKelvey," the mayor says, motioning them to sit down, although there is only one vacant chair. "Thanks for joining us this morning. You especially, Mr. McKelvey. Constable Nolan here says we're fortunate you decided to return home when you did. I guess we'll see about that."

"Constable Pete Younger can't join us. He's down to the hospital in Timmins to get a statement from Mark Watson.

Kid had a four-inch blade perforate his bowel," Gallagher says, and shakes his head.

McKelvey is surprised to see Levesque here, but he supposes that Levesque could be considered a significant stakeholder in the community, in that he owns a good number of the old Carver Company houses and has plans for the future. Both McKelvey and Nolan stand, moving to the sides of the room so they can lean against the walls.

"Constable Nolan, you interviewed Scotty Cooper early this morning about his altercation with Mark Watson," Gallagher continues. "He's to be transferred to Monteith later this morning. Second local kid we've shipped down to the detention centre in a week. He say anything of value, Ed?"

Nolan pulls his black notepad from the side pocket on his winter jacket. He flips a few pages, scans his writing quickly.

"He's despondent." Nolan raises his head to look around the room. It is as though he has never had to use that word applied to any situation here in Saint B. "Suffering the effects of narcotics. Coming down, his eyes are red and dilated, and he's not making much sense. He goes from ranting about Mark, to just crying and rocking. He's scared. I asked him where he got the drugs and he said the arcade. I asked from who, and he said from nobody. I asked him again, who sold you the drugs, and he said, quote, 'they were just there,' end quote."

"He won't finger the seller," says Gallagher. "This generation and their bullshit code. Don't snitch. Well, anything else of note?"

Nolan scans his writing and closes his book. "Maybe in a day or two when Scott Cooper has detoxed we can talk to him again."

"We've got a serious issue here, boys," Danny Marko says, and shakes his head slowly to punctuate the gravity of the moment. He is a squat man with a small pot belly and a round face. He wears a moustache, which comes in too thin, giving him the appearance of a teenager trying to look older than his years. "Mark Watson is in critical condition. They've got him stabilized but he's not out of the woods yet. And Scotty Cooper, I know his family. I hunt with his father, for God's sake. What the hell is happening here?"

Chief Gallagher sets his coffee cup on the edge of the desk. He leans back in the chair and folds his arms across his chest. He is dressed in khaki pants and a cable-knit sweater with a thickly coiled roll-up neck. The moustache he wears is thin and trim and silver. McKelvey thinks the man looks more like a mutual fund adviser than a cop.

"Best we can tell, it was a drug deal gone wrong," Gallagher says, as though this sort of thing happens all the time in a small town. He looks down at his own hands and shakes his head. "Methamphetamine," he says quietly, as though in speaking the word he might better understand its power.

"Drug deal? Methamphetamine? This is Saint B, not goddamned *Toronto*." Marko's eyes flash to the visitor, the politician careful not to offend. "No offence, Mr. McKelvey."

"None taken. I was born here."

"True enough," Marko says. "We're glad you could spend some time with us this morning. Constable Nolan here suggested your experience in the city could be of benefit under these, uh, less than ideal circumstances."

"I don't think we need to be pulling any alarms here, Danny," Gallagher says. "This is something we can and will deal with from the inside. What we need right now is strong, steady leadership. Not kneejerk reactions."

Marko rests back in his chair and smiles. "Well, Gallagher, when you're sitting in this seat one day, you'll get to provide all the strong, steady leadership that you want." He then pulls upright and the smile falls from his face. "Until that day, I'm the mayor and you're an employee of this township. I won't be undermined, not in here and not out on the street."

Gallagher nods once. He uses a thumb and forefinger to smooth his moustache.

"The Crown is coming in this week," Gallagher says. "There's some buzz down in the city about the Lacey attack and now this stabbing. Two attempt murder charges in a week. We'll need to have a briefing ready for this woman. Nolan, you up to the paperwork?"

"Consider it done."

"The truth is, this isn't just a drugs or a teenage problem for us," Marko says. "Saint B is hanging on by a thread. The provincial police have been taking over the policing in small towns all over the province. It's cheaper than running your own small force. Our days may be numbered. We need to be able to show the people of Saint B that we can protect them better than outsiders with no roots in this town. We've got some economic development opportunities that could change the fortunes of this place and turn things around one-eighty. Kids stabbing each other isn't good for business."

Levesque wipes a dab of lemon jelly from the corner of his mouth with the back of his hand, and says, "I couldn't agree more. We need to nip this in the bud before potential investors get scared and run down the road to Kirkland Lake or some fucking place like Cobalt. What about a search of the lockers up at the high school?"

"You leave the policing to us, Carl," Gallagher says.

"What policing is that again?"

"You just remember who's got your back around here."

"Enough with the pissing match," Marko pipes up. "I'll expect an update on this in twenty-four hours. Let me know what you've found out, where this shit is coming from, and what your plan is."

The men all begin to move, standing from their chairs, uncrossing arms. McKelvey follows Nolan to the door, and Marko says, "Hey, Eddie, you make sure our guest here has whatever he needs. We can use all the help we can get."

Gallagher shoots Marko a look, but the mayor just smiles, pleased with himself.

"Nolan," Gallagher says, "wait up there a minute."

Outside the air is cold and clean. Flakes melt on contact with warm flesh, bead like drops of rain. Gallagher looks agitated.

"Listen, Nolan," he says, and then looks over at McKelvey. "I didn't want to say anything in front of Marko and Levesque, but I got a call right before this meeting from Harry Griffith. You know Harry Griffith, right?"

Nolan nods. "Scumbag defence lawyer for all the reprobates of the North. Garson family has him on speed-dial, I bet."

"My point exactly. Harry goddamned Griffith called me not fifteen minutes ago." Gallagher leans in closer, and his volume drops by half. "Seems he got a call from Wade Garson about you and your new partner here abusing him in his home without so much as a warrant."

"Abusing him," Nolan repeats. He can't stop the small smile from turning his lip.

"Wipe that grin off your face, Constable." Gallagher's eyes flash with anger, the veins on his temple rise like turgid worms beneath the flesh. "I'm in enough of a jam these days without having that scumbag Harry Griffith climbing up my ass. Now smarten up."

Gallagher looks over to McKelvey, who has taken a few steps to the side to offer some space.

"That knock on the head must have driven out some common sense," Gallagher says, and then shakes his head. He has nothing else to say. He looks up at Nolan and his face folds on itself, a father who is not angry, but disappointed. "You best head on over and talk with Miss Laney at the arcade. Go easy, Eddie. And keep an eye on your friend here."

*   *   *

The snowfall is gaining strength, the flakes coming down thick and heavy. An inch has covered the cruiser during the twenty minutes the men gathered in the mayor's office. Nolan brushes the vehicle clean while McKelvey sits inside, the engine running, his mind running. He has little interest in this turn of events. Rather, he wants to get back to the Station Hotel and talk to the old-timers about the strike and the violence that came with it, that dark year in Saint B's history. He wants to understand once and for all his father's place within a past unspoken.

He watches as the world around him becomes clear, as Nolan brushes away the snow from the windshield. The day is bright but grey as gun metal and he finds himself squinting. This thing right now, sure, what he would do is talk to the most connected teacher up at the high school, get a lay of the land. Talk to the local pharmacist. Talk to whoever runs the arcade, talk to the kid who was stabbed ...

Nolan jumps in, removes and sets his gloves between the seats. He claps his hands together and blows into them. McKelvey can feel the younger man's eyes on him.

"So," Nolan says. "What are you thinking?"

"I'm thinking your boss and the mayor have opposing views on my involvement here. I'm also thinking Chief Gallagher sees himself running for mayor in next fall's election. Neither thought makes me overly eager. I don't have a good track record for — how would you say it — playing politics."

Nolan nods and puts the cruiser in reverse. Main Street is empty. The snow is coming in on an angle, the plump flakes hypnotic framed through the windshield. Space and time cease to exist as they shuttle through the swirling white labyrinth. McKelvey remembers now how quickly the snow can obliterate the world up here, how it can become both the alpha and the omega, north and south. He recalls storms that seemed to be alive with energy, almost a human character, tricking mortals by slowing for a time and then surging back. It is for this reason the people of Ste. Bernadette became accustomed to holding an emergency stock of non-perishables in a cellar — cans of soup, crackers, tuna and sardines, candles, matches, batteries.

"I don't trust Carl Levesque," Nolan says. He is sitting straight, hands at two and ten o'clock. "This deal he keeps talking about, land for a casino and resort. I heard he's been meeting with the chief and economic officer over at the reserve. He wants to run shuttle buses from all the smaller communities and reserves into Saint B so folks can feed their pension and welfare cheques into slot machines."

"Where is he getting the seed money?" McKelvey asks. "He'd need into the seven figures to get a venture like that off the ground."

"I guess that's why I don't trust him. Guy like Levesque, I mean, come on. He's a comb salesman. Where would he get that kind of backing unless it was dirty money?"

"There are ways to look into his business. Discreetly. See if he's up to date on his income tax, how many bank accounts he's got in his name, that sort of thing. What they used to call skip tracing. The collection agencies have these guys who are bad or worse than cops. The good ones can sniff shit on a shoe from a hundred miles away."

"Skip tracing," Nolan repeats, and nods. He stares into the swirling white void ahead. "You be able to help me with that sort of thing?"

"I know a guy down in Toronto. Real dirtbag, but probably the best skip tracer in the world. I'll give him a call and introduce you. It'll cost you, though. He works by the hour, regardless of what he finds."

"Let's start there," Nolan says. "If there's dirty money coming around Saint B, I don't think it's a coincidence that we've got this meth coming in, too. For all I know, Carl Levesque could be backed by the mob out of Thunder Bay."

McKelvey smiles. He likes what he hears from the young cop. He turns to the side window and rubs the fog with his gloved hand. His work reveals a world of pure whiteness. He squints against the brightness. There's Main Street, the main artery of his hometown. And it looks for an instant like the idyllic scene in a snow globe. He's a kid again, standing in his pyjamas at the kitchen window, mesmerized by the innocence and simple joy of falling snow. For a fleeting moment he is filled with what he believes must be a sense of gratitude. For this life, this moment. *He is alive.*

"Just to be clear," McKelvey says, looking out the window, "I'm not working with you. My police days are done."

"I can respect that," Nolan says, and nods. "I'll get you home now."

They drive in silence for a long moment, cruising down Main Street.

"You don't mind if I just make a few stops on the way," Nolan says, and he can't hide the smile.

Thirteen

T he machines ping and whir in the dimly lit arcade while lights flash and snap like technicolour paparazzi. It's mid-morning, and despite it being a school day a dozen kids stand or sit or slouch in front of the video games. These places have always depressed McKelvey for some reason he can't quite put a finger on. It's the same with carnivals, and he wonders now if this notion has stuck with him ever since he was a boy and the fall fair would come through town. Strangers arriving in their old trucks hauling dented chrome rides, these filthy and bedraggled men falling out of vans and old school buses to set about constructing a temporary fun-land in some empty field. There seemed to be no genuine delight on the faces of those hung-over and dark-eyed workers as they barked out the rules and chances for their games — *three balls for a dollar!* — and McKelvey's father would always say just under his breath how it was all rigged. The workers were mostly ex-cons down on their luck, Grey McKelvey would say, and the rides were probably all missing important parts.

"These games all a dollar?" McKelvey asks, checking out a machine by the door that features some sort of alien robots under attack from other alien robots.

"Mostly. Some are two bucks."

"Jesus, kids must get some allowance these days."

McKelvey has opted to join Nolan rather than sit in the cruiser as it cools off. One street behind Main, the arcade is sufficiently tucked away from the eyes of parents and teachers seeking truant students. The teens look over at the two men now and whisper as though they are seeing Halley's Comet, a once-in-a-lifetime spectacle to behold.

McKelvey is used to this treatment, and then some. Walking into an after-hours club up in the hornet's nest of Jane and Finch in Toronto nets a cop more than dirty looks, it's taking your life in your hands. For some reason he thinks of the murder of Constable Todd Bayliss, shot to death by a Jamaican who had been scheduled for deportation. His mind flashes with images of that hot summer of 1994. The racial tensions were high following the killing of a white woman at the hands of black robbers at the Just Desserts Café in Yorkville, then the killing of the bright young cop.

He and Nolan make their way over to a middle-aged woman reading a paperback behind a counter stocked with candy bars and licorice that looks as dried and tough as leather. She sets the book on the counter. The title on the spine is *Evening Snow Will Bring Such Peace*. McKelvey isn't convinced.

"Laney," Nolan says, and gives a little nod.

The woman smiles and nods and shrugs at the same time. Laney is a compact woman — or "petite" if McKelvey were using the vernacular of the day — but she exudes a strength within her small frame. She wears no makeup and is pretty in a sort of tomboy fashion. Her brown hair is tied back but some strands have escaped and fall loose at the side of her face. The fine wrinkles engraved across her upper lip tell McKelvey the woman has likely smoked for the better part of her life.

"Officer Nolan," she says.

"Back in business, I see." Nolan turns to survey the room.

"Can't afford a day off. I don't have a town pension. Every buck popped into one of those machines means there's a chance I might clear my rent this month, and who knows, maybe even eat."

"This is Charlie McKelvey," Nolan says with some pride, a boy showing off a new friend to the neighbourhood. "He's a friend of mine."

McKelvey nods and holds out a hand, which Laney grips with the strength of a dock worker. Her eyes hold him in a confident gaze that is venturing toward defiant.

"We just wanted to come by and ask a few questions," Nolan continues. "You were understandably upset the other night."

"Having kids stab each other in your business tends to be upsetting."

"Scotty Cooper said he got drugs here, from the arcade," McKelvey says, jumping straight in. He can't help himself.

Laney turns her whole body to regard McKelvey for a moment.

"Imagine that," she says finally. "Drugs in an arcade. Like doughnuts in a police station. It comes with the territory, guys. Cut me some slack. I don't strip-search the kids when they come in here. But I sure as hell don't allow them to smoke dope or sell it within eyesight. I'm one person. What they do in the washroom is beyond my reach. Why don't you ask their parents what they're doing?"

McKelvey looks around. He catches and holds the glare of a tall teenage boy. The boy stares back with eyes of pure hatred. McKelvey recognizes the look, understands something of the philosophy that drives this attitude. As he did with his own boy, with words that fell on closed ears, he could tell this kid the truth about life. The unalterable fact of the matter is that life and man work in reverse of each other, in that a man owns more swagger when he knows nothing of the world than once he has tasted the bitterness of longing and loss, despair and defeat. McKelvey supposes there is no magic to this; it is simply the power of humility to remind a man of his insignificance. Teenagers are not only the centre of their own narcissistic universe, they are the sun and the moon and the gravitational pull all at once.

"They sell dope in the washrooms, sure," McKelvey says, turning back to Laney. "A few grams here and there. But what about adults? What about strangers? Anybody strike you as out of place coming or going from the arcade in the past couple of months?"

Laney thinks, chewing her bottom lip a little.

"Wade Garson?" Nolan offers.

McKelvey cringes inside, for the young officer is leading. It is akin to putting words or memories in the mouth of a witness. He makes a mental note to point out the behaviour once they are alone. A good cop never corrects his partner in public.

"Sure," Laney says. "Wade comes in two or three times a month, I guess."

"We know he does," says Nolan. "We know he moves marijuana around town."

"And she knows, too," McKelvey says. "Don't you? I'd say Wade Garson even gives you a cut off the top. Either in cash or in product."

Laney looks over to the group of kids huddled at a racing game. She looks back to Nolan and McKelvey.

"I don't sell drugs," she says. "I don't allow kids to smoke in here."

McKelvey leans in and folds his arms across the counter. He has been here a thousand times before. Working the Hold-up

Squad, it was always a variation of the same interview, the same perp, the same stupid lies that always led to the same places.

"It's how it works," McKelvey says. "You're a business owner who can hardly make ends meet. Catch as catch can, right? So you take a few grams or a few bucks and turn your back while Wade heads to the men's room. No harm done."

Nolan seems now like a spectator at a duel. He is no longer on the inside of this, but on the periphery.

"Mark Watson was stabbed right over there in that washroom," Laney says, visibly upset. "You think I want anything to happen to these kids? Jesus Christ, Eddie, you knew me when you were a little kid around here. I went away, you know, I got out of this shithole. But I came back to work in the lab at Carver. Stupid me. And when I lost my job, well, what was there to do? This place was sitting boarded up for more than a year. I went out on a limb to get it up and running again. So you ask the kids around here, Mr. McKelvey. Ask them where they go when they're cold or lonely or just want to get away from the fighting that goes on in their homes. They come here, that's where."

McKelvey is about to comment on the touching nature of the monologue, something about the woman's altruism, when Nolan steps inside the circle once again.

"Laney, you're not in trouble here. We just want to know what's going on around Saint B. Where do you think the kids are getting the meth from?"

She sits back and sighs, and folds her arms across her chest.

"I wish I knew. I mean, there haven't been any strangers around that I know of. There's that Italian-looking guy from the U.S. He's been in a couple of times to kill the hours. Doesn't talk much. He changes like fifty bucks at a time and plays the shooting and hunting games over there. And, of course, locals. There's Carl."

"Carl Levesque?" McKelvey asks.

She nods.

"He comes by every couple of weeks. Pathetic, actually. He thinks he might have a shot with the girls. It's like watching a train wreck, how he comes out of the washroom with his comb-over all slicked back. I'm pretty sure he smokes pot and shares a joint once in a while with the older kids. But I can't prove it."

Nolan gives McKelvey a sideways glance.

"Thanks, Laney," Nolan says. "We'll give you a call if anything else comes to mind."

They take a couple of steps and then McKelvey pulls a classic Columbo tactic. He stops and turns back as though he has suddenly remembered an important question.

"You went away," he says. "To school?"

Laney nods. "University of Toronto. The big city."

"Do you miss it?"

"Toronto? It's like an old boyfriend, I guess. I only miss it once in a while, and always for the wrong reasons."

McKelvey smiles at her.

"I hope your dad's doing okay," Laney says to Nolan in a softer, friendlier voice. It can be no other way in a small town. Once official business is conducted, they are free to be their real selves once again.

"Thanks," Nolan says.

The daylight is nearly blinding as they step outside. The silence rings in their ears now that they are removed from the constant hum and thrum of the video games.

McKelvey stops and glances back. "I don't know how she sits in there all day and all night."

"She's right, though," Nolan says. "If this place closes, where will they go?"

"I'm sure Carl Levesque would take them in ... the girls, anyway."

They climb into the cruiser and Nolan turns the engine. "You think she's in on this? Moving the drugs?" he asks.

McKelvey certainly believes the woman allows Wade Garson to peddle marijuana with impunity, likely for a kickback of one form or another. At the very least, she knows full well what goes on under her roof, and in this way she is morally, if not criminally, implicit.

"She knows the arcade is the place for drug deals," he answers, "but whether she knows anything about the movement of meth, who knows. When you interviewed Scott Cooper, he said the drugs were just there."

Nolan nods. "That's right. He did. Verbatim. 'They were just there,' he said."

"Maybe someone left the drugs in the washroom," McKelvey offers.

"By accident or on purpose?"

"Maybe both. Dealers in the city who work the parks and malls and high-school hangouts usually give kids one or two freebies; a little baggie to whet your whistle. When you go looking for more, there's a cost."

"Makes sense. Laney probably only checks the washrooms once or twice a week. Would be easy enough to leave some packets out where the kids would be sure to find them. And I know for a fact Wade Garson has left marijuana in the can for some of the boys."

"We'll suppose that for now. Until something else makes sense."

McKelvey then turns to the younger man and asks, "So, did Laney babysit you when you were a kid or something?"

Nolan blushes a little.

"Actually, yeah, she did."

*   *   *

Their next canvass takes them to Gaylord's Drugs on Main Street. They could have walked over in five minutes from the arcade, but McKelvey has Nolan park the cruiser right in front of the drug store.

"Mr. Gaylord won't like us taking up a spot in front like this," Nolan says. "He tries to save it for the older customers who pull up like it's a drive-thru."

"We want the good people of Ste. Bernadette to see you out doing your job, Nolan. Police work is one part process, one part luck, and one part optics. This is their tax dollars at work. Makes them sleep better at night."

Stepping into Gaylord's Drugs — which as far back as McKelvey's own childhood has been a source of giggles and endless variations on poking fun at that name — is like stepping into a time machine. It is the 1950s again, and McKelvey is standing just inside the door, smelling the perfume of this place: *freshly rolled gauze, pine floor polish, a top note of something bitter and chemical, like the powder from crushed pills.* The layout is the same. Four aisles of bandages and cold medicines, feminine products, hair dyes, toothbrushes, a turning rack of dime novels at the front, the drug counter along the back. McKelvey pauses at the book rack and gives it a slow spin. Zane Grey. David Goodis. Elmore Leonard. Pulp fiction and westerns and war novels, romances with torrid covers painted in glossy oils. This is the very place McKelvey whiled away long hours as his mother got snarled up in local gossip during her "quick stop in" to fetch a prescription.

McKelvey is surprised to find that Ethan Gaylord, the grandson of the founder, Harold Gaylord, has followed in the family tradition. He is thirty-five years old and the spitting image of his father and grandfather. Tall, thin, with stretched, blanched flesh that is nearly alabaster. You can see the blue veins spread beneath his temples and cheeks like a road map.

He wears his blond hair longer than his previous generations, and it is combed back.

"Officer Nolan," he says, standing three feet above them on a raised platform. Dressed in a white smock, with his pale skin and golden hair, he looks like a member of the choir hovering above the masses. The counter is accessible by entering a swing door that locks from the inside. Behind Gaylord there are shelves upon shelves of drugs in boxes and large bottles. McKelvey does the same thing he did when he was a kid, which is to scan those shelves, wondering what in the hell all these different drugs are for, imagining grotesque afflictions, picturing old Harold Gaylord grinding powders in his bowl for Mrs. Tavistock's bulging goitre, this bizarre and mysterious world of the apothecary.

"Ethan." Nolan nods. "How's business?"

Gaylord continues to count pills, dividing them three at a time with a wooden tongue depressor. "The same," he says in a voice eerily similar to his grandfather's. "I'm down to one assistant two days a week. I would close if I had any sense. But then where would that leave the seventy percent of Saint B that happens to be over the age of sixty-five?"

"Tough times all around," Nolan says.

"We need our damned mayor to step up to the plate." Gaylord pauses in his work and raises his eyes to his guests. "This idea that we can wait until hydro contracts are signed and all these thousands of linesmen come up here to build new transmission, well, I'll be retired or bankrupt by then. We need immediate action."

"I hear you," Nolan says. "Listen, this here is my colleague, Charlie McKelvey."

McKelvey nods. Gaylord scans the face and nods his familial recognition.

"Your father was Grey McKelvey, yes?"

"That's him. I remember coming in here when I was sick

and my mother talking with your father or grandfather. They were both working behind there at one time. I'd always leave with a lollipop."

"Not many kids around these days," Gaylord says.

"Speaking of kids," Nolan breaks in, seeing his opening, "what do you think about all of this news about meth going around Saint B?"

Gaylord is finished counting the pills. He sets his hands on the counter and looks down on his visitors as though he is about to deliver Mass. He takes a moment to gather his thoughts. He is a man used to measuring, counting, ensuring all the proper steps are followed.

"With all due respect, I'd have to question the effectiveness of our local constabulary," he says. "I'm not an expert in recreational drugs, but I can tell you, from what I know, the production of methamphetamine is dangerous but easy. And once entered into a society, especially one as closed as Saint B, it is very difficult to root out."

Nolan's cheeks have turned a deep shade of red in response to the pharmacist's admonishment.

"One of the key ingredients in meth is cold medicine, is that correct?" McKelvey asks.

"Specifically, pseudoephedrine."

"In English?"

"Sinus medicine. Sudafed and Contac and the like."

McKelvey scans the rows of lozenges and throat sprays and boxes of over-the-counter cold and sinus medicines that fill the space along Gaylord's drug counter. He picks out a box and holds it up to read the ingredients on the side.

"So, like this right here?" McKelvey shakes the box.

"Correct."

Nolan reaches into his coat and produces his notepad and short pencil. He makes a few notes and then says, "So Ethan, you notice any missing stock in the last few months? I mean, of this sinus medicine."

Now it's Gaylord's turn to blush a little. He sighs and his lips work for a moment as he prepares his statement.

"I don't have the help I need," he says. "So my inventory leaves something to be desired of late."

"Surely you'd notice a few dozen boxes going missing," McKelvey says.

Gaylord stares, and then blinks, but he has nothing to say.

"We could help you go through your orders, check against sales," Nolan adds.

"I'll poke around, see what I can find for you."

"I appreciate that," Nolan says. "Be in touch."

Nolan and McKelvey turn for the doors and Gaylord clears his throat.

"One thing, at least," Gaylord says. His face is drawn serious, intense. "Maybe this meth problem is the final straw that we needed in order to get some action around here. Maybe people will sit up and notice this dying little town."

"Let's hope you're wrong about that," Nolan says gravely.

"Mr. McKelvey," the pharmacist calls after them as they turn to leave. He produces a red sucker and holds it out. "For old times."

"Thanks." McKelvey reaches for the sucker, the past flooding back through his body in a physical vibration. He turns the sucker in his fingers and then tucks it in his jacket pocket. How simple life is when you're young, he thinks, the simple and grateful joy of a proffered sweet.

Outside on the sidewalk, standing in the day's strong sunlight and cold, McKelvey turns to Nolan. "If the drug business fails, that guy could always double as an undertaker."

Nolan slips his notepad into his coat and shakes his head. "Gets more depressing around here every day. I'll drop you at home. I have to go and check in on my dad."

They slide inside the cruiser. Nolan picks up the radio and hits the talk button so that the cab fills for a quick moment with a burp of squelch. He lets Shirley Murdoch know that he is booking off to tend to his father.

"Ten-four, doll," the woman replies.

Nolan hangs the mic and pulls away from the curb. "I'll drop you at home," he says. "Since you're not working with me."

McKelvey turns to the young cop and smiles. "Thanks, doll."

Fourteen

McKelvey sits on the edge of the bed and dials Jessie Rainbird's number. It rings seven times and then flips to voicemail. Hearing her recorded voice makes him feel lonely and guilty, and he could almost cry. He hesitates at the beep which announces his invitation to leave a message.

"Uh, Jess …. Yeah, it's just me. It's Charlie, okay? I got your messages there and you shouldn't be worrying about me, kiddo. I'm doing real good. I'm good. I miss you and little Emily there. You tell her that Grandpa said hi, okay? I'm just back up home for a bit but I'll be back soon. Maybe you guys, you know, maybe you could come down to the city for a visit this summer. Anyway …"

It is both a cruel and laughable irony that now, on the precipice of his sixth decade, sick as he is, McKelvey feels he finally owns enough wisdom to make this conundrum not only workable, but probably even enjoyable. That is to say that, within those first bleak hours of sitting in the waiting room at the oncology clinic, or the endless hours spent alone in his apartment within the prison of his thoughts, he came to believe with a genuine confidence that he could, if given the chance, finally be the father, the husband, the cop, the man he was meant to be all along. Two minutes left in the hockey game and McKelvey wants the coach to put him in. All of the insecurity which gets disguised as indifference, the impatience that belittles those we love, these rough edges have been weathered down and replaced, through no conscious effort of his own, by a sort of quiet acquiescence. There is, within the acceptance of his predicament, a noble surrender to the innate powerlessness of man against time. McKelvey has simply lived long enough to come all the way back around, this boomerang of cosmic education.

Like most men his age, McKelvey sometimes wakes in the middle of the night. He is disoriented in the darkness and he hears his ragged breathing, the sound of a stranger in the room. He sits up and he marvels at the cold, hard truth of his situation. *Here. Now.* The only part of the whole that we all face alone, the ending. He moves to the bathroom and flicks on the light. He stares at himself in the mirror, the curls now grey, the crow's feet deepening like grooves worked into wood. This is his father's face …

Goddamn, he thinks, *I'm just a kid.*

* * *

The black vehicle follows the tail lights of the snowplough ahead, the driver's knuckles white on the wheel. The huge steel blade pushes the snow to the side of the highway as though it is weightless. Sheaves rise and catch the wind, blowing back in gauzy curtains that momentarily shroud the world. At times the driver of the black vehicle hears and feels his tires find the deeper snow and ice of the shoulder, and he fights to pull the vehicle back from this seemingly magnetic force that wants only to see him in the ditch. It is twilight and all he can do is follow these brake lights, beacons in the wilderness.

As he is sure he will, he blindly sails past his destination. It is pitch black out here, everything lost to the smear of treeline, the sky, shadows thrown across the endless snow. He bets a man could drive these roads a million times and still feel like a stranger. Everything about the North is designed to confuse the viewer into believing he is always seeing things for the first time. It is no wonder this man has heard the stories of the local hunters who get lost for days in woods they claim to know "like the back of their hand."

He catches a glimpse of a mailbox jutting from the furling blankets of white. He engages the brakes on the large vehicle and watches as the snowplough charges forth, swales of snow blowing back in its wake. The driver suddenly feels more alone than he has ever felt in his life. The wind whistles and he wonders if cold has a sound. He is still not used to being in the centre of vast open space like this. He wonders sometimes if man has evolved to the point where the rural landscape, from whence we were born and reared as a species, now runs counter to biology and physiology, psychiatry and spirit. Man now manoeuvres best in the tangled life of the always-moving, always-on city. Out here in the middle of nowhere on the edge of town there is only a brief and sudden reconciliation of his own insignificance. The driver reaches and pops open the glove compartment. The sight of the handgun in its holster provides him with the confidence and comfort he needs.

He puts the vehicle in reverse and slowly makes his way back up the black and deserted highway until he reaches the mailbox. He leans over to read the name on the box. It is too dark, there is too much snow, and so he sets the vehicle in park and gets out. He curses loudly as the first bite of the wind chill stabs at his open neck, his uncovered hands. He bends and squints and reads: *Garson*. Satisfied, he hurries back, jumps inside, and slams the door. He blows warm air into cupped hands. God, he thinks, who would ever try to populate a place like this? He sets the transmission in drive and begins to navigate his way up the laneway, headlights bouncing across the wall of trees.

Fifteen

At the Station Hotel, seated at a round table beneath a dartboard, Carl Levesque finds the two men he has come to meet. The men, both Native, do not smile when Levesque grins and reaches out to shake their hands. He keeps smiling despite the cold greeting. He stands there for a moment, fishing in his jacket pockets. He finds his cigarettes and finally has something to do with his hands. The municipal ban on smoking indoors is a law on paper only. He lights up and takes a draw, blows a plume like a steam train pumping smoke. Randy Travis's baritone swoons from the juke on the far side; tortured declarations of regret that seem right at home within these old walls.

"Sorry for running late, Chief," Levesque says. "Got tied up with an errand."

"I'm not your chief," says the older of the two men. He is in his late fifties, a broad-shouldered man with long black hair laced with grey. The hair is tied in a ponytail. His eyes are narrow and severe. His hands remain calmly folded in front of him, both sets of knuckles tattooed with faded blue lettering that is difficult to decipher.

Levesque takes a seat, his salesman's smile beginning to dim. He taps the cigarette and knocks ash to the scuffed floor.

"What the hell's going on down here in Saint B these days?" the younger man asks. He could be the son of the older man, or perhaps more likely a nephew. There are similarities in the set of the eyes, the cut of the jawline, which suggest a shared pool of genetics. Where the older man is thickly built, the younger man is lithe, lean. Skinny, they would have called him in school. His dark hair is cut short, combed back. It shines black as midnight.

"Little crime wave is all," Levesque says. "Just some bored teenagers."

"Kids getting stabbed over drugs ain't good for tourists coming in by bus," the older man says. "My council gets worried. They think maybe this is not the best place for our casino and resort. Kirkland Lake, maybe. Or Elliot Lake. A lot of retired folks there."

Levesque pulls a last drag and drops the cigarette to the floor, kills the ash with a twist of his booted foot.

"Good for property values though," Levesque says. "People start running scared, they sell at low prices. Eventually the kids will find something else destructive to do, you know, and life will move on. Nothing lasts forever, not even the plague."

"Glad you see the upside in all this," the younger man snaps.

The older man nods once, stares at Levesque.

"Say, can I get you a drink, Mr. Whitehorse?" Levesque asks.

"Don't drink," the older man says.

"Pepsi? A ginger ale?"

"Levesque, listen to me." Whitehorse leans close. His eyes are hard and locked. "I don't like you. I don't need a new friend. I came to talk about the work you were supposed to do for us about the land leases and killing this Detroit landfill deal. That's all I'm interested in. I want to get back on the road up to Big Water before another snow squall rides in."

Levesque settles back and folds an arm across the back of the chair. He sighs.

"I'm working on it."

*   *   *

In Room 16 of the Station Hotel, almost directly above the table where Carl Levesque sits with his guests in the tavern, Chief Gallagher watches as Tony Celluci stands at the bureau and pours two fingers' worth of Canadian Club into a Dixie cup. The ice machine in the hotel is broken, has been broken for years, and so Celluci has opted for a can of club soda to cut the drinks. He fixes a second drink and then turns and hands one to Gallagher, who sits on the edge of the bed because there is nowhere else to sit.

"Sorry, Chief, no ice."

"Enough of it out there." Gallagher nods toward the window. He then stands and moves to the same window, as though drawn there; he parts the thin lace curtain and looks outside. The lights on Main Street glow yellow, but only every second post is lit. "That's what you call a symbol of rural decline right there. Town can't even pay to turn all the lights on these days."

The Chief drinks some of his whisky. It runs from his belly to his heart to his head like a natural gas mainline, changes the man's mood almost instantly. His body feels as though it has sighed, sloughed off the weight of these last few days. With his free hand he spreads thumb and forefinger across the neatly trimmed moustache he has worn since he could grow it, having watched it change from auburn to dark brown to grey to silver.

"We can change that, you and me," Celluci says. "We can make the Carver Company mines look like amateur hour. Saint B will not only have all the street lamps shining, Main Street will be paved with gold, Chief."

Gallagher turns and leans back against the windowsill.

"Marko doesn't want Detroit's garbage up here," he says. "He's clear on that. The little prick has no vision. He's got his hopes set on this goddamned transmission line they've been talking about building for twenty years. He's waiting for those good line jobs and dollars to come while the town rots from the inside out."

Celluci is about to respond when a snap of squelch pops. A muffled and disembodied radio voice, or voices, buried within the wood of the bureau. Celluci opens a drawer and fiddles with something.

"Radio scanner," he says over his shoulder, and closes the drawer.

"*Police* scanner you mean," says Gallagher. "What the hell do you need that for up here? Are you keeping tabs on us, Tony?"

Celluci smiles, and his arms and hands come out in a marketer's soft welcome. He is the vision of a harmless schoolboy caught listening to a transistor radio during the playoffs.

"I use it on the highways from the Sault on up," he says. "Cuts down on speeding tickets if I know where the speed traps are set. Listen, Chief. Detroit has a problem, and it looks and smells like four million tons of garbage a day." Celluci swishes the whisky in his cup but he does not take a drink. "That's four million tons every day, seven days a week. We're running out of space to bury it, and we can't burn it fast enough, and you can only float so much of it around the harbour on a barge. New York tried that and they're fucked. Look at this place up here, Chief. The first time I came up here I couldn't believe my eyes. You've got the one resource we don't, and that's miles and miles of space. You're in the middle of nowhere, away from the eyes of the hobby environmentalists, the Greenpeace maniacs. We cut some trees and make a road in off the highway, and you've got yourself a twenty-year landfill agreement. The train starts running more regular again, hauling loads in nondescript cargo boxes. And a few years in, once all that shit has started to decompose, we pop in some gas turbines to generate electricity from all that trapped gas. Maybe by then your pal Marko has his transmission line built and we can sell our gas-powered electricity back to the grid."

Gallagher takes another sip of his drink. He grimaces, his palate unused to the strong flavour of rye, liquid smoke. He has been a small-town sheriff; he knows well how deals are made, whether for horses or hay. Men stand in barns or in back rooms and they share a drink because it somehow puts both buyer and seller on equal footing; it lubricates the negotiation. He saw his own father take this ritual to a different level, however, so that he was selling cars down at the lot with a steady glow, the veins coming out on the top of his nose, always ready for a drink before, during, or after a deal was made. Gallagher supposes this is why he has owned this argument with alcohol his whole life, as though he remains nervous in this woman's company despite having been near her and with her hundreds of times.

"You don't have to convince me, Tony. I'm the one your friends in Detroit put you on to, remember? I worked with your friends on that solid waste deal down in Pawhuska, Oklahoma. Talk about learning more about shit than I ever hoped to. Jesus Christ, a lifetime in public service and this is where I end up."

Celluci nods. He swishes the Dixie cup and looks down into it. He drains the contents like a shot, winces, and sets the empty cup on the bureau.

"Marko will come around to your way of thinking because he has no choice. There's nothing else he can do. The mine is closing. He can't keep the lights on. And all the kids are turning into meth junkies. There's a virtual crime wave out there. The timing couldn't better to put Marko right across a barrel."

Gallagher looks over at Celluci. The younger man is all city, dressed in his good suit, with his hair cut not by a barber but by a stylist in a place that smells like shampoo and nail polish. But the clean hands and fancy pants are not to be mistaken for a man incapable of getting business done in whatever manner required. Gallagher knows of the lineage at play here, the front door connection with the City of Detroit Department of Sanitation, the men behind the unions and the back offices. Tony Celluci is a made man.

"People will almost think we planned this," Gallagher says. "Detroit comes to Saint B and presto, we've got a meth problem. Now we're even more desperate to make a deal to take your garbage."

"Coincidence or luck." Celluci shrugs. "Either way, I'll take it."

Gallagher takes another sip of the whisky. He looks into the Dixie cup as though he is reading tea leaves, looking for a sign. Then he remembers something and smiles. Setting the cup on the windowsill, he says, "My dad used to say luck is what happens when preparation meets opportunity."

*   *   *

The snow has ceased. The sky is black and peppered with stars like the targets they used to shoot at back when Ed Nolan was in the army. He shivers with the notion of wasted time, those years he searched to find the core of himself, some sort of motivation or even a keen interest to propel him toward schooling or a trade. The army in those days seemed to gather the lowest common denominator as though this was precisely the intent of their recruiting. These sharply dressed soldiers sent to stand in the shopping malls and gymnasiums of high schools in small towns in Newfoundland, Quebec, Northern Ontario. The recruiter looked upon the faces before him and nodded, hands on his hips. His eyes seemed to convey all that the young men and sometimes women were themselves coming to accept with a sense of both failure and relief: *we are your last best chance; we are your new family.* This was in the mid-1990s, and the forces were floundering under budget cuts, stretched across too many peacekeeping missions without adequate resources. The same few thousand had cycled through multiple tours in Bosnia, Croatia, Somalia, and they exited in droves once the futility of their work was made evident. There were no parades, no ceremonies to welcome them home.

Constable Ed Nolan has just pulled into the rear parking lot of the Station Hotel. Whether this is a stakeout, he is not sure. But he is watching Carl Levesque's movements and recording them in his notepad — *Carl's Cadillac is right now parked beside a dumpster and beneath the single lamp that hangs loosely from a hydro pole.* Nolan supposes this is what it means to "tail" someone. He smiles to himself at the notion of conducting real police work up here in the middle of nowhere. Or perhaps, more accurately, not even the middle of nowhere, but the far edge of it.

Nolan has come to see that places like Saint B truly do not exist for the people of Toronto, Montreal, Vancouver, except as oddities. Urbanites insert these places as adjectives into conversations as they sit in trendy coffee shops and bistros. They use these places as the punchlines for jokes. Or as mock threats for some sort of corporate transfer — *we're sending you to Amos, Quebec, or Pickle Lake, Ontario, ha ha ha.* Who would freely choose to live in these places, they wonder. What do people do for fun, culture, sushi, international films? Places like Saint B don't make the news until a mine or a paper mill or a shoe factory closes and the flow of a resource to the city is threatened. Even the federal and provincial politicians don't care about a place like Saint B, because the votes of its constituents just don't matter on election day. It is for these and many other reasons that Ed Nolan believes he made the right decision to come home again, and to stay. To stay despite the loneliness, the state of his father. But there are things which need fixing here, and he wants to make a difference.

Nolan is anxious to share with McKelvey news of his skip tracing efforts. He has made inquiries, turned over a few rocks, run some checks against a series of names. Carl Levesque, he has discovered, carries with him an old conviction for drug trafficking, busted in the mid-1980s in Winnipeg with twenty grams of hashish and half an ounce of marijuana. The man also has a series of arrests on file from his younger days, minors for sailing bad cheques at grocery stores, a drunk driving incident. A shark in a cheap suit, this is how Nolan has always viewed him. He knows Levesque is an opportunist, it is in his marrow, but this revelation of a criminal past has added to Nolan's understanding of the man.

The snap of static makes Nolan jump as Shirley Murdoch's voice comes over the radio.

"Reports of an explosion and a fire just outside of town," she says. "Sounds like it could be the Garson place. The caller is a long-haul trucker. He's pulled over to the shoulder."

Nolan closes his eyes for a moment and tries to conjure an image of the scene. The flames, a curling ball of choking black smoke. Wade Garson's trailer, exploding like a grenade, the air sucking in on itself. A propane leak, perhaps, or more likely some sort of illicit activity. Nolan has read about this, these small towns in the U.S., amateurs cooking batches of meth until the smallest misstep leads to Armageddon. This is, he believes, the fault line which is threatening to split wide open and swallow his town.

Younger's voice comes on the line.

"I'm not far," the young cop says. "Just heading back from the hospital. Over."

"Trucker says the flames are twenty, thirty feet high," Shirley Murdoch says. "Fire station's notified. You want me to call the ambulance or wait for your word? Over."

"Wouldn't hurt to have them ready. Over and out."

Nolan is about to respond when the back door of the Station opens. A band of yellow light gets painted across the parking lot, the packed snow made dirty from tires and big-rig highway slush. Nolan watches as Carl Levesque comes down the stairs, pauses at the bottom to fish cigarettes from his jacket pocket. He cups his hands to light a cigarette and then the door opens again. A few bars of the country music bleed into the frozen air, this wailing refrain of lost love that makes the dark night seem darker, lonelier. Two men join Levesque at the bottom of the stairs. Nolan believes he recognizes them from the Big Water First Nation. He is parked at an angle and far enough away so as not to draw attention, but the distance also makes it difficult for him to make a positive ID. The men all shake hands. Nolan must wait now until they are in their vehicles and driving away. Levesque is the last to go. His interior dome light reveals his movements against the blackness. He is leaning over, fiddling with something in the glove compartment. Finally he turns the engine and navigates the big black Cadillac out onto Main, a sleek yacht that appears out of place in the North, in a land of half-tons and SUVs.

"Nolan here," he says into the mic. "I'm on my way. Over and out."

He starts the cruiser and pulls out of the parking lot. There is no need for lights or sirens. He will move quickly, but given the report, there is little hope of finding anything more than ashes and bones.

Sixteen

There is strange comfort to be found in sharing a woman's company in the absence of anticipation of reward. This fact seems to allow McKelvey to remain focused on the moment, for there is no hyped prize waiting at the end of the game — *this is it.* The smile on Peggy's face, the sound of her laughter, the black humour in her jokes, the way she moves the hair from her forehead. He notices everything, and he fills yet again with a foreign sense of gratitude for life and all of its tiny moments, the real magic that he and most of his kind fail to appreciate in the ignorance of their youth. He believes he could seduce this woman, pry open and climb through the window of her northern loneliness, say whatever it is that she wants or needs to hear, and he could be with her.

He could be with her, or at least he believes the odds are in his favour. And he would. His equipment still functions — despite the dire warnings in the pamphlets of a potential doomsday to come — and he certainly has not yet lost his drive where these matters are concerned. He still dreams of

Hattie and her lithe body, the nipples of her small breasts that felt so perfect against his tongue, the softness of her lips and the strength of her muscle, those hours wherein they got tangled and lost together, the sheets twisted, his heart outside his chest. He thinks of Caroline, too, but mostly this is guilt for the worry he has caused her, how he stood and watched her simply slip away — the unalterable fact that he was not there when she needed him, when their boy died and he got lost in anger. Yes, he has the ability and the drive and certainly the desire to lay down with this woman. But he has finally come face to face with the cold, hard truth of his predicament: *he is dying*. If not soon, then sooner than later. If not from the cancer percolating in his prostate, then it will be cancer of something *else*. Or his heart. Or one of those falls you hear that stupid old men take, tripping down a flight of stairs while rambling around to take a piss in the middle of the night. This thing is waiting for him down the line like a car pulled off to the side of the highway, engine running, signal flashing.

It is not male ego on his part that whispers he could become entangled with this woman; rather it is the history of humankind. Men and women, these situations, an ancient and unnameable tension, the spark and the chase, the dance with all feathers preened on jubilant display. This is what the sexes have always done and will always do, but McKelvey lacks the energy to lie or pretend, or to pretend to lie, and so it is that he accepts an invitation to enjoy a home-cooked meal with Peggy from Coffee Time with the complete absence of ulterior motives. So it is that he sits across from her in her small house, hardly touching a glass of red wine. It has been a long time since he has had a drink, or it seems like a lifetime anyway, and the first swallow rushes straight to his head. It comes back to him why he quit, this haunting refrain, jerking flow of images: the disgrace of an elderly gentleman sprawled on the floor of his bathroom, waking from a blackout, sick as a dying dog, addled brain clicking in desperation to piece together those last hours. He pushes the glass farther and farther from his reach.

"So what are you running from, Charlie?" She wears a mischievous smile. "Woman trouble? Taxes?"

"Just like that, eh? Right to the point. I like that."

He sits back and thinks, at ease in this room, within himself. It seems the older he gets, the less he feels a need to ensure his voice is heard — his point of view, his thoughts on a particular subject. Anyway, a man could make everything up as he went along and it wouldn't make any difference.

"But you're not going to answer," she says. "You're evasive."

"It's supposed to be sexy," he says, and smiles. "Mysterious."

She takes a drink and sets her glass on the table.

"It's annoying more than anything. But I'm not pushy."

"Nothing mysterious about it," he says. "I'm separated. We've never really gotten around to discussing what comes next. We're probably too old to bother with divorce. She's a few thousand miles away from me, which is almost a safe distance. I decided to come back up here, I guess, to see if it looked any different."

"And does it look different, Charlie?"

He thinks for a moment about this place where he came from, the place that made him. He knows he has carried parts of Saint B with him every day he lived in the bustle of the country's largest city. Whether it was fear of becoming his father, he doesn't know, but he does know that he did not leave this place, he *escaped*. It comes to him now, the truth he has searched for all these years: he has carried a sense of guilt for leaving, for being one of those who turned away from the work and the life that was offered, as though he wanted or needed more.

"It's changed a lot," he says, "and it looks exactly the same."

Peggy smiles and takes a sip of her drink.

"You mentioned something a few days ago, about your father and his old friends. Something you were hoping to find. Have you found it yet?"

McKelvey is still unsure whether he wants to know the truth about that violent year here in Saint B, less so his father's specific involvement. The darkest days of the labour movement. He was a little boy when his father was thrown out of work for months. What he remembers of that time is less food, his mother stretching groceries, more arguments in the house. But mostly a stark image of his father sitting alone at the kitchen table. The police had been by to ask questions. McKelvey watched his father from just inside the living room, a voyeur. His father sitting there at the table staring at the wall and smoking, just smoking, lighting one cigarette off the ember of the last. It was a scene that scared the boy in way that he could never quite describe. He remembers that much, anyway. Seeing your father so lost and idle, it was shattering.

"There was a strike," McKelvey says. "That's how it goes in a mining town. Years of peace fractured here and there with unrest. Collective bargaining, wildcats, walkouts. You have no idea how a strike affects a town like this until you're in the middle of it. That particular year things got ugly fast. The company brought in scabs, unemployed hicks from the nearby towns, a bunch of guys from the Big Water reserve. A lot of the miners had served in the Second World War, and some of them, like my father, had just come back from a year of combat in Korea. They weren't in the mood to roll over."

"You have unanswered questions about your dad's role in the strike?"

"A scab worker was killed in an explosion. Nobody was ever charged. It was something people whispered about for years. Back then, the death of a scab — and a scab who happened to be Native — didn't exactly result in a major police investigation. It was a different time."

A silence falls between them, but rather than awkward, it feels right. A moment of silence for the dearly departed perhaps.

Finally, Peggy breaks the silence. "You've always wondered about your dad, haven't you? If he was capable of committing an act of violence — a murder — and living with it. Do you ever wonder if that's why you became a cop?"

The revelation hits him with the force of a blindside. The doorway to his entire life swings open. *My God*, he thinks. *If that is in fact the truth, this thing I've sought all these years, this notion I have wrestled with daily — good men who commit desperate acts, justice and revenge, right and wrong.*

"I'll leave that one to my psychologist." He chuckles to lighten the mood, switch the channel. "I have one on retainer back in Toronto."

He reaches out and touches the stem of the glass, turns it, and settles back.

"You don't like the wine?" she asks, having noticed his reticence.

"I'm not much of a drinker these days." He finds himself amused with the sound of those words coming from his mouth. He half expects a sudden fluttering of locusts, perhaps the sofa to erupt in flames.

"Why didn't you just say so," she says with a laugh. "I'm drinking red grape juice myself. I haven't had a drink in nine years. Nine and a half, actually. I keep a bottle of wine on hand for my rare guests. It's probably stale as hell."

They are sitting in the living room on a love seat. The room is spare, with a leather club chair, a coffee table with a few old magazines on a rack below, three large framed photos of ocean vistas on the walls. McKelvey smiles back at her, both amazed at the subtle hand she has played, and also at their seeming inability to be completely honest even at their age. *Absolute beginners*, he thinks.

"That's funny," he says. "I thought you'd be disappointed if I didn't take a glass."

"Societal rituals and peer pressure. Here, I'll switch you over to grape juice. It's full of the same antioxidants as red wine, only it doesn't kill brain cells or result in demoralizing behaviour."

"Probably too late for me on the brain cells."

She laughs and gets up and takes his glass into the kitchen. He listens to her movements. The fridge opening, closing. A glass bottle set on a counter. A top being unscrewed. It seems as though suddenly everything matters, every detail, the painting in of all the lines that he was always so happy to leave blank for so many years. And then his mind breaks free of this unnatural sense of peace and he thinks of the pills. *The pain pills*. Oblong capsules of bliss, tiny torpedoes of transcendence. He has wondered, increasingly, about the validity of the pain which necessitates the ongoing prescription. The twinge of shame he feels when he visits old Dr. Shannon, how he can't meet the eyes of the pharmacist when he is asked whether he understands the significance of the medication. *Yes, yes,* he assures them, already shoving the bag in his pocket, shuffling toward the checkout, *I know all about it …*

I am not addicted, he thinks. No. Reliant, perhaps. A crutch. But addicted?

McKelvey has been a frontline worker in the field of addictions. As a detective on the Hold-Up Squad, he came face to face each day with the ceaselessly shocking things a human will do in order to ensure an uninterrupted flow of dope. Junkies holding a jagged piece of glass to the throat of a taxi driver for the sake of twenty or thirty dollars, shooting a convenience store clerk in the face for a garbage bag of lottery tickets and cartons of cigarettes to be sold for one-tenth their face value on the street. The whores who roll their johns, the strippers who slip wallets from pant pockets with the liquid fingers of a magician. And the worst, always the worst and the most unpredictable, the crackheads and the tweakers.

Heroin is a drug of sloth, the ancient domain of jazz musicians and cerebral poets, mats scattered on the floor of funky and dimly lit Chinese dens. The men who trade in heroin are for the most part highly organized in terms of business structure, highly intelligent, and thereby highly dangerous criminals who view their import-export trade as simple economics, the supply and demand of replacing life's misery with instalments of joy. Marijuana is the culprit in many street-level gang deaths, to be sure, but use of the drug itself is in many ways actually an aid to the police, in that its users are most often rendered slow-witted, dumb and lazy. It is the street nature of coke and speed — blow and crank — the easy access and affordability of a five-minute high, that combine to make the vortex of its peddlers and users such an insane and volatile labyrinth.

Are you using these pills because you can't cope with life on life's terms?

Within the otherworldly hierarchy of drug addicts, speed users are the bottom feeders and also the most dangerous. A crack cocaine high lasts about twenty minutes; speed lasts ten or twelve times longer. Tweakers run for days on end, smoking foils of meth and angel dust in filthy rooms, soaring and jabbering through the long-lasting high, then riding the rough shoulder of the come-down. It is in this final phase of the use and abuse that junkies appear as aliens who have just landed here. To refer to them as *otherworldly* is not inappropriate.

Peggy comes back in the room and sets his drink on the coffee table.

"You quit drinking," McKelvey says. "Like cold turkey?"

"I used to go to meetings," Peggy says. "Twelve Step meetings. There's only one in Saint B, on Tuesday nights, and I haven't been in a while. It goes from three people to a dozen on any given night. When things got bad between Davey and me, I knew what I had to do. Stop drinking and drugging. Wake up to my life. Be here, *really* be here."

"Takes a lot of balls," McKelvey says, and it comes too quickly. He wishes he could change his choice of words. But he watches Peggy. She smiles at him. He adds, "Most people aren't capable of being that honest with themselves, is what I meant."

And he is about to talk about his boy. His Gavin, and the fall to drugs. How it seemed he was one day just a kid with a skateboard and cowlick and the next he was lying on that steel bed in the morgue. But he doesn't have the strength to rip those stitches and begin again. The story from start to finish. He will not wake that dog.

"You get older and you look back through your family," Peggy says, "and you realize all those uncles and aunts and grandparents you thought were these real free spirits were just drunks. A bunch of alcoholics gathered for a family celebration is like putting a stick of dynamite on the kitchen table and setting a candle beside it. You just stand back and wait."

They are quiet for a little while. McKelvey welcomes silence, the warmth of the small house, this sense of connection that he can't quite name. He understands this is perhaps what it means to be still. His mind is not turning, obsessing on a problem real or imagined. He closes his eyes. The blood hammers in his ears. *This is his heart pumping blood through his body. And his body is well worn and abused, but sitting here now with his eyes closed, he could just as easily be a kid again ... fully alive and young, just starting.*

"I can't change the past, but I can change today," Peggy says, and her words reach McKelvey like a sacred doctrine. "I can make a difference in some small way, even filling coffee cups all day. Just do the next right thing. That's all I want, Charlie. To close my eyes at the end of the day and know that I didn't intentionally hurt anyone or play games with them."

McKelvey opens his eyes. Peggy is smiling at him. He feels as though he has slept for a hundred years. He thinks for a moment that perhaps if he sits here, if he makes no move to leave, then time will cease. He does not want to open the door. He does not want or need to step outside, to the world, The Diagnosis, the calls from his worried family.

"I want to give you something," she says. "I think you could use it."

*   *   *

McKelvey's old family home is dead quiet when he returns. He pauses just inside the door which opens onto the kitchen. If he squints he can see his mother standing there with her back to him, busy at the stove — she glances over her shoulder and smiles that smile that delivered the family through good times and bad. And over there at the kitchen table, his back to the wall, his father sits with his legs stretched out, workboots untied, the tongues sticking out, running fingers through his hair made messy from wearing a hard hat all day. He turns a stubby bottle of beer with his fingers, a hand-rolled cigarette smouldering in an ashtray, package of Drum tobacco next to a Zippo lighter.

McKelvey smiles to himself as he fills the upstairs tub with hot water, the steam fogging the mirror. The tub, an old-style claw-foot, brings him back to his childhood, those Sunday night baths whether he needed one or not. He liked them best in summer when he would sit in the cool water and his mother would wash his hair and the air coming in the open window smelled of newly cut lawns, and he could hear the crickets singing at twilight. Now he drops his clothes on the old white tiles and steps into the tub. He eases back and lets the water envelope his aching body, accept his aged vessel like a hand to a glove. He looks down at his body in the water, and he smiles again. An old man's body. But he feels like a boy inside. Is this how it is for everybody, he wonders. He remembers Peggy's words, about doing the next right thing, about putting your head on your pillow with a clear conscience, and an image of the young cop comes to his mind. Eddie Nolan. A good young cop trying to make a difference in this dying town. He knows then that he will help the young man. Though he is not given to the notion of karma and cosmos, he does contemplate the coincidence of his arrival, the breadth of experience he can bring to Nolan's virgin work.

He towels himself dry and then wraps the towel around his waist. His hand reaches out and opens the medicine cabinet above the sink. His fingers move the deodorant, the shave cream, the Preparation H, and find the pills. Peggy's words enter his brain like a telegraph. He holds the pill bottle for a full minute, gears shifting, his mind conjuring various scenarios, and then he raises the toilet seat and sprinkles the pills. This is not the first time he has done this; he has been here before. He has twice flushed the source of his nagging doubt and the very next day called Dr. Shannon for a refill. But he wants to make this change in his life once and for all. Wants to, needs to, *has to*. He stares down at the floating capsules, tiny tablets of heaven and hell. And he flushes.

He smiles for what seems like the hundredth time that night as he climbs into bed and pulls the covers up, and he recalls the mischievous grin on Peggy's face as she kissed his cheek at the door and said "I hope you didn't think you were going to get lucky tonight, Mr. McKelvey. But I'm not that kind of girl …"

To which his face burned red, and he stood at her door, stammering through some adolescent reply. She smiled and closed the door. And now he looks over at the card she gave him before leaving. It sits on the closed toilet seat. The Prayer of St. Francis of Assisi.

Lord, make me an instrument of your peace
Where there is hatred, let me sow love;
where there is injury, pardon;
where there is doubt, faith;
where there is despair, hope;
where there is darkness, light;
and where there is sadness, joy.

It's all good, he thinks. Despite the current state of his blood cells, the fact he has very likely run away from his life, the likelihood both his estranged wife and doctor are searching for him right now, despite the flushing of his lifeline down the toilet, it's all good.

Seventeen

"Consider yourself deputized," Nolan says over the phone.

Nolan says he is at the station, has been there all night. Everything has changed, he says, and McKelvey hears the exhaustion and fear in his voice.

"Chief Gallagher got special approval from Mayor Danny Marko in the middle of the night. You're on the force, Charlie. A special constable. Limited authority, but a step up from an auxiliary officer."

Special constable. McKelvey turns the phrase on his tongue. He both likes and dislikes the sound of it. What it means exactly, he can't be sure. Perhaps "auxiliary officer" is more fitting. He was certainly an auxiliary husband and father. But he has already decided to help the younger cop. Titles are meaningless to him now.

"What happened?" McKelvey asks.

Nolan runs through the high-level details. Wade Garson's trailer exploded just before eleven o'clock. Constable Pete Younger arrived first on scene. The rookie got too close to the fire. He was taken by ambulance down the highway to meet the Medevac to Sudbury.

"He's not in good shape, Charlie. They're talking about flying him down to Toronto. I was second on scene. The trailer was beyond fully involved, it had blown apart by then. Insulation and metal siding sprayed all over the woods like confetti. When I got to Younger he was barely breathing."

"They find Wade Garson's body?"

"We'll need to run dental records on this one. God, I can still smell it. I can't get the taste out of my mouth …"

McKelvey knows what Nolan is talking about. He can see and smell the first body he ever responded to as though it were only yesterday. This homeless man who drank himself to death and was left to swell to the point of bursting in his room at a King Street flophouse. It was during an August heatwave. Maggots crawling from the ears and nose, the smell a strong and sickly sweetness of pus and vinegar. The landlord was absent and the other tenants were drunkards themselves, oblivious to the rotting corpse down the hall. It marked McKelvey for life, this notion that in the end we die alone.

"Garson must've been cooking the meth after all. I think I smelled ammonia or something like that. The Chief is there now holding the scene until the fire marshal arrives. Gallagher sounds like he's about to lose his mind. He found out the provincial police are sending a senior investigator from HQ in Orillia. He's going to pick him up at lunch and meet back at the station for a briefing. I'll swing by and pick you up."

"I'll be ready in twenty minutes."

He hangs up. Something is bothering him, digging at his mind. He stands there at the phone which Levesque has finally activated with the telephone mafia at Bell Canada. He has a phone listing here; he is apparently an auxiliary — or special — member of the police force. He is back home, or so it seems, and yet his home is in the city. Toronto the clean, Toronto the dirty.

And then it comes, like the name of a song recalled in the middle of the night. Wade Garson's place didn't smell of ammonia. A lingering pong of stale marijuana, perhaps, but not the chemicals required in the production of methamphetamine. If Nolan is right, and he did smell something strange in the fire, then what has changed, McKelvey wonders, in the last twenty-four hours?

*   *   *

McKelvey slides into the cruiser, which is warm and smells of smoke from the fire which clings to Nolan like a fingerprint, and on top of this there is the pungency of Nolan's young-man's cologne — something loud on the senses, too aggressive. McKelvey is reminded of the younger men on the force, how much care and attention they put into their appearance compared to the old days. Gelling their hair, frosting the tips, playing games with their facial hair, reading magazines in the lunch room that gave tips about which red wines to buy, which exercises to employ in order to achieve Hollywood abs.

When it came to doing sixteen hours of dead-time in a ghost car for a winter night stakeout, or God forbid, getting down to business in the darkest corners of the dark world they policed, McKelvey sensed a subscription to a new law of diminishing returns from this generation. This young cop at his side reminds McKelvey more and more, not of himself in his own rookie days — for he was much more brash and balls-out, for better or for worse — but of the cop he wishes he had been. Nolan's eagerness to learn, to in effect be the best cop he can be, leaves the older man with a sense of remorse.

"It'll take you a few showers to wash that smoke off." McKelvey looks over and sees Nolan's hands are blackened with soot.

"Chief's wound up like a top," Nolan says, putting the cruiser in motion.

The day is bright and clear. It doesn't seem possible that problems could find a place like this as they navigate the quiet streets, roll past simple homes with snow-covered roofs. Hard-working people living simple lives of low expectation. In fact, McKelvey recalls, the only base expectation seemed to be that a life of hard work, of attending church on Sunday, of helping a neighbour when they were sick, that a life lived by these rules should necessarily result in less pain and suffering. McKelvey looks out the window at the sleeping town and thinks, *but there are no rules, no promises to be kept or broken*.

"We've got some extra uniform shirts I can get you, and a weapon and some cuffs," Nolan says, "and we can get you set up with Younger's cruiser."

"I don't need a gun," McKelvey says, still looking out the window. He sees but does not register the passing landscape, his vision clouded with stark images of the old factory down by the Toronto harbour — the shootings there, the gunfire that echoes still. If he closes his eyes he can see the body of Detective Leyden splayed on the catwalk, he can smell the gunpowder; can see it hovering in the air like a horizontal mist. And he watches, too, as the man he shot gets pulled backward out the window to the green-blue water below. He hears the broken glass from the window hitting the concrete floor below as though a chandelier has crashed. He hears it most nights when he closes his eyes.

Nolan shoots him a glance. "You don't *want* a gun or you don't *need* a gun?"

"I don't need it," McKelvey says, then adds, "Don't want it."

"Fair enough, I guess. Saves paperwork with the Chief. You take a baton at least?"

McKelvey nods once, then asks, "Who's the coroner in these parts?"

"Doctor Nichols at the clinic here. He doesn't get much practice with this sort of thing. Mostly old people dying in their sleep." Nolan says this as though he himself has dealt previously with this sort of predicament, examining charred bodies pulled from an exploded trailer suspected of being a meth factory. "He's at the scene with the Chief right now. We should catch them before the Chief picks up this OPP investigator. I'm not looking forward to that, to be honest."

"The OPP riding in to save the day? Not much chance of them staying out of it once you have a local officer hurt and this rash of crime. Just make sure they know you're leading this. Don't take your hands off the reins for a minute. Those assholes think they invented investigative procedures. Just be thankful it's not the RCMP coming in."

They are out on the highway now; it is as though the town has simply dissolved behind them. The pavement is scraped clean of snow and ice. The steel guard railings are caked with brown from salt and dirt kicked up by the big rigs, but the treeline set farther back is dusted with white snow, pristine.

"I'm glad you're here," Nolan says. "I've never attended a scene for something like this." He turns and gives McKelvey a small smile. The gratitude is genuine. McKelvey can't help but think of the card he has tacked to his fridge door: The Prayer of St. Francis. What is he blind to in himself that Peggy was able to see? What does she know about him?

Nolan has to hit the brakes as he comes around the slight bend in the road. They are suddenly at the turnoff to Wade Garson's trailer. Before McKelvey can respond to Nolan's comment, something occurs to him.

"Stop," he says.

He pops the door latch and climbs out. He walks over to the mouth of the snow-packed lane leading into the trailer. He looks down at the ground. He crouches and touches the snow in various spots. Another door swings shut and boots crunch across the frozen ground.

"Tire tracks?" Nolan says, standing to the side.

"The OPP will photograph, set casts, and generally sniff up and down this lane six ways to Sunday," McKelvey says. "We don't want them throwing evidence in our face like we're amateurs or something. You ID any tires here that look fresh?"

Nolan leans in and squints into the snow. The brightness of the day does not help their work. He clamps a thumb and forefinger like a vice across his forehead.

"My head," Nolan says, and he shakes it to clear his vision.

"Wheelbase, tread wear patterns. Just like a thumb print," McKelvey says.

"This one," Nolan says, and he stands up, pointing. "This is a truck or an SUV. Something bigger than the Nissans we drive. What do you think?"

"Could be the paramedics, or anybody who came through here last night." McKelvey stands and takes a haul of the fresh country air into his lungs. He feels good. He is working on something here. Small, or nothing at all really, but it's a start, and he can feel it starting again, this thing that happens when he stands at the very edge of an investigation. "We'll get some pictures of these tracks, Nolan. Find out what the paramedics and the coroner drive, start running some checks."

Nolan heads back to the cruiser. "I've got a digital camera in the glove compartment."

"Next time," McKelvey calls after him, "your Chief should know better than to leave the entrance to a crime scene unattended like this. Anything ever makes it to court, the defence will have a field day. A break in the chain of evidence collection is grounds for reasonable doubt."

McKelvey looks over and Nolan is taking a picture of him. "What are you doing, making a fucking scrapbook?"

"Sorry," the younger cop says, and he shrugs. "I'm a little excited, I guess."

* * *

The trailer looks as though it has been blown apart with the industrial grade dynamite they use in mining. The roof and three walls have been shredded, twisted, peeled back like the top of a Jiffy Pop, but strangely enough the far side wall still stands. It is an eerie sight. Curtains still hang from blown-out windows on that wall, everything scorched and smouldering. The remnants of Wade Garson's life exist only in outline now, a fridge leaning sideways, the skeleton of a favourite La-Z-Boy. Though the fire has been doused for hours now, small spirals of smoke still curl and rise from the soggy mess of ashes. Dressed in a lumber jacket and hip waders that he likely uses for fly fishing, standing up to his knees in the centre of what must have been Wade Garson's kitchen, can only be Dr. Nichols, the only physician within the town limits, the only coroner in perhaps the region.

Nolan and McKelvey leave the cruiser at the mouth of the laneway and walk in. Gallagher gives a little wave. He is sitting sidesaddle inside Younger's police cruiser, door open, legs outside. He could be a man enjoying himself at a tailgate party, McKelvey thinks. But as they draw closer, he sees the man's face is haggard, the worry written deep in his eyes. Gallagher drinks from the lid of a steel Thermos.

"This is a real goddamned jackpot, boys." He motions toward the remains of the trailer. He takes another drink, flicks the cup lid toward the snow, and then screws it back on tight. "Should've run these Garsons out of this town a long time ago, pulled a Texas lynch mob on their asses. Now look at us. I got a good young cop in the hospital with his lungs burned to hell and the OPP is coming in. That'll be the end of this police force, all on my watch."

McKelvey notices Gallagher's glassy, rheumy eyes. He catches a whiff of rye in the air and understands the Chief is not consoling himself with coffee. This will make matters even worse when the provincial police arrive on the scene. He knows from experience that despite best efforts, big-city cops necessarily doubt the talent and abilities of their small-town colleagues. He has held this view himself, following the trail of a bank robber from Toronto to a town like Brockville. He supposes it's this way with most professions, this notion that if you were any good at what you did, you sure as hell wouldn't be content to work in some backwater for half the pay. He is reminded of some of the shoddy dentistry that had been performed on him by old Doc Finton when he was a kid up here, this miner's town dentist who reeked of body odour and had hair sprouting out of his ears and nostrils like he was using fertilizer to grow the stuff.

"You look tired there, Chief," McKelvey says.

Gallagher rubs his jaw. He looks up and stares at McKelvey for a minute.

"You wanted to get your nose in this, well here you are," he says. "Welcome to it. You're with us now, McKelvey. A special constable. Congratu-fucking-lations."

"He didn't ask to help," Nolan says. "I asked him. And with Pete in the hospital, well, we can sure use the extra body."

McKelvey thinks of pulling the older man aside, as he would do if he were back home in the city and smelled booze on the breath of a colleague. Tell him to head home for a shower and some rest, a bite to eat. Let a man exit with grace.

But he believes it would not go this way with Gallagher. The man has this notion of McKelvey, big-city cop looking down his nose at the local force. He decides to take a longer route to the same endpoint.

"That the coroner over there?" McKelvey asks.

"Dr. Nichols," Gallagher says. "He's not the best, but he's the best we've got. Body, or what was left of it, was bagged and tagged and brought by the paramedics to the medical clinic."

McKelvey watches as the coroner stoops, rummaging through debris like some collector at a flea market. The coroner is afforded certain privileges, access to the scene where a body is found, but this probably borders on destruction of evidence. In the city, the forensic officers would be booted and suited to avoid cross-contamination. *But this is not the city*, he thinks.

"We should string up some tape to close off a perimeter on the scene," McKelvey suggests. "The OPP find the place wide open like this, your coroner digging through the scene in his hip waders, they'll have all of us removed from the investigation."

"You got some yellow tape in your truck, Eddie?" Gallagher asks.

"Shit," Nolan says, "I think we ran out a while back. Pete was supposed to order some more."

Gallagher shakes his head and sighs. His breath taints the air with an almost visible cloud. It is the strong and sour smell of liquor half-digested on an empty stomach. McKelvey looks at Nolan and Nolan looks at McKelvey. The younger man looks pained, perhaps let down by this father figure.

"Listen," McKelvey says, "if you guys want to take Dr. Nichols back to the station and get ready for the briefing, I can run and pick up the investigator at the airport. When is he due to arrive?"

Gallagher glances at his watch. "Twelve twenty. Just under an hour." He scratches his cheek and neck, which is covered with white stubble that adds a decade to his age. He looks like a man who has not slept in a day and a half. "I'll take you up on that offer, McKelvey. I need some time to get my head on before I meet this provincial asshole. And in case you boys haven't heard the good news, there's a fucking storm heading in."

Gallagher gets up out of the truck, stretches, and moves a hand to his lower back. He straightens and walks over to Dr. Nichols, who is still bent at the waist and staring into the debris.

"Hey, Doc," Gallagher calls. "You done fishing? We need to head back into town to get our story straight."

McKelvey uses the moment to turn to Nolan.

"Make sure he eats something and brushes his teeth," he says. "He smells like a fucking distillery. Does he have a problem with the booze?"

Nolan looks like a kid left disappointed by a weekend father.

"Hardly ever touches it," Nolan says. "He has no tolerance for the stuff as far as I can tell. You know, a few swigs here and there on a special occasion. He seems really stressed lately, out of sorts, ever since this Celluci guy came up from Detroit, selling his landfill paradise."

"Well, his timing for a breakdown is impeccable." ·

Nolan digs into his coat pocket, pulls out the keys to the cruiser, and hands them to McKelvey. "The OPP contact is Inspector John Churchill."

"I'll take the scenic route back, buy you some extra time."

"There's only one way to Saint B from the regional airport."

McKelvey smiles. "I'll drive slowly."

Eighteen

McKelvey enjoys the open space on the highway and the time alone, but most of all he enjoys being behind the wheel of a police cruiser again. He knows he will never admit the fact to anyone, but once he has cleared the town limits, he glances in the rear-view to check for traffic and then he hits the lights. He scans the dash console and finds the switch for the siren, too, and lets it wail for a few seconds before deactivating. The sound of the siren and the strobe of the lights does something to his insides — like electrodes hooked to his heart, the amperage shocks him back to life, real life, the here and the now, the stuff that matters.

He sits up straighter, grips the wheel with both hands, and the first thing that crosses his mind is his duty here to help Nolan, and even Gallagher, however he can. (And he can't get Peggy's goddamned Prayer of St. Francis out of his head. He is neither religious nor particularly spiritual, so he is left wondering if he is going soft as he contemplates illness and loneliness and an end he has for so long now convinced himself he will embrace.)

The second thought to cross his mind concerns Caroline and the call he owes her. He is an asshole, to be sure. That much has not changed, at least, whether in sickness or in health. *Oh, Caroline, sweet Caroline …*

He is enjoying the freedom of the wheels rolling beneath him when it swings back and hits him with the force of a sucker punch: this rising tidal surge snaking through his intestines, cold chills that make him shiver with an instant malevolent fever. He clenches his teeth and rides the nausea that makes his mouth water, and he thinks for a moment it is possible he may need to pull over to the side of the road. To shit or vomit, it's a coin toss. But he swallows the wave of malaise, takes a deep haul of air. He glances in the rear-view and sees the sheen of sweat shining on his forehead. *Fucking pills.* The throat-clutching, ball-kicking strength of this stuff. And for the first time in a long time — perhaps not since the day of the shootings at the harbour — McKelvey is truly afraid of what lies in wait around the next corner.

He shakes the unease and gets his mind back on the situation at hand. While the latest developments would seem to indicate a neat and tidy closure to the issue of meth in Saint B, McKelvey knows from experience the mistake of making assumptions before the last card has been placed face up on the table. If the body found at the trailer is indeed identified as that of Wade Garson; if Garson was indeed manufacturing the drug in his trailer, which led to the explosion and his own death, then chances are good Nolan and Gallagher have found the root cause of this recent surge in crime. With the key producer and dealer out of the picture, the local cops will be free to implement an enforcement program and an educational campaign going forward to ensure meth does not again find a foothold in the town.

The question is, did Wade Garson act alone?

Is the dead body Wade Garson or someone else?
If Garson didn't act alone, the root problem still exists.
If the body isn't Garson, then who is it?

A ways to go yet before Nolan will get to stamp CASE CLOSED on this one, McKelvey thinks as he spots the highway sign for the airport: five kilometres ahead and to the right. He is slowing to take the turn as he hears and then sees the small passenger plane coming in from the southwest for landing, this graceful steel bird that seems to simply get swallowed by the treeline. McKelvey is lost in thought, scanning the woods for sight of the plane, when the radio squawks. The sudden trill of white noise causes him to startle and he jerks the wheel a little, almost hitting the snowbank that wants to suck the vehicle into its unforgiving mass.

"Base to McKelvey, over." Nolan's voice fills the cruiser.

McKelvey keeps a hand on the wheel and fiddles with the mic.

"McKelvey. Over."

"I took the Chief home like you said. He lay down on his couch and fell asleep right away. He said he'll catch up with the investigator after he gets some rest. I poured a bottle of rye down the kitchen sink. He had an empty one and a mostly full one out on the table with a gift card from Celluci. Over."

"That's good, Nolan. Looks like the flight just landed. I'll give you a call when we're fifteen minutes from the station. Listen," he says, and pictures this woman he has never met, Shirley Murdoch, listening to their every word as she sits at her kitchen table dressed in a housecoat, dispatching police business from the comfort of her home. "Never mind. I'll talk to you offline. Over and out."

He hangs the mic back in its clasp. As the cruiser rounds a curve, the woods open up to reveal the regional airport. Located about half an hour south and west of Ste. Bernadette, it is a single swath of clear-cut forest serving the nearest four municipalities. There is a large hangar built of gun-metal grey siding, three or four garages and sheds painted orange, a three-storey air traffic control tower, and a terminal about the size of two family bungalows pushed together.

McKelvey pulls up to the front of the terminal where six or seven cars are parked at an angle. He leaves the cruiser running out of habit from his years in a patrol car. They had it drilled into them to keep the car running when you stepped into a coffee shop, just in case you had to take a call. Nowadays this is frowned upon because the hundreds of vehicles in the Toronto Police fleet running around the clock collectively produce enough greenhouse gas emissions to end all life on the planet. He steps outside and stretches. The day is growing warmer. It could be early March, and he wonders if the storm will pass them by. He makes his way to the front doors and reaches into his coat pocket for the piece of paper that Nolan handed him with the name of the OPP investigator.

Inspector John Churchill, the note reads in Nolan's neat block printing.

But as he comes through the doors, as he lifts his head, it is not Inspector John Churchill he sees crossing the terminal with a garment bag slung over one shoulder and a thick black briefcase clasped in the other arm. In fact, it's not a man at all, but a woman of perhaps forty-five. McKelvey stops. She looks around the terminal, empty save for a young man reading a paperback at the only airline counter. She looks at McKelvey. He can't see her hair beneath the OPP black sheepskin trapper hat, and her form is well concealed beneath a black heavy parka with yellow flashing and insignia. It matters not that she is wrapped from head to toe, that only her face and clear eyes are visible. McKelvey knows that she is beautiful.

Perfect, he thinks. *Just what I need.*

*   *   *

McKelvey is putting the investigator's bags in the back of the cruiser, taking his time, wondering if it is really possible that she does not remember him after all. Her face betrayed not even a hint of recognition. Perhaps he is a victim of his own grandiosity, this notion that she would certainly recall having worked together, albeit briefly, when the bank robber D.J. Chasson wound his way from Toronto up through Barrie and then Orillia, eventually holing himself up in a highway motel in the Muskokas. It was in Barrie that he worked with this woman for about a week. He believes she had just made the Major Crime Unit on that growing city's force, and she was green but steady and had a good instinct for the work. He is not mistaken, for her name is unique — Euphenia Madsen, but she "goes by Finn," as she would always say. He closes the back hatch and gets in the cruiser where she is fiddling with a cellphone.

"I can't get any service," she says.

"Comes and goes," he tells her. "Out on the highway you might catch a signal."

He sets them in motion. She rummages through the thick black briefcase at her feet, riffling through papers, pulling out file folders, and he sees from the corner of his eye that her bag is a mess. It looks like a teenager's school backpack in there. She pulls a paper from the quagmire and smoothes the wrinkles.

"I've got a few questions I wrote down on the flight, if you don't mind running through them. Are you the lead up here?"

He turns and looks at her, really looks at her. She has removed the ball of sheepskin from her head and unzipped the parka. Her hair is shorter now, and perhaps even a different colour, a deeper chestnut. He can't recall the specifics. It is driving him crazy that she doesn't remember him at all, as though he could be so utterly forgettable. Or perhaps he has become one of those people he likes to mock, the sort who pretend they are not balding or gaining weight. But more likely, he realizes, she has no reason to place him up here in the Far North, a thousand miles and years removed. The context is all wrong.

"You don't remember me, do you?" he says. He feels better right away. Like opening a valve. He can feel the pressure leaving his body in a slow and silent leak.

She looks at him and squints. And then she smiles a little and shakes her head.

"Sorry," she says. "Should I?"

And so he tells her about his visits, two of them, to her small city on the lake. Seven or eight years ago now. The overachieving bank robber D.J. Chasson, who robbed twenty-six banks in eighty-four days, two of them in Barrie, and his last in Orillia. How it was the guy's M.O. that got him snagged in the end.

"He was obsessive-compulsive, had this thing about jacking the same colour of car before every heist," McKelvey says. "We set him up with a navy blue Ford Escort we had wired so we could track him. Found him holed up in that crappy motel out on Highway 69."

"That was my first serial bank robber," Madsen says. And she looks at him again. She squints as though she is trying to read the words on a sign that is too far away. And then her eyes light up.

"Oh my God," she says. "*Yes*. You were the Toronto cop. The Hold-up Squad. Oh my God, I'm so embarrassed. I'm sorry. McKelvey, you said. Of course. Yeah, I remember. God, what are you doing up here?"

"I grew up in Saint B. This is a temporary assignment, you could say."

"Sounds like the local guys could use all the experience they can get. Three times in a week this little place came across the provincial wire. Police officer assaulted, kid stabbed, and now a suspected meth lab blown up. The body, it was in pretty bad shape?"

"It'll be a dental ID. They've got a good cop, Nolan. He's on the ball."

"And the chief? This Gallagher?"

McKelvey has lived and breathed the Blue Code so long that his response comes instinctively. The same response he would provide to the Special Investigations Unit or Professional Standards. He doesn't say a word.

He looks down at the speedometer and eases off the gas. He is bringing them back to the station too quickly. Nolan needs the time to straighten things out, get Dr. Nichols on the page, and let Gallagher freshen up. "So you switched from city force to provincial, eh?"

"Nine years with Barrie, I had an opportunity to try out for the OPP's Criminal Investigations Bureau. Pay increase, better pension. And anyway, I like the uniform pants. The yellow stripe really does it for me."

She smiles at him. And then she frowns. "Are you feeling all right?"

"Oh, sure," he says, and he glances in the rear-view and sees his face is blanched.

His palms curl into the wheel as he swallows down another rivulet of this torment.

Nineteen

Chief Gallagher comes to on the couch in his living room. He opens his eyes and blinks at the ceiling. His mind is addled, groggy, thick with the booze he drank foolishly on an empty stomach. He is not a boozer, never was. Something he has turned to only and always at exactly the wrong time. He can't handle commotion, that's the thing. He has sought to control the weather, the temperature of things, since he was a boy in a home of chaos. And now the dial has moved right around to the other side, and sooner than later they will find out how he has been running this small operation. The books are a mess. Expenses have been padded, petty cash has been abused. He doesn't need foreign eyeballs rummaging through his business; he's been a sheriff for Christ's sake. Sat on the executive of the Oklahoma Sheriffs' Association, four thousand members. This place was supposed to be quiet, good fishing, better hunting, little more than a paid retirement. He saw himself moving into the little mayor's office. Sign that deal on the landfill with Celluci, and Jesus, the municipality wouldn't know what to do with the infusion of tax dollars. A hero, that's what they'd call him. A new recreation facility: Gallagher Complex. Closing on seventy years old and he rides in and saves a goddamned shit-ass town from closure, from a drug epidemic, from the clutches of hell itself.

He lifts up and swings his still-booted feet to the floor. He holds his head in his hands and steadies himself. A hero. Sure, and with money in his own pocket to burn. What was so wrong with a plan like that? Public service for a lifetime ought to result in something more than a paltry pension less deductions. Celluci had taken him on that fully-paid trip on a fishing boat out on the Gulf; yes sir, bobbing out there in the blue water with the sun and salt burning his eyes, catching kingfish, mahi, amberjack, barracuda shooting like silver muscle from the water. He didn't feel a bit guilty about accepting that gift, or others to come. He will pay for that trip one way or the other, anyway, for Celluci and the men he works for always get paid in the end.

It's the drugs, he thinks, the goddamned scourge of the lazy and the weak-minded. *Methamphetamine.* And now it has come to this small and isolated place, an island on dry land, and choices have been made, the wrong ones. On his watch. He has been so busy with his own plans, people will say he has lost touch with the community. He can admit that much, and it is a sin for any sheriff. Perhaps he should have hung up his badge years ago. He looks at Eddie Nolan sometimes and he doesn't know whether to be proud or jealous. He knows that Nolan waits for him to lead, to step out and show the way. Wear a big star on his vest like some goddamned vision of Wyatt Earp. But it doesn't work that way. He has tried to teach the kid as much as he can. Being a sheriff, being a chief, isn't about wearing a gun on your hip and throwing people in jail. It's about managing expectations. It's about delivering the illusion of safety and comfort, prosperity and peace. Knowing when to chew and swallow that mouthful of shit with a smile on your face. Is this the hill you're prepared to die on, he asks Nolan three times a week.

And anyway, he left the Midwest not for any of the reasons the townies here had whispered upon his arrival. No sir, just a story as old as the Bible. A man broken in half by a love turned sour, a man lifting his eyes to some new horizon. He thought of her all the time in those first long weeks and months adjusting to the Canadian winter that was beyond a definition you could put into words for the few friends he still talked with back home. He grew to respect and even embrace the cold, hard change that winter brought each year. Standing in the open, that biting ice and northern wind was strong enough to scour a man right clean, blow away the parts of himself he didn't want to keep fastened down.

It is rural men like Wade Garson that Gallagher best understands. The same version of a slightly different model found down in the small towns of Oklahoma, Kansas, Iowa. Men born of desperate families boiling with bad blood like a poison in the DNA, rich histories of violence and bred-in disrespect for the law and order of so-called square society. That Garson's place has blown up, that it appears to be the centre of production for this new entry of methamphetamine, it is so utterly predictable that it makes Gallagher wonder. It is the intelligence of Wade Garson, not the criminal motivation, which he has to consider. What it boils down to, there is no way in goddamned hell that Wade Garson has the wherewithal to mastermind the production and quiet distribution of meth on his own.

The phone rings from the kitchen. He lifts himself and gains some new energy as he puts himself in motion. He grabs the receiver, speaks his last name.

"Chief," Nolan says. "McKelvey's here with the investigator."

"Does he look like an asshole?" Gallagher asks.

"Uh, no. Not really," Nolan says. "She looks nice enough."

"She?"

"Correct."

Gallagher whistles. He spreads his thumb and forefinger across his moustache.

"Well, I'll be there in a tick," he says. "I need a shower and a shave, throw on a clean shirt."

Twenty

The squad room in the police station is sombre, the mood palpably dour as McKelvey walks in. Finn Madsen lingers just behind, briefcase in hand. Mayor Danny Marko and Dr. Nichols are slumped in chairs, heads bowed, and Nolan stands against a wall, arms crossed at his chest. The room smells strongly of the fire, wet cinders and a thick taste of burnt metal that settles like a coating on the tongue. Dr. Nichols is still wearing the hip waders, mucky with a milky grey ash that he has tracked across the floor. He is a tall and wiry man of sixty-five, silver hair thinning across a shining dome, and his round face is daubed in soot like a kid who has been playing in the mud. He looks up and blinks from behind thick wire-rimmed spectacles.

"Mark Watson died early this morning," the doctor says. "Septic shock settled in from the stabbing." His voice, weary from the long night and this recent news, make the words sound more like a question, as though there might be some room yet for negotiation. "Scotty Cooper will face charges for killing his best friend."

"Jesus," McKelvey says. He is yanked back to the middle-of-the-night phone call, sitting in the darkness on the edge of the bed with his wife just waking, clawing her way from the last good sleep she will ever know, the death of his own boy, this chain reaction of drugs to blades to bodies. "Where are the parents?"

Nolan uncrosses his arms and stands tall, almost at attention. "I just got off the phone with them," he says. "They've been at the hospital since he was admitted. The father said they were planning their first family trip to Mexico this March, and now they're planning a funeral."

The room falls silent for a time. Madsen finally clears her throat and sets her briefcase on the floor.

McKelvey says, "I'm sorry. This is Inspector Finn Madsen of the OPP."

The men stare for a moment, hardly hiding their indifference, and then introduce themselves and one by one they stand to shake her hand. There are no attempts at phoney welcome or small-town charm. This is uncomfortable for all, and the mayor, Danny Marko, looks as though he might cry. His eyes are red and welling. If McKelvey feels like an interloper, he can only imagine how awkward this must be for Madsen, cop or no cop. This is a small and closed room in a small and remote community.

"I know the Watsons well," Marko says, sitting up. "This is insanity. Mark Watson was an *A* student six months ago. What the fuck is happening to this place. Excuse my language."

He sits again, or more truthfully wilts to the chair.

"I hope I can help with that answer," Madsen says. "I have some experience with methamphetamine in the rural context. I took an extensive training course offered by the Drug Enforcement Agency. They're cutting their teeth on this issue in small towns all over the middle west. "

The men simply stare back at her.

"I sure hope your fancy courses can help us, miss. You'll have to excuse me, I need to go and help the Watsons with their arrangements," Marko says. "They've got to bring their boy back home here to be buried. And little Scotty Cooper can head off down to Kingston to the penitentiary instead of going to college."

The mayor takes his coat from a hook, pulls it on, and walks slowly to the door. Madsen moves aside to let him pass. Nolan follows the mayor and is about to close the door behind him when he hears the outer door open. Marko and Gallagher trade a few words and then the Chief comes in. He looks better, though not entirely well. His eyes are tired and his cheeks are red where a blade has just moments ago scraped away the silver stubble. The smell of half-digested booze has been masked with a good splashing of strong cologne, something manly, cedars and boot leather.

"Chief Gallagher," he says, and extends a hand with his politician's smile.

"Inspector Madsen," she says. "Finn Madsen."

"I could use a coffee there, Eddie. Why don't you put on a fresh pot while we all sit down and meet Miss Madsen here."

"*Inspector* Madsen will do just fine."

She smiles to warm the comment a little, but the frosty edge remains.

*   *   *

If murder is still front-page news in the world's largest and most dangerous cities, then in a place like Ste. Bernadette it must be a seeming force of nature or *anti*-nature, a foreign organism blown in on the winds of something evil, capable of forever altering the landscape and social fabric. For one thing, it invariably means at least two families have come together in the most violent and base way within the circle of humanity, the effects of which reverberate for generations. McKelvey is thinking of this notion, prying his memory of the wildcat strike and the explosion at the utility shed, the death of that scab worker, how the old guys at the Station Hotel had mentioned his father was somehow implicated. And then Duncan, the night manager, had said something cryptic a few days later. He'd bumped into McKelvey at the Coffee Time and he said, "Don't believe everything George Fergus says about your old man there." And that was it.

Now he re-focuses on the here and now.

"They'll need to be sent for proper analysis," Dr. Nichols says, "and I'm no forensic pathologist, but those aren't human bones up there. No sir. Deer likely."

Nolan's eyes flash. "So Wade Garson is still out there somewhere?"

"I didn't want to say anything in front of the mayor," Dr. Nichols continues, soft-spoken and measured, the same voice he uses when explaining some untreatable illness to his elderly patients. "I couldn't find any other remains in there. The explosion and fire were intense, but you'd need heat sustained at 700 to 800 degrees for several hours in order to turn bone completely to ash. There'd be the femurs for one thing, the skull for sure. So, yes, I'd say there's a good chance Wade Garson wasn't in that trailer when it blew."

Madsen makes notes in shorthand in a small notebook with a black cover, something that looks department-issued. McKelvey stirs sugar into his coffee and pictures the scene. Someone dragging a dead animal into the fire. No, it would be too risky. The animal being dumped in there prior to the explosion. Either way, it was obvious the carcass had been set there with the purpose of confusing the police, at the very least buying some time.

"He set the whole thing up," Nolan says. "He knew we were circling in on him."

"We don't know that," McKelvey says. He wants to push farther, give a short lesson in the consequences of making assumptions too early in a case. God knows he learned that lesson the hard way many, many times. "We've got to stick with what we know, which isn't much. No living relatives of Garson we can call, check to see if he's made contact?"

Gallagher shakes his head. "Got an older brother, Hank, that's all. And he's doing time at Monteith. Worth a call, though. Nolan, you can add that to your list."

"I'd like to speak with the family of this boy, Mark Watson," Madsen says.

"I should be the one to do that," says Gallagher. "They might be a little sensitive to an outsider during this difficult time."

"I'll have to insist, Chief," she says. "This is now a murder directly related to the sale of methamphetamine. You've already got a teen sitting in the detention centre for his meth-induced attack on Constable Nolan. Whoever manufactured the product, whoever sold it, may not be criminally responsible for Watson's murder. But they are responsible for introducing it to this community. The one thing I learned from my work with the DEA, we need to trace this back to the very root and cut it out. I'll start with the boy's family. Find out who he was hanging with, any new behaviours they noticed. And someone needs to get in to see the accused, this Scotty Cooper. Push him to reveal where the dope was coming from."

"I'll be there when you meet with the Watsons," Gallagher says. "And that's not negotiable."

"Fine. I'd also suggest we get a bulletin posted on Wade Garson to all local and provincial police within a hundred kilometres. And it wouldn't hurt to talk to the principal at the high school, maybe the teacher that the kids think is the coolest of the bunch, most likely to have an ear to the ground."

"I can do that," McKelvey offers.

"Sounds like we've got a plan here," Gallagher says. "I'll take you over to the Station Hotel, get you checked in. I'll get the Watsons on the phone and see if they're coming back to town tonight or tomorrow."

"First thing, though, I'd like to visit the scene of the fire," says Madsen, "and then go and see these bones for myself. Dr. Nichols, are you able to accompany us?"

The doctor nods. "You'll want some rubber boots."

Twenty-One

Having anticipated the moment she would slip inside and close the door to this confined and anonymous space, find herself easing into a deep tub of hot water, Finn Madsen is beyond disappointed when she sees her room at the Station Hotel. In fact, she stands there at the threshold of the doorway for a long minute. *Crap*, she thinks. She is reminded of western movies, and can't help but conjure images of scenes played out in this very space. Lonesome nights of desperate acts. She closes the door, sets her briefcase on the bureau, and hangs the garment bag in the small closet. The room smells as though it has been sealed shut for months.

She sits on the edge of the bed and sinks deep enough to feel the metal from the coiled bedsprings. It has been a twenty-hour day. Up long before dawn for one final argument with her husband, not speaking to one another on the drive to the airport, the flight in the Dash-8 that bounced and burped all the way from Orillia to that field in the middle of the thickest woods she has ever seen. Flying in low, the regional airport appeared like a concentration camp tucked away from civilization. A long day of enduring the cold and the male jackassery of this silver-haired cowboy, Chief Gallagher. Treating her like she is his granddaughter. Miss this, dear that. She knows she will tell him to piss off pretty soon. She thinks she could detect a lingering smell of booze on the man, and that would be just par for the course for these small-town coppers. The old man is a living, breathing cliché.

She moves to the bathroom, runs a hand in the darkness across the wall. She finds and flicks the light switch. A sixty-watt bulb flickers, hesitates, and then glows steady. The weak lighting does nothing for the room or her mood. There is a toilet, a sink stained brown at the drain from brackish water, and a shallow tub with a shower spout that is crusted with calcium and lime. The tub is also stained and scratched, dark gouges pocked like scars against white enamel. A bath is out of the question. As is room service, she imagines. She is starving, but the hunger has moved from growls and pangs to that place where she can focus again and ride it out, so hungry she is no longer hungry. The body is strange, she thinks, how we get used to pain or discomfort, how we learn to adapt to changing environments and conditions. She knows, for example, in a day or two the sight of this room will summon feelings of rest and privacy. It will become hers, for better or for worse. This is the greatest trait of humanity, she thinks: *we adapt and we survive.*

There are reports to file, and so she moves to the bureau and flicks on the small desk lamp. She opens the briefcase and pulls out a laptop and her notepad. She has a slim digital voice recorder, too, which she used when she and Gallagher spoke briefly with Mark Watson's father, David Watson, on the phone from the hospital in Timmins. The father was grief-stricken and exhausted, but managed to confirm that his son's behaviour had changed drastically in the past couple of months. Mark had experimented with marijuana, David was sure of that, and had skipped classes here and there. But there was a marked change after Christmas. The boy seemed to withdraw, became defiant, spent entire days away from school, and his behaviour grew increasingly erratic, staying up all night playing video games in the basement, irritable, no appetite.

She hits the play button and David Watson's voice fills the spare room, weary and hoarse from lack of sleep:

"We thought it was normal teenage stuff at first. But I see it now. The difference. We had no idea, no clue. We're both working, we're one of the lucky families, both my wife and I still have jobs. For now anyway. We assumed he would pull out of it. I guess we were just too busy. Now he's dead ..."

"Who is his best friend?" she hears herself asking, all of their voices disembodied across the telephone lines. *"The one person he would trust?"*

The recording picks up movements and voices in the background at the hospital. She closes her eyes. She pictures the room where he is calling from, a respite area for families. Soothing paintings on the walls, benign landscapes of Canadiana. She has never met the man, but she pictures his face, eyes closed, holding back the tears.

"Scott," he almost whispers. *"The boy who stabbed him."*

She stops the recorder and jots a few notes down. This will be her first interview. The murder suspect. She reviews her other notes from the day. The scene at the trailer was a disaster. The locals traipsed back and forth as though it were a fairground. The coroner is correct, however, in that the bones he discovered are most certainly not human. There have been no reported sightings of Wade Garson. In the morning she will request a ride to the correctional centre to interview the boy, Scotty Cooper. And she will attempt to interview the young officer wounded in the explosion, Constable Younger.

This town, it seems to her, is an icon. A dying way of life. A place carved from a single resource, and now the resource is in decline, and there is no backup plan. This nation was born and raised rural, she thinks, our tradition is in farming and exploiting the land, and yet today that connection is lost. We live in cities, or more accurately, we live in sprawling suburbs, we work in cities, and we buy our food in anonymous warehouses. She has been here a dozen hours and already she can tell there is no hope, there is only a sense of quiet acquiescence to this evolution. For now, there is nothing she can do. She is exhausted. And hungry again. She pulls her parka on and leaves in search of potato chips or jujubes, anything to fill the empty space.

*   *   *

He is dreaming that he is trapped in a large house, running a maze of hallways, and there is a phone ringing and ringing, and each door he opens only leads to another door and the sound of the phone ringing seems always to be coming from the next room down the hall.

When McKelvey opens his eyes and holds his breath, he hears the jangle of the telephone in the kitchen downstairs. It sounds like a dentist's drill, and he jumps out of bed and scrambles. *Caroline has found him.* She is on the line, he knows, and she has set up a conference call with Dr. Shannon and probably a team of psychiatrists. He takes the stairs two at a time, slides on the tile into the kitchen, snatching the receiver in mid-ring.

"Yes," he says. His heart hammers in his chest and he is winded.

"This McKeller?"

The man's voice is gruff, rough from cigarettes. McKelvey gets his bearings and realizes it is the middle of the night. Dark outside.

"McKelvey, yeah. Who is this?"

McKelvey hears sounds in the background, engines, big rigs gearing down, whining in the distance.

"Wade Garson."

McKelvey is still breathing hard. The sudden waking and the flight down the stairs have his T-shirt visibly undulating over his heart. He is sweating again, too, his face suddenly slick. The snake is back, curling through his lower intestines, forcing its evil into his belly, up to the back of his throat. He could puke. *Will* puke.

"How did you get my number?" he asks, and swallows the bile.

There is the sound of a lighter sparking, the caller drawing air.

"Fucking hard, that's how," Garson says. "Had to call the goddamned operator for new listings. Three times. Starting with your name, Mc-Something, and then down to who got a phone hooked up."

McKelvey can hear the mechanics of the man's smoking. The lips, the draw of air, the exhalation. The distant sound of an engine gearing down. Calling from a phone booth out on the highway somewhere. The truck stop. The only real possibility. Open around the clock.

"Where are you now?" McKelvey says. He eyes the sink and the faucet and wants to stick his head beneath a flow of cool water that smells and tastes of the earth, burn the fever to a steam.

"I don't trust no fucking cops, but you're the only one of the bunch not from here. So I got no choice, see. You're not *from* here and you don't know me and maybe that means I stand a fucking chance."

"What do you want from me?"

"I been set up. This is *bullshit*. I heard what they're saying, and it's a lie, a fucking lie. But who's gonna believe Wade

Garson, right? The Garsons can't hardly spell their own names, bunch of fucking redneck losers. Well you know what, asshole, I sell pot and hash and pills when I can get them, that's right, and I'll get you parts for your car, no problem. But you think I'm cooking goddamned *meth* out there? I never even smoked that shit myself."

McKelvey clears his throat and he blinks. The kitchen is still and quiet, and then the fridge clicks on and begins to hum with electrical current. The new sound is strangely soothing, and his fever ebbs. He takes a deep breath and feels well again.

"I can help you, Wade. Let me come to you and we can get this figured out. You're going to get picked up sooner or later. They've got a bulletin out on you."

"How the hell are you going to help me with Sheriff Smiley and that dipshit Nolan? That rookie Younger thought he'd be a hero, jumping in like that. I saw it, you know. I was coming through the woods. I almost got myself blown to shit. Lucky for me I was off jacking a whitetail. Everything I got was in that place, mister. I hauled ass after I seen Younger fall over from the smoke, Mr. Hero gonna save the day. And I cut through the woods and caught a ride out on the highway a few miles south of my lane."

"You can't run forever. You don't know me from a stranger. All I can do is give you my word. I'll come to you and we can talk. If you don't think we can fix this together, I'll let you take off to wherever you want."

"Bullshit," Garson says. And he draws mucous from the depths of his sinus, and he spits. "You'll just let me ride off like that, I bet."

"I don't have a gun, Wade. I don't even have handcuffs. I'm not interested in being a hero here, riding you back to town. You've got my word on that."

"I'm at the truck stop. I know the waitress and she'll cover for me if the highway cops come by, but not for long. I'll be in the washrooms at the back of the building. Middle stall. And you better say who you are, 'cause I've got a blade here, man. I'm not doing time like my brother Hank on some trumped-up charges."

"It'll take me half an hour, but I'll be there."

McKelvey hangs up the phone and moves to the sink. He turns on the tap and he stoops and scoops water and pours it over the back of his neck, cups it and splashes his face, finally drinks a mouthful. It is the cleanest, coldest water he has ever tasted. Earth, rocks, and minerals.

"Fuck all mighty," he says, and wipes his face with the bottom of his T-shirt.

The fridge stops, its final hum a reverberation in the empty room. He feels horrible. He is shocked and ashamed. He has underestimated the strength and grip of those seemingly benign pain pills. Once begun, one is obliged to maintain a baseline, a sort of maintenance level. Besides some rare moments of stupefaction when he has unwisely pushed beyond the regular daily amount of four pills — *morning, noon, dinner, and bedtime* — he recalls no jarring or unsettling effect beyond the obviously desired numbness. Once the flow has ceased, and done so with a cold and sudden halt, this is another matter altogether. He understands with a new sense of humility what he has done to himself, how he has meandered to this very place through his cynical philosophies, a belief in his ability to fight anything if given a fair shake. It is difficult to determine, here at the sink, whether he has been trying to kill himself or save himself.

Despite the promise to Wade Garson, he knows he can't meet the man alone. Perhaps in his younger days he wouldn't have thought twice about heading into the night on a mission like this. It was only this past September that he found himself criss-crossing the city in search of Tim Fielding, and he remembers all too well how that came to end. He is not unwilling to admit that he has lost some of the fool's courage he once owned, believing his actions at least partly responsible for the death of Detective Leyden. There; he has admitted it. This lump in the back of his throat has finally got a name: *Leyden*.

He will call Nolan and update the constable, recommend they arrive in separate cruisers. And this is what he does when he raises Nolan on the telephone.

"Give me a fifteen-minute head start," McKelvey says. "See if I can talk some sense into this guy, get him to come back to town and answer a few questions."

"I don't know, Charlie. Wade Garson is a loose cannon."

"I can handle myself. If he figures something is up, we'll lose him for sure. We can stay in touch by radio."

"Chief won't like this. But I'm in. I'll back you up."

McKelvey hangs up. And for the first time he regrets not taking Nolan up on the offer of a service pistol. He will be unarmed and without immediate backup as he faces a dangerous man backed into a corner, a man who has nothing left to lose. And that, McKelvey thinks as he heads up the stairs to pull on jeans, might be the only thing he and Garson have in common.

* * *

Finn Madsen has a can of Pepsi and a bag of Hickory Sticks open on the bureau when she hears voices bleeding through the thin walls from the room next door. She pauses her crunchy chewing and listens. The voices are not here in person, but coming across a radio, scratched with static. A man's voice. Followed by a woman's voice. Short, declarative exchanges. She gets up and moves to the adjoining wall, presses an ear to the fibreboard. She closes her eyes, as though this somehow enhances her hearing, and she makes out bits and pieces.

"... *Garson* ..."

"Truck stop. Over."

The conversation comes to a sudden stop. There is movement within the room next door. And then a door opens. She hears footsteps in the hallway. She goes to her door, opens it, and looks out in time to catch the backside of a man descending the stairs. She can't judge the height from this distance, and she instantly searches for a point of reference — the man's head, dark hair cut short, passes at the same height as a light mounted on the wall of the hallway. Dark dress pants. Long black coat. Or dark navy. Probably wool. And he's gone.

She puts these observations in her notepad, and she smiles to herself as she remembers working that bank robbery with McKelvey from the Toronto Hold-Up Squad. She remembers him now, of course she does, and she feels some embarrassment for her failure to make the connection earlier. She remembers how driven he was, tenacious, a dog with a bone. It seemed almost personal, the idea that this serial thief might slip between his fingers. She learned a few things from him, too. Like this. The importance of noting even the most seemingly insignificant observation — the scent of bubble gum, a brand of cigarette, a conversation heard through the thin walls of a cheap hotel.

And then she returns to the paperwork and her dinner of Hickory Sticks.

Twenty-Two

Now McKelvey rides the dark highway in the middle of the night. He replays his visit that afternoon to the high school. "Officer Grandpa," the kid had called him. Waiting outside the principal's office like he was back in school, sitting there in his jeans with a Saint B police uniform shirt buttoned up. Half a cop is what he felt like. No gun belt, no cuffs, not even a Maglite. The teen sitting across from him, his shaggy hair covering the tops of his eyes, cheeks dotted with acne, laces undone, some breakfast still stuck to the corner of his mouth, it brought McKelvey back to the worst days with his own son. When Gavin became openly defiant, daring McKelvey to … to what? *Hit him?* And he had, too, in that final and explosive encounter which resulted in Gavin running away, Caroline turning inward, the spark that set the whole wilderness of their lives ablaze. He wanted to tell this kid that, while it may seem hard to believe right now, in a few years he would gladly cut his hair and throw on a necktie in exchange for a girl who loves him and the promise of a steady paycheque. All of this posturing and posing will seem like it belonged to someone else, a stranger you hardly knew.

"What are you in for?" McKelvey had asked.

The kid raised his head a little and just blinked. McKelvey recognized the look. He may as well have been a slab of cheddar cheese carved into a duck. A strange and foreign object requiring of simultaneous translation. When the receptionist had called the boy, he rose and pulled his sloppy jeans up from his knees and slunk toward the vice-principal's office for trial and sentencing. It was on his way past that he mumbled that line — "Officer Grandpa" — and it made McKelvey smile now.

The visit to the school had confirmed that a select number of students — those already known or suspected to be marijuana users — seemed to have taken a nosedive over the recent months in terms of attendance and grades. McKelvey convinced the principal that Mark Watson's death made clear the need to circumvent privacy legislation in this instance, and he got a non-official list of five names scrawled on a piece of paper. Mark Watson, Scott Cooper, Travis Lacey, Steve Ridge, and Casey Hartman. These were the students whose behaviour stuck out the most. And three of those students were either in jail or dead. The visit also confirmed the fact that despite being with them and around them every day, even the school administrators seemed caught by surprise. They were in shock.

"I can't believe Mark Watson is dead," the principal had said with the door to his tiny office closed. McKelvey had been here before, forty-five years ago, a lifetime and just yesterday. A middle-aged man with plain features, the principal seemed an every-man, the sort of actor you'd get to play this very role, a small-town principal. "I've failed these kids," he said, and his eyes welled. He stared down at the paperclip he was absentmindedly unwinding. "We're supposed to not only *educate* them, but *protect* them as well. We're just like their parents, too busy and caught up with our own lives to notice them, *really* notice them ..."

McKelvey grips the wheel now and wishes it could be different, this trip through the strange landscape of adolescence. His mind moves forward to Wade Garson, who waits with what he imagines is an elaborate and far-fetched story he hopes will exonerate him. The explosion at the trailer, he will say, and the eventual discovery of materials used in the production of methamphetamine, well, he had nothing to do with either. He will lawyer up with this shady defence attorney the Chief so detests, this Harry Griffith, and anyway, the cops have nothing of value. Dr. Nichols, with a second opinion provided by Madsen, has confirmed the bones discovered belong to a deer and a large dog. The stabbing and resulting death of Mark Watson cannot be directly linked to Garson, regardless of whether he sold the dope that eventually contributed to a psychotic episode. It is one of the frustrating grey areas of law, and McKelvey has long desired the ability and authority to hold the pimps and dealers of the world accountable for the spinoff misery they cause.

That they must collectively find the source of meth production and distribution in Saint B is without question. This is the task at hand. The boy who stabbed Mark Watson, Scott Cooper, will face the consequences of his actions, to be certain. But McKelvey grips the wheel tighter and his jaw clenches as he relates the predicament of these two boys — the victim and the accused — to the fate of Gavin. And maybe his son would be alive today if he had never tried drugs. He would be alive today if he had never met a member of the Blades bike gang and started selling drugs for him. A bullet took his life, but drugs pulled the trigger.

A big illuminated sign for the Rest-Rite Truck Stop glows like an apparition in the dead darkness of these thick northern woods. Red lettering promises showers, hot meals, laundry, and diesel fuel. McKelvey turns in and drives past a few cars parked out front. The lights are on inside the restaurant, which is empty except for two or three people sitting alone at tables nursing coffees, reading the paper. He slows the cruiser and comes around to the rear of the truck stop. Half a dozen rigs are lined in neat rows on the far side of the building.

He steps from the vehicle and into the chilly grip of the night. The cold makes him shiver and his breath is visible in condensation that hovers in the air like mist. The lot is illuminated with the garish yellow of three tall light posts. As he approaches the back door with the symbol of a man tacked to it, he again second-guesses his quick refusal of Nolan's offer of a gun. He is utterly defenceless as he turns the knob and steps inside.

The washroom is tiled white from floor to ceiling. Four urinals and three stalls, a hand dryer and a metal box dispensing condoms and breath mints bolted to the wall. The room smells of disinfectant and old piss.

McKelvey bends over to look, spots a pair of booted feet in the middle stall.

"Wade," he says in a loud whisper.

There is no response. He moves closer and pushes the door of the middle stall. It swings slowly to reveal Wade Garson propped on the toilet, fully dressed, leaning back with his eyes staring, mouth hanging open, what looks like a full jar of strawberry jam splashed across the white tiles behind his head. The blood is mixed with bits of hair, white flecks of bone fragment, the glop plastered there and sliding down the tile like a mess made by a kid with craft paint and glue. McKelvey's insides constrict and he steps back. He turns on instinct to the row of sinks and bends to expel a mouthful of nothing. His stomach is empty and he rides the thrum of dry heaves, standing there with his hands gripping the old counter splashed with water and bits of paper towel. He spits, the best he can muster, steps back and wipes his mouth. He stands there in the silence of the truck stop washroom, looking over at the dead body of Wade Garson. And all he can think is *what a lonely goddamned place to die ...*

McKelvey is contemplating the body and his next move when he hears the door. Nolan steps in. His eyes go wide when he sees McKelvey, and he takes three steps and looks inside the middle stall.

"Oh, Jesus," he says.

And then, just as McKelvey has done, Nolan pivots and grips the counter in time to gag and spit into the sink.

*   *   *

The glowing white dome light of the ambulance illuminates the round face and hazel eyes of Inspector Madsen. The paramedics have been sent in to get a coffee and keep warm while Dr. Nichols climbs out of bed to attend his second crime scene in twenty-four hours. Chief Gallagher has arrived in his own four-by-four Jimmy with Madsen, and he secures the washroom while Nolan searches the immediate perimeter. McKelvey and Madsen sit in the back of the ambulance reviewing the facts of the situation.

"Gallagher called me after Nolan called him," she says. "Chief was on his way out here before he thought to loop me in. I told him I'll need a vehicle of my own. I'm not going to be dependent on some ..." and she searches for words, frustrated. "Some silver-haired misogynist."

Misogynist. McKelvey rolls the word on his tongue. He understands the notion, for he himself has been guilty of the charge. Sure he has. In those days when the first women started appearing like an alien species inside the sanctum of the squad room. The environment, the jokes, everything changed. It would be a lie to say otherwise. But it was only now, in his old man's hindsight, that McKelvey could see the change had been for the better. He believed that men and women saw the world through a different lens, and it was by combining these views into the same set of glasses that their collective work was heightened.

"Gallagher's a small-town sheriff at heart," McKelvey says. It is not an excuse, simply a statement of the facts. "He feels threatened with the provincial cops coming in. Even more so that it's a woman. He's all bark."

McKelvey looks around at the boxes of bandages, clear IV lines, tubes, tapes, chrome parts shining, and he feels too close to *infirmity*. The sense of vulnerability he has always found in hospitals, doctor's waiting rooms, it feels to him like suffocation. He is not dizzy, but he feels a little off-centre. This is the fog he still carries thanks to the pills, or more rightly, their absence. He still feels a little like a tube of toothpaste that has been rolled and squeezed in the hope of coaxing one last dab. He looks at Madsen and she sort of smiles at him, but not quite. For some reason she reminds him of a cub reporter on the police beat, sitting there with her back straight, eyes wide to the world, notepad peeled.

"So you arrived here at, what, midnight or shortly after?"

"Five past midnight," he says.

"Constable Nolan responded at 12:13," she reads. "Found you in the washroom, the body of Wade Garson in the middle stall. Nolan secured the scene and called the Chief at 12:20. Nolan called for paramedics at 12:21. Nolan then gathered the restaurant staff and the three customers at a table. You secured the scene until the Chief and I arrived."

McKelvey gets up and opens the doors of the ambulance, lets in the night air. He sits back down on the stretcher and steadies himself. He is lightheaded, a little dry of mouth.

"Garson called me," McKelvey says, and glances at his watch, "an hour and twenty-five minutes ago."

"How did he have your number?"

"Said he had to call directory a bunch of times. We could check the records on the phone booth out by the highway. I'm pretty sure that's where he called from. Said he couldn't trust the local cops, so he took a chance. He wasn't home when his trailer exploded. Felt he was being set up. He must have been desperate, because my only interaction with him didn't go in his favour."

Madsen makes notes. The deck of the ship is swaying, and so McKelvey closes his eyes a moment and imagines his feet planted firmly on the ground. He opens his eyes and the world is still.

"How long did it take you to get out here?" she asks.

"About thirty-five minutes. I had to wash my face and throw on some clothes first. I wasn't feeling very good."

"It hit me when the Chief called and told me about Garson's murder here at the truck stop. Someone in the hotel has a police radio or a scanner," Madsen says. "I heard the call through the wall. The guy left right after the call was dispatched that Garson was seen at the truck stop. I'll need to see who's staying in the room next door."

"So who was here in the truck stop in the last hour?" McKelvey's brain is beginning to work again, finding the old slots and grooves. It's like riding a bike. It all comes back to him as he sets in motion the line of questioning, the trail of evidence to be checked and eliminated.

"Travelling salesman, a trucker, and some fellow from Detroit," Madsen says.

"Guy named Celluci by any chance?"

She regards her notes. "That's it. You know him?"

"We've met. Where's Nolan now?"

As though on cue, Nolan comes around the side and stands there in the wide band of light cast from the ambulance. He holds between his gloved thumb and forefinger a small silver revolver with a pearl-grip handle.

"In the trash can by the side of the building," he says.

"Bag it," Madsen says. "Where's the Chief?"

"He's securing the body," Nolan tells her. "Dr. Nichols is just pulling in."

"I've put a call into HQ requesting a forensics officer, likely from the Timmins detachment," Madsen informs them. "But it could be late morning tomorrow before they get here. That's if this storm they're calling for blows over. I have a little video camera in my bag. I can shoot a three-sixty of the scene."

She steps down from the ambulance, then pauses to regard the revolver still gripped between Nolan's fingers.

"A .38 Smith & Wesson," she says. "Six-shot, four-inch barrel. It's cute."

Madsen walks over toward the restaurant doors. Nolan watches her go. When he is sure she is out of earshot, he says, "Charlie. This gun, I've seen it before."

McKelvey lifts himself up and steps down from the ambulance. He does not want to spend another minute in the back of that place, that transporter of the infirm, the dead, the dying. He wants to wash himself, cleanse himself of bad karma.

McKelvey says, "She's right. It is cute."

"It's the *Chief's*," Nolan says in a loud whisper.

McKelvey stares at the younger cop.

"His personal weapon," Nolan says. "Keeps it at the station in the lockbox."

Nolan's face betrays a mixture of bewilderment, fear, confusion, and disappointment. McKelvey thinks Nolan looks like a father who has found contraband in his son's bedroom.

"You're positive?"

"As sure as I can be. I'd have to go and check the locker, of course, but this is the only gun like it that I've ever seen. Jesus, Charlie. What does this mean? What do we do now?"

McKelvey sees the paramedics coming out of the restaurant doors with steaming Styrofoam cups of coffee. They could be a couple. They are both in their late thirties, the man stocky like a high-school football player and the woman is wide at the hips and shoulders, her pretty face glowing with health. Both of them are built for lifting and delivering bodies of all sizes and shapes.

"We've got to tell Madsen," McKelvey says.

Nolan looks over at the paramedics, who are halfway to the ambulance now.

"Shit," Nolan says. "What if it really is the Chief's gun?"

"We'll deal with that if and when the time comes. Right now you don't have any allegiances, Ed. Your only loyalty is to the crime scene and the collection and preservation of evidence."

McKelvey is surprised by his own rousing soliloquy on the stoic nature of police ethics delivered in the cold dark lot of the Rest-Rite Truck Stop. The paramedics step to the back of the ambulance. McKelvey moves fast, and he takes and slips the revolver into his coat pocket.

"How bad is the coffee?" McKelvey asks, flashing a phoney smile.

The male paramedic takes a sip from the Styrofoam cup and offers a grimace.

"Slightly better than no coffee," he says. "Hey, is Dr. Nichols coming, or what?"

"Any minute," Nolan says.

"There's a big storm coming in from up north, eh," the woman paramedic offers. And then she leans in close to the two cops and says, "So, you figure there's a hit man on the loose? Organized crime?"

Nolan goes to answer but McKelvey cuts him off.

"Can't discuss the case," he says.

And then McKelvey steps away, walking toward the cruiser he has been loaned. Nolan catches on and follows. McKelvey turns to him. "Go on in and send Madsen out here, okay? You stick with Gallagher. Don't let him out of your sight. And don't say anything about finding the gun. You good with that?"

Nolan nods. McKelvey stops and watches the young officer turn and walk back toward the doors leading to the washrooms. Nolan walks like a robot. McKelvey knows the kid is in shock from the sight of Garson's body; seeing the blood and guts up close like that, it's something they can't train you for. And someone you know, like Garson, brings home the fact of your own mortality all the more. Here one second and gone, just like that. The fragile nature of this strange arrangement has been made all too clear to Officer Nolan. What exactly is happening here, McKelvey is not sure, but he knows there is bad business afoot in Saint B. And he hopes the Chief and Nolan can keep it together long enough to save their town from sliding off the map into a new modern hell.

But even as he thinks this, he hears the whisper of his own heart: *It's too late …*

Twenty-Three

The day crawls forward to reveal itself in a sky of scratched and unpolished silverware. Light snowflakes fall, or more accurately, meander to the ground, and the air hangs heavy with the chill of threatened precipitation — the storm so promoted may be coming after all. The body of Wade Garson has been inspected, photographed, and removed to a temporary storage unit at Chapelle's Funeral Home in town, where Dr. Nichols can keep it sufficiently cool until, in his mind, the "proper authorities" arrive and rescue him from this sudden late-career thrust into criminal forensics. He has offered to stay at the funeral home and "guard the body," as it were, but mostly he is looking to hide for a few hours. The notion that he will eventually testify, indeed that his medical notes and expertise may be deemed crucial in a criminal trial, fills him with a dread that reminds him of exam day back in school, that sick feeling that seemed to drape over his shoulders like a wet wool blanket.

Madsen discovered in a corner of the washroom a spent .38 calibre shell casing which she bagged as evidence. All those in attendance at the crime scene were interviewed, with not one having registered the sound of the gunshot. This information had been put into context by one of the kitchen staff, who said it was common for big rigs to backfire or otherwise emit loud expulsions of burning diesel. One of those interviewed has been identified by both Madsen and McKelvey as a "person of interest." There is no interview room, and so Tony Celluci sits in the centre of the squad room of the Saint B police department. McKelvey sits at the Chief's desk and Madsen occupies a third chair directly across from Celluci. Officer Nolan and Chief Gallagher have returned to Wade Garson's trailer to check for anything that might have been missed, including, at Madsen's instructions, footprints through the surrounding woods leading to or from the trailer. McKelvey plays with a paperclip, content to have Madsen open the game.

"Midnight snack is all," Celluci says in response to the first and most obvious question. He is dressed in dark jeans and a blue button-down Oxford, his long black wool overcoat hanging on the hat tree by the door. "Nothing open in this shit town after nine o'clock."

Madsen studies her notes and then closes and sets the book on the edge of the desk. McKelvey watches her, and he notices the small change to her face. Her eyes narrow and her jaw sets. She is ready.

"Let's cut the crap here, Tony," she says.

Celluci likes something about this new direction, and he can't hide a small smile.

"You're staying in a room beside me at the Station Hotel. I heard your police scanner go off last night when Nolan informed dispatch he was heading to the truck stop. You left your room immediately after that call. I saw you go. Are we to assume that within seconds of receiving the transmission from Nolan your stomach began to growl?"

Celluci doesn't say anything. He sits as though he is getting a haircut, shoulders back. His hands move from his lap and clasp together in a final display of ease.

"I checked with the Michigan State Police and you have a CPL — *concealed pistol license*," Madsen says.

"And so does half of Detroit," he says. "Maybe even three-quarters."

McKelvey clears his throat. If he were at home in a stuffy interview room back in Toronto, he would fall into the easy role of negotiator here, the good old cop who understands how this terrible thing has happened, how a situation can run out of control and anyway, sometimes a man can't be helped. Here in this antiquated squad room, in this suffocating town, he feels off his game, part western-movie sheriff, part Andy of Mayberry.

"Why do you have a police scanner, Tony?" McKelvey asks.

Celluci shrugs. "Use it to watch for speed traps."

"Use a radar detector for speed traps, not a scanner. A scanner catches the dispatch calls. You know, like a bank robber uses one to know how much time he has before the heat arrives on-scene."

"It's a toy, nothing more. If they're illegal up here, you can take it."

"This landfill site you're shopping around up here," McKelvey pushes on, "I understand the best access point to the land cuts across Wade Garson's country estate. They're dumb and bad as hell, but those Garsons managed to hold on to a lot of land on the edge of Saint B. They wouldn't sell?"

"There are always other options, other ways to get the same result," Celluci says. "You should ask your Chief about his views on the landfill. I understand he feels quite confident the deal is in the best interest of the town."

"This town needs a life preserver, that's for sure. What do you make of this recent spike in crime, Mr. Celluci? I'm sure you've heard we've got a bit of a problem with meth."

"I'm not a sociologist, I'm just a businessman. But I'd say the same principal applies here in Ste. Bernadette as it does in business."

"And what principal is that?" McKelvey asks, already forming a severe dislike for this man's smugness and bottle-tanned face.

"Survival of the fittest. The weakest succumb to the promise of instant gratification — like pacifying kids with candy. The winner has a plan for the long game. It's all about spiking the ball in the end zone."

"You don't look like you're used to losing very often, Mr. Celluci."

"I can spot a sucker from a mile away. Doesn't make me a killer."

Madsen sees her opening and she turns to Celluci. "You won't mind if I swab your hands for a gunshot residue test, then?"

Celluci holds both hands out like a child awaiting an inspection. His hands are well tended, the nails clean and trim, and they do not shake. Madsen opens the black case at her feet and rummages around. When she comes back up she holds a test tube and swab kit, something reserved for DNA tests, and a balled pair of blue latex gloves. She pulls the gloves on quickly, something she has obviously done many times, like putting socks on while she sits on the edge of the bed in the morning. McKelvey watches as she runs the swab over Celluci's fingers and palms and then returns the swab to the tube. Next she opens a small packet and removes what appears to be a hand towelette. She wipes his hands and fingers and places the soiled tissue in a second vial.

"That's all for now, Mr. Celluci," she says. "I'd ask you to let me know if you plan to leave town in the next few days. We may have some follow-up questions."

Celluci stands and moves to the door. He pulls on his long coat, smoothes it with his hands, and nods before leaving.

"Prince Charming," Madsen says.

"Not the first narcissist to make his way in the business world."

McKelvey leans back in the Chief's chair. Grey daylight streams through the front windows, the sort of dead-of-winter light that is for some reason harder on the eyes than blaring sunshine. He has not pulled an all-nighter at a crime scene in about three years. Hard to believe it has been that long since he was in the game, and yet everything comes back to him as though his muscles and cells remember how this works. He will be sixty years old in less than two months. He is unsure of where he is headed, where his next move will take him. Everything is strange to him right now except for the process, the procedures, the age-old strategies to be implemented, and so he does what he has always done when the world is too loud and he feels as though he is being poked by a hundred unseen hands: he holds his breath and dives in head first.

"He's been interviewed by the cops before, that much is obvious. Guy was slick as hell. I have to ask, Madsen. Do all provincial investigators carry a mini lab around for GSR and prints and stuff?"

Madsen sets the vials out on the desk and then leans down and picks out a small spray bottle that could easily be perfume or air freshener. She writes on each vial with a marker, recording Celluci's name, the date, time, and place.

"This one we'll save for the lab," she says, and indicates the swab in the test tube. "This other one we can check right now in the field. The towelette applied diluted hydrochloric acid to his skin and this spray will indicate the presence of antimony, nitrate, sulphur, or lead. It's not admissible in court, but it can help weed out the number of POIs."

"We used to do the paraffin wax job," he says. "Just dip and send to the lab."

"It's still used, but time is of the essence, as you know," she says. "We're an instant gratification society. We'll have a drive-thru lab one of these days."

She finds a pair of tweezers in her case to hold the towelette and shoots a mist of spray. She waits a beat and then shoots a second blast of fine mist. McKelvey watches with interest. On the big-city force, these duties fall entirely to the forensic officers. It gets harder each year to get away with a crime, he thinks. Soon there won't be any fun in police work at all.

"Interesting," she says, holding the towelette which has changed from white to a light pink. "Definitely traces of potassium nitrate. That's the key ingredient in black powder cartridges."

"That's old school," McKelvey says. "They use smokeless powder these days."

Madsen retrieves the small plastic baggie with the spent shell casing. She uses the tweezers to extract the casing and hold it up. Squinting one eye shut, she appears like a jeweller examining a diamond.

"Remington 14 GRS thirty-eight cal," she reads. "This is vintage. And the firing pin has left a very deep and clear impression, about as good as a fingerprint. I imagine it'll be a perfect match with the .38 Nolan found in the trash can. Speaking of which, we need to lock all of the evidence down."

McKelvey sighs and reaches behind his chair where his jacket hangs. He has bagged the .38. He pulls it out of his pocket and sets it on the desk.

"Introducing new information," he says. "And before you freak out, I had my reasons. Nolan says this looks like the personal weapon of Chief Gallagher. In fact, he's quite positive the gun belongs to Gallagher."

Madsen stares at him. She does not blink.

"Says he keeps it in the lockbox right here, by his desk," McKelvey continues.

Madsen blinks finally, but her expression remains stony.

"I get the distinct impression you're mad at me," he says.

"When were you good old boys going to bring me into the loop? I mean, it's not like it's potentially the murder weapon or anything."

McKelvey sits up. "Listen, the kid is scared, okay? He's shitting his pants right now. This is his *chief*. The only cop boss he's ever had. And anyway, I'm telling you now. You know, Inspector, not every motive is underwritten by your jaded perception that all men in law enforcement necessarily discount their female counterparts."

He smiles at her. She busies herself collecting the various baggies and vials and storing them in her black case. She picks up the bag with the revolver and weighs it in her palm.

"I'm sorry," she says. She lifts her head, and uses the back of her gloved hand to move stray strands of hair from her face, and she sighs. "I'm having some home issues. Let's just say it's starting to affect my view of all men. You don't deserve that. And I do remember working with you, you know. You were a good detective. I learned from you."

"Forget it," he says. And he thinks, *I probably deserve my share of it, to be honest. All of us do.* That too-long look across the squad room, the drop of the glance to chest level when all eyes should be on the job at hand. He can work with a beautiful woman and has done so, there is no doubt, and he can respect her experience and her authority without hesitation or question. But what he can't get past is the smell of her from across this desk, the plain beauty of her face without sleep or makeup, the seemingly insignificant gestures that reach him and tickle something that feels dead. How something inside of him ached as he watched her standing in the headlight beams of the cruiser in the parking lot of the truck stop, how she reached up and tied her hair back with her two hands, working quickly because it is an action she has performed a thousand times without even thinking. That's what they don't understand about us, he thinks; how they can kill us by simply crossing their legs.

"The way I see this, we've got two problems, Charlie. First, why would someone purposefully leave behind a spent shell casing from a revolver when they could have simply disposed of it at a later time. That requires a specific and deliberate effort. To shoot someone in the head and then take a moment to crack the revolver and pull out the casing and set it on the floor. A pistol, sure, you have to deal with auto ejection and look around for the casings. Even then, only the pros remember to pick them up in that moment of fear and adrenalin. Fingerprints on casings are hard to come by because the oil from skin gets burned off during firing. So it is obvious our perpetrator wants to leave behind some evidence for us. Is this a game to the killer? And second, whose gun is this?"

"Nolan said Gallagher keeps the key to the lockbox on him or he forgets it at home," McKelvey says. "So we've got no choice but to come at him straight on. Would be better if we knew for sure it was his gun when we corner him on this. I hate going in with half the information. It'll change our relationship, that's for sure."

"Well," she says, and smiles a little, "what if I keep Gallagher and Nolan busy with some things and you take a little poke around the Chief's place?"

McKelvey looks at her in surprise. Perhaps it is the long night and lack of sleep, the fact his body is still fluttering in the absence of the pills, but he finds her so incredibly attractive right now that a physical loneliness rises in his chest in a balloon that he can't swallow. He almost smiles to himself as he imagines her pulling her sidearm on him when he says *Hey, did you know you're beautiful.*

So instead he says, "I like how you think, Inspector."

Twenty-Four

The Coffee Time is busy with locals alternately discussing the murder of Wade Garson, the memorial service to be held for Mark Watson when the weather breaks, and debating whether the storm will be sufficiently ferocious to close the main highway. There are mentions of food reserves, canned goods and liquor and cigarettes and bingo cards, all the necessities of life. Outside the snow is picking up steadily. A bitter wind howls in from the northeast on a sharp angle that lifts and holds the flakes in mid-air, sometimes creating a momentary horizontal blur of pure whiteness. McKelvey smiles at Peggy as he comes in the door, tails of snow sneaking in with him. A dozen and a half heads turn in unison to watch him, and the place goes silent for a full second. He steps through the tables to the counter as conversation resumes. He hears his name whispered, and that of Wade Garson, Gallagher, Nolan, all of them mixed up in this together.

"Hello, stranger."

Peggy smiles at him, and for the second time in less than an hour his body flushes with desire. He sees the two of them in back, bags of flour sending dust in the air like the snow outside, his hands on her hips, all over her body, her uniform shirt open to the fifth button, doughnuts in the fryer and a line of customers at the counter. He's not sure whether this is normal, or whether it is a side effect of drug withdrawal, but he feels like a teenager again, buzzing with strange hormones.

"Charlie?"

McKelvey snaps out of it and says, "Sorry, I haven't slept yet."

Peggy pours coffee in an extra large take-away cup.

"It's the talk of the town, as you can imagine," she says. "People are really starting to wonder if you and Gallagher and Nolan can handle this. Not that anyone's mourning the death of Wade Garson, exactly."

"It's under control," he says, and takes the cup and pours sugar from a glass dispenser. He has only started adding sugar since he began drinking the pitiful coffee here, trying to sweeten the bitter chemistry. "Listen, I wanted to thank you for that little saying you gave me. It made me think of things in a new way. My life in police work and my life today. What I'm supposed to be doing."

He wants to tell her about his son and his loss and what he has learned, about the pills and how he feels like a man who has been wandering in a storm for years, simply putting one foot in front of the other, walking blind. He wants to tell her that the words in that poem are true, perhaps the truest words that ever described who he was and what he had tried to do all his life. *It all turned out wrong,* he wants to tell her, *but I meant to be a good man.*

"A couple of old-timers were in here yesterday asking about you," she says. "Said they were friends of your father's. I hope you don't mind I told them you were staying at your old place."

"I don't mind. Listen, I've got a favour to ask you. Something that you either say yes or no to, but you can't really ask any questions. Okay?"

Peggy stands straight and she waits, smiling with her eyes.

"Can you leave here, take a break for an hour?" he says.

She looks over her shoulder at the big round clock hanging on the wall.

"Sure. I can get Pauline in back to watch the counter," she says. And her hands are already working behind her back to undo her apron.

*   *   *

Peggy sits in the cruiser. Like a bank-robbing duo, she has instructions to honk the horn if Gallagher pulls into the drive.

"This is the most fun I've had in two years," she says, and grins like a schoolgirl. "And I know, I know, I can't ask any questions."

McKelvey opens the door and slides out of the driver's seat.

"If I'm not back in ten minutes, you need to get out of here," he says.

"Seriously?" she says, and her smile disappears.

He turns back, leans into the cruiser.

"I added that for dramatic effect," he says. "Just honk if anyone pulls in."

Inside the Chief's home, McKelvey is unsure what exactly he's looking for. Perhaps some obvious clue to the increasingly likely fact the Chief's gun was used in the killing of Wade Garson. Why the chief of police would kill Wade Garson is the question. Opportunity, sure. Anyone could have slipped in and out of that washroom at the back of the truck stop at that hour of the night. Motive is the thing. What motive would Gallagher have for shooting Garson? And then to toss his own handgun in a trash container at the murder scene. But before doing that, he takes the time to crack the revolver, pull out the spent shell, and toss it on the floor. The shooter is either Gallagher, and he wants to get caught. Or the shooter wants to frame Gallagher.

The home smells of oil heating. McKelvey has gained entry with little effort. It is a known fact that these old homes settle and shift as the ground freezes, so that doors and their locksets are often just slightly off-kilter. He gave the door a hard push above the doorknob and it opened. Had this not been the case, he was prepared to employ other measures, namely a butter knife pocketed from the Coffee Time.

Gallagher keeps a tidy home for a bachelor, but then McKelvey supposes an intruder would say the same about his condo in Toronto's historical Distillery District. He enters at the back and steps into a clean and sparse kitchen. There is a small table and two chairs, some toast crumbs and a couple of coffee mugs left on the counter. He opens the cupboards and finds plates and glasses, then checks below the sink. There are two empty whisky bottles standing by the drain pipes. These would be the bottles Nolan emptied when he fetched the Chief.

The living room is just as sparse; however, this room owns a little more character, a taste of the man. There is a painting on one wall of a western scene — a couple of faraway riders crossing a sun-baked prairie on horseback — a small TV on a chest, a long coffee table that appears to have bull horns for legs. McKelvey can't help but pause a moment to admire the gleaming polished horns, four of them, holding this tablet of wood upright. On the coffee table there are two or three copies of a glossy magazine, *Cowboys and Indians*. There is the corner of a manila envelope sticking out from underneath them. McKelvey sets the magazines aside and sits on the couch to check the mail. The envelope is letter-size, addressed to Chief Gallagher. The postmark says DETROIT, and the date — McKelvey squints to read the smudged ink — looks like late December.

The envelope is already ripped open, so he pulls the contents free with his index finger and thumb. Two or three tickets are paper-clipped to a letter.

> *Chief —*
> *Remember, ashes to ashes and dust to dust!*
> *Let's see this through to the end.*
> *Come on down to Motown to celebrate.*
> *Tony*

There are two tickets to a Red Wings game — dated for a Saturday in February — along with a plane ticket from Sudbury to Windsor. McKelvey files the material back into the envelope and stands. He is moving down the hallway when a horn blast makes him jump. His heart pounds as he takes fast and long strides to the kitchen, to his boots which are by the door.

He has trouble shoving his feet into the boots, and he swears and feels like a goddamned kid again wrestling with footwear instead of taking the time to unlace. He finally manages to crush the leather and lining sufficiently to accommodate his feet, and he opens the door and slips outside. He locks and closes the door behind him and comes around the side of the house to see Constable Nolan standing by the driver's window of McKelvey's cruiser, talking to Peggy.

Nolan steps back and gives McKelvey a searching look.

"What were you doing, Charlie?"

"Stopped by to see if you and the Chief were back yet. We interviewed Celluci, and Madsen ran a GSR on his hands. He tested positive for black powder."

Nolan nods and blinks. The younger cop is not convinced, McKelvey can tell.

"Black powder," Nolan says, "like they used in older ammunition."

McKelvey nods. "Where's Gallagher? I thought the plan was you would stick by him, keep an eye."

"He drove over to the funeral home to talk to Dr. Nichols."

The two men stand there in the Chief's snow-packed laneway, Peggy in the cruiser trying not to look at them. It is snowing steadily now, and their shoulders and Nolan's ever-present toque get dusted with flakes that exist for a moment and then dissolve.

"So," Nolan says, seeming shy to ask, "what were you *really* doing over here? I mean, after we found the Chief's gun at the scene and everything. You must have some ideas."

"Well," McKelvey says, "probably the same thing you were doing coming over here if the Chief was headed to the funeral home."

"Spying?"

McKelvey shrugs. "Spying sounds so … *dirty*."

"Surveillance?" Nolan offers up.

McKelvey considers this and nods, as though it is in fact the exact word he has been searching for to complete his crossword. For now, he will keep his discovery of tickets and the letter from Celluci to himself. Alone it proves nothing more than perhaps the fact the Chief is open to accepting a bribe. As a non-elected public official, McKelvey isn't even sure it would count as anything more than a gift accepted in bad taste. It is the strange wording in the note that has his mind working — *ashes to ashes and dust to dust.*

"So what's next?" Nolan asks.

The snowfall is increasing in intensity by the minute. If the much-hyped storm delivers as advertised, then their work will become all the more complicated. On the plus side, McKelvey thinks, nobody will be able to leave town.

"I'll take Peggy back to the shop," McKelvey says, "and then we should sit with Madsen and start back at square one, starting with the Travis Lacey attack on you. Work our way forward. Throw all of our cards on the table and see if we can get a few pairs."

"And what about the Chief?"

McKelvey tilts his head back and looks up into the stone-coloured sky. The flakes are mesmerizing, a pattern that blurs all relation to sky or ground, and he can't keep his eyes open. But the snow is wet and cold on his face, and he feels like a kid again, and it crosses his mind that he wants to live, he does indeed, and maybe that has not been made as clear as it could have been.

"I guess we hope he doesn't have a matching card."

Twenty-Five

Madsen sits in the police station alone, the compilation of evidence and notes spread before her. She has a cup of Earl Grey tea, something stale rummaged from the poorly stocked kitchen. The fridge is a horror show of old yellow mayonnaise dried and cracked like plaster inside a nearly empty jar, some ancient cheese slices sprouting patches of wispy grey fur, an opened box of Arm & Hammer baking soda for no apparent purpose, a jug of water, a Tupperware containing nondescript leftovers that were in their original life a stew, perhaps chili or meatloaf. Boys, she thinks, and their mess.

What she has before her is also a mess.

"Good Lord," she mutters to herself as she regards the file of notes recorded by the municipality's so-called coroner. There are no admissible tire tread casts from the Garson fire, the scene itself ruined for evidence by the trampling of Dr. Nichols. The fire marshal's early report indicates some sort of accelerant was employed in the blast, but the heat was sufficient to burn away all other useful evidence. The truck stop is visited daily by a hundred different people leaving prints and DNA behind, especially in a washroom. What she needs is a continuum of evidence putting Tony Celluci closer to a motive and an opportunity to kill the small-time drug and junk dealer Wade Garson. But the blowing snow outside means her promise of forensic assistance is delayed another day.

She is looking at the spent shell casing in the plastic evidence bag when McKelvey and Nolan enter the station. They kick snow from their boots and the sound reminds Madsen of being a kid in school, coming in from recess with red cheeks, a snowsuit soaking wet, the smell of wool mittens drying on a radiator.

"You boys out making snowmen?"

Nolan sets a box of doughnuts on the desk. "Breakfast of champions," he says.

"It's way past breakfast where I come from."

"Brunch of champions?"

He opens the box and, like a big kid, puts his tongue to his upper lip as he peruses the varieties. He chooses a Boston cream and takes a big bite.

"Do you ever take your toque off?" Madsen asks him. She leans over and peers into the box of doughnuts. "You should let that injury breathe a little. Not good to keep it wrapped up like that all the time."

Nolan reaches up with his free hand and absent-mindedly touches the toque.

"I think I fell asleep with it on last night."

Madsen decides against a doughnut and turns back to the papers before her. She has compiled all of the various notes into a one-page synopsis.

"These are all the subjects interviewed," she says. "The names circled indicate subjects with opportunity and or motive."

McKelvey takes the page and sits with his back to the window in the Chief's chair. Madsen watches him reading, thinking. Nolan stands with his back to the wall, finishing his doughnut.

"You gravitate naturally to that chair, did you know that?"

McKelvey looks up at her. His face is innocent, a boy's, and it is obvious he has not thought about this — taking the Chief's chair.

"We've got Laney the arcade owner, Gaylord the pharmacist, Celluci from Detroit, Carl Levesque, and ... we need to add Gallagher," he says.

"These are people of interest for Wade's murder or for producing the meth?" Nolan asks. He has finished his doughnut and is wiping his hand down the side of his dark uniform pants.

"Let's pretend for a moment the two are connected — which seems obvious to me, but maybe not," Madsen says. "If we're looking at Celluci, the issue with Wade Garson may have been around his land, period. If we're looking at this as a connection, I'd suggest we're dealing with a partnership that turned sour. Someone — maybe someone on this list — was producing meth and distributing it with Wade Garson."

"Laney may know her arcade is used for deals," Nolan says. "But I can't see her working with Garson, and she sure as hell isn't a killer."

McKelvey nods. He regards the list again. "Who had access to the murder weapon besides Gallagher?"

Nolan looks to his boots and thinks for a minute.

"Gallagher, me, Constable Younger ... and Celluci. The Chief was having a drink with Celluci a few days ago in here and I remember the drawer being open, the lockbox sitting right there. Who knows, maybe the Chief showed it to him. He liked to do that every once in a while. Show it off. He'd say how it was a modern version of the gun Doc Holliday used to carry around to poker games, except Holliday used a .32, not a .38."

Madsen makes notes, updating the profile sheet on Celluci.

"In terms of the meth production, your creepy local pharmacist would have the professional ability, he certainly has access to some of the ingredients, and his general attitude toward the recent spike in crime seems alarming," McKelvey says.

"He was in bed with his wife when Wade was killed," Nolan says.

"And Levesque?" Madsen asks. "Who knows this guy?"

A loud banging on the front door startles all three of them.

"Who's out in this weather?" Nolan wonders as he slips down the hall.

A man's voice, loud and angry, fills the hallway, interspersed here and there with Nolan's voice trying to calm him. The voice grows louder as it draws closer to the squad room, and then the voice has a body, a large body, a towering man dressed in big snowmobile boots and a brown canvas work jacket covered in snow, his jaw covered with a trimmed red beard, his eyes sparking high voltage.

"You better find Carl Levesque before I do," he says. "I swear to God, I'll kill that son of a bitch. I swear to God I will ..."

Nolan puts a hand on the man's shoulder.

"Mike, it's not a smart thing to do, uttering death threats in the middle of the police station. Have a seat. Calm down for a minute."

The big man slides his shoulder so that Nolan's hand falls away, but he takes the advice and sits in a chair by the door. He leans forward, clasps his massive hands, and rocks a little to burn away the energy running through his body.

"What happened, Mike?" Nolan asks, sitting on the edge of a desk.

"I just found out my daughter, Casey, my sixteen-year-old daughter, has been over to Carl Levesque's place. I found a joint in her backpack and this," he says, and reaches into his breast pocket. He hands over an inch square of foil. "He tried to fool around with her, the scumbag."

Nolan accepts the foil, examines it, then passes it to Madsen. She finds an evidence baggie in her black case and drops the foil inside.

"Is that the meth stuff everybody's talking about?" Mike asks, and suddenly the anger and threats are gone, and he looks smaller slumped in the chair, a worried father.

"We'll have to test it," Madsen says, "but it looks like it could be. There's powder residue. We'll need to speak with Casey."

He nods. "And what about Levesque? You gonna arrest him, too?"

"Nobody's being arrested, Mike, not just yet," Nolan says.

"That's what people are saying, that you guys don't have a goddamned clue what you're doing. Wade Garson gets his brains blown out and kids are stabbing each other high on meth and nobody's in jail yet."

"It would be good if we could talk with Casey alone," Madsen says. "I could come over to your house so she doesn't have to come in here."

Mike stands, and his long frame is once again revealed. He turns for the door but stops and turns back. "Threat or no threat, I'm telling you. You better find that piece of shit Carl Levesque before I do."

The father turns and slips down the hall. The front door opens and chimes, and a blast of cold air rolls like a tumbleweed all the way back to the squad room.

"Looks like we're splitting up," Madsen says. "I'll go talk to Casey."

"I've got Levesque," McKelvey says.

Nolan looks between the two of them, the kid picked last for the ball team.

"Nolan, I think you should go talk to Celluci," Madsen says. "You weren't there when we interviewed him. It'll keep him on edge, knowing we're still asking questions. Maybe find out if he has any plausible explanation for the GSR on his hands."

Nolan nods but it's obvious he has something on his mind. Madsen and McKelvey wait.

"And the Chief?" he finally asks.

Madsen looks across the desk to McKelvey.

"I've been avoiding the subject," McKelvey says with a shrug. "I don't know what to make of the guy. I was hoping we could move this forward a little bit before we threw this in his face."

"You know him better than we do," Madsen says, looking straight at Nolan. "You should be the one to go and talk to him."

"Do I just go and say, 'Hey, Chief, we think we found your gun'?"

Madsen leans back in her chair. She sighs and brushes hair from her face. "You're a big boy, Constable. Get your Chief to come in here and open his lockbox for you. Tell him we found a gun that looks like his and we need to discount him so we can move on down the list. Unless you want me to come with you and hold your hand, I suggest you buck up and do your job."

Nolan's face folds in on itself like a boy who has been scolded. What makes matters worse is the fact he has a dab of chocolate icing in the corner of his mouth. Madsen doesn't know whether to go over and smack him or wet a tissue with her tongue and clean his face.

"Be better if you guys aren't here," he says. He moves to the phone on the desk and cradles the receiver while punching in a number from memory. "Dr. Nichols. It's Ed Nolan. I know, I know. It's really coming down. Listen, is Chief Gallagher there?"

Madsen and McKelvey are standing now, zipping their coats. They both watch Nolan's face in an attempt to decipher the one-sided conversation. Nolan hangs up the phone and turns to them.

"Chief never showed at the funeral home."

"I thought you said he was going to see Dr. Nichols after you checked on Wade Garson's place," McKelvey says.

Nolan shakes his head. "That's what the Chief told me. But Dr. Nichols said he's been alone all morning. Just him and Wade Garson's body."

Twenty-Six

*A*shes *to ashes and dust to dust.* McKelvey is trying to recall a biblical verse that he likely never even learned in the first place. His parents were not religious, despite the fact that like most of the mining families, getting dressed up to attend Sunday services was just another part of life. It was like going to the grocery store, a weekly routine. His parents never read the bible or said prayers or even talked about the *concept* of God. McKelvey remembers how his father hated putting on a shirt and tie, standing there in the bathroom at the mirror, cursing a cloud of blue as his thick fingers attempted to create a knot. Inevitably, his mother would gently insert herself into the situation and close the loop on a knot that Grey McKelvey would then rip open the moment they sat in the car following the service.

What does the saying mean to Celluci and Gallagher, he wonders. *Dust to dust*; this can't be a reference to methamphetamine. Or could it be? It could mean anything. McKelvey thinks about the pieces of the puzzle as he drives the cruiser over to Carl Levesque's address. It is not yet noon and the sun burns somewhere behind a quilt of misty grey gauze. The streets are thickly packed with snow, and due to budget cuts the plough has only been out once or twice. The driving is slow. He gets stuck twice on Main Street and has to reverse and take another run. The snow has stopped for now, but there is more in the air. This is just the storm stopping to catch its breath. McKelvey figures a foot and a half has fallen so far.

He pulls in behind Carl Levesque's big black Caddy. He watches the curtains closed across the front windows for signs of movement. Nothing. McKelvey looks around the cruiser for something, anything, to hold in his hands, a prop. He feels like a man half-dressed, the uniform shirt and police jacket against his blue jeans. He pops the glove compartment and finds a six-inch flashlight in metal casing. It will do.

McKelvey is about to open the door when he remembers the radio. He decides to follow protocol and call in his location, as much out of curiosity to hear this unseen woman's voice.

"McKelvey here," he says, depressing the talk bar on the mic. "At 26 Hard Rock Way. Over."

The radio snaps and pops. Then silence. He hangs the mic on the hook, wondering if this Shirley Murdoch woman is off duty. He is standing outside the cruiser adjusting his jacket when her voice booms eerily from the ether.

"Well, howdy there, good to meet you, Mr. McKeller."

"McKelvey," he corrects, leaning across the seat.

"I've heard all about you," she almost sings.

"Only the rumours, I hope."

She sniggers. "Welcome aboard. Ten-four on your location."

He hangs up the mic again and heads to the front door.

* * *

Carl Levesque has no hair. That is to say, he has even less hair than the thinning hair he presents to the world. Having roused him from bed with repeated pounding on the door, McKelvey discovers a man who is almost unrecognizable from the character he plays each day on the streets of Ste. Bernadette. Levesque opens the door and squints bleary-eyed into the day. He holds the door with one hand and the edges of a ratty, worn housecoat — closed almost, but not quite — across his girth with the other.

"Charlie, Charlie, well what's the pleasure?" he says. His voice is thick with phlegm, and he is not wearing a partial plate. He is missing three front teeth. "I hear you're working for Saint B's finest these days. I sure hope I don't have some unpaid parking tickets you want to talk to me about."

It is obvious now the man wears a piece of false hair to cover the biggest area of balding. Without it, he looks somehow stark and sickly, a cancer patient. The sparse hair that remains is wispy as a baby's down.

"Can we chat inside," McKelvey says, but it is not a question, and he's already pushing his way in.

Levesque retreats into his messy living room as McKelvey moves forward. Empty beer bottles and ashtrays and dirty dishes fill every possible free space, from shelves to the coffee table, the tops of the speakers from an old RadioShack stereo system. The house reeks of cigarette smoke so thickly that McKelvey feels once and for all cured of the habit for life. The room makes McKelvey's sparse and spartan bachelor existence back in Toronto all the more appealing.

"You look so serious there Charlie, Jesus," Levesque says, and tries to laugh his salesman's laugh as he fumbles in his housecoat pockets for cigarettes and a lighter.

"It's pretty serious, Carl. You should sit down."

Levesque tosses some old newspapers and magazines to the floor and sits on his couch. McKelvey stands, both because he doesn't want to make contact with any of the filthy furniture and because he wants the physical supremacy here. Levesque lights a cigarette with a shaking hand and draws hard.

"You nervous about something?" McKelvey asks.

Levesque laughs, but it doesn't work. He can't even convince himself.

"Casey Hartman." McKelvey says just the name. Then he watches for the truth in Levesque's eyes, the way he has done a thousand times as a beat cop, working Hold-Up, asking the questions and watching for the physical reaction. Everything, the truth of the world, is in the eyes.

"What's that little cock-tease saying?" Levesque says.

"First of all, her father wants to kill you," McKelvey says. "You can thank me for getting here first. Second, she said you gave her pot and meth. We've got the evidence back at the station and we're interviewing her as we speak."

"She gave *me* meth, more like it, brother. Or tried to. Listen, don't believe the whole innocent-little-girl routine. I never made her do anything she didn't want to do. So sue me for taking what I can get, if you know what I mean." As he says this, he pokes his tongue against his cheek in a crude gesture.

McKelvey has the flashlight from his pocket in one liquid motion, the same response and action as though it were his sidearm. He pushes Levesque's head back with one hand and jams the flashlight into the man's mouth with the other. Levesque's eyes bulge just like the eyes of Wade Garson's dog when McKelvey shoved the rock in his yap. Levesque's arms flail as he attempts to push McKelvey off, but he has no strength; he is as weak as a child.

"Do you like that?" McKelvey says, and he is on top of Levesque now, pushing down, his own teeth clenched, the anger rushing forward, the injustice of his son's death, Jessie and his granddaughter Emilie, all the girls of this world unsafe as long as predators like Carl Levesque roam the streets, and it's not fair, it's just not goddamned fair.

It is within the heat and the flash of this anger and violence that McKelvey finds he is above and beyond himself, looking down at the scene, and the world is muted — there is only the rush of blood in his ears. This is who and what he is. This, right here, is the very gist of Charlie McKelvey. The propensity. The ability. The willingness. The lapse between spark and fire may have grown with the years, but it hardly matters. It has defined him, this aspect of his nature, it has frightened Caroline and Gavin, it is responsible for the lack of advancement in his long career. He sees within this moment something new, or at least something old seen from a new angle, and the words from Peggy's poem come back to him. He wants to help, not hinder, educate rather than annihilate. It is to pause and do the exact opposite of a man's very nature that requires true strength. And he wonders if it is too late to change …

McKelvey eases back, releases his grip, pulls the flashlight from Levesque's mouth like a dentist finished with a difficult procedure. Sweat has formed on McKelvey's forehead and runs down his cheek to his chin. His heart throbs. As always, he is left thrumming once the adrenalin begins to ebb.

"I should sue your ass off, sue the whole fucking municipality," Levesque spits, a hand moving to his split lip, blood staining the teeth that aren't missing. "That chick is sixteen or seventeen, so you've got nothing on me."

"Shut up, Carl," McKelvey says. He spots a coiled white tube sock on the floor by the couch and picks it up. He tosses it at Levesque. "Wipe your mouth," he says.

Levesque dabs the dirty sock against his lip and holds it out to look at the blood like a kid fascinated with his own nosebleed. He reaches with a shaking hand for the cigarette burning in the ashtray and takes a long haul.

"Fuck this town, man." Levesque laughs, and this time the laughter must be genuine, for it comes with a new darkness and weariness. Gone are the false singalong clichés of success and positivity. "I should be almost retired, and here I am in Shitsville getting assaulted by a tenant-slash-geriatric part-time cop, getting reamed by the town on taxes, the Indians circling around ready to scalp me …"

McKelvey moves to a La-Z-Boy across from the couch and pushes a few magazines to the floor. He sits and gets his breathing back in rhythm. The arms of the chair are pocked with blackened cigarette burns where he imagines Levesque has fallen asleep in his underwear on so many nights.

"Tell me about the girl," McKelvey says. "Before her father shows up here and removes your head from your body."

Levesque squashes the cigarette, knocking a few old butts out of the ashtray. "I've got a little gun, so I'm not too worried."

McKelvey levels a dead stare at him. "Show me," he says.

"Well, maybe I'm just joking, who knows."

"The girl," McKelvey says. "What happened?"

"I saw her at the laundromat with some friends. We all shared a joint on a cold and lonely night." He raises his hands in mock arrest. "I told her if she wanted to, you know, smoke a little more some time, to give me a call. And she did. And we did."

"What about the stuff in the foil?"

"That was hers, buddy, not mine. I'll swear on three fucking bibles. She showed me that stuff. She seemed to be bragging and scared at the same time. Said she got it from that kid who stabbed his pal. Scotty Cooper. They smoked some of it in his garage. She didn't really want to smoke it, I could tell. And I've done a lot of stupid things, but I'm not gonna try that shit. So I dumped the powder in the toilet. And she went home."

"With one of your joints in her coat pocket," McKelvey says. "That her father found."

"Just my luck," Levesque says, and shrugs.

McKelvey watches the man, and he leans toward believing him.

"You're in a lot of trouble, Carl," McKelvey says, "and I'm the friendliest guy you're going to see for a while. Why don't you tell me about your troubles. And tell me where you think these kids are getting meth around here."

Levesque runs the fingers of a hand over the top of his head, and the fingers work to gather what remains of the hair, a farmer searching for wheat in a field of drought.

"It's no secret I'm working on a land deal with the folks at Big Water. With the chief there and his nephew, the economic development officer. I'm a little over-extended. I told them I had all the land leases for the two hundred acres they've got their eye on for a casino and resort."

"They spotted you some dough?"

Levesque nods. "Finder's fee and whatnot. The rest is due the day I transfer over all the deeds to those little shitboxes your people lived in for half a century."

"And you can't deliver because you don't actually hold all the deeds, right?"

"I'm working on it," Levesque says, and now beams his old salesman's smile. It comes off as creepy and sad, what with the bloody lip and lack of dentures. "As for where the meth is coming from, you got me, brother. I admit it, I smoke a little of the weed, probably drink more beer than I should. And Christ knows I smoke too many of these goddamned things," he says, and lights a new cigarette. "You ask Laney down at the arcade? She's got her eye on those kids closer than anybody. You ask me, that place is a hub of all kinds of illicit action."

"Wade Garson," McKelvey says. "What do you make of his death?"

Levesque finds the sock beside him on the couch and dabs at some fresh blood forming at the split in his lip. He tilts his head a little to the side, considering the question.

"Well, that's for you and your tag-along Nolan to figure out, isn't it?" he says. And then smiles his ghastly smile, and adds, "One silver lining in all of this seems to be that the more crime we have, the more inclined folks are to sign away their homes to dependable old Carl. And at bargain basement prices, too."

McKelvey stands. He bites back against the surge of impulse to give the bald-headed bastard one more shot on the chin for all of Ste. Bernadette.

"Thanks for your time," he says. "We'll be in touch if we have more questions. And listen, Carl. Do yourself a favour. Stay under the radar while we talk to Casey Hartman and her father. It might just save your life."

Levesque looks at the bloodied sock in his hand and nods.

"You might not have broken any laws by chasing after that girl," McKelvey adds, "but there's the moral issue. The kids in this town are lost. The last thing they need is someone preying on them."

"Save your sermon, Charlie. And next time you come over to give me a wakeup call, you better have a warrant and a gun."

"Is that a threat, Carl?" McKelvey says, and stares.

Levesque spreads his hands wide in a benign gesture, and says, "Forewarned is forearmed."

Twenty-Seven

Constable Ed Nolan sits beside the bed with a bowl of steaming vegetable soup and a cloth napkin to catch the liquid that inevitably dribbles from his father's mouth. The room is so stale, so ripe with his father's sour body odour, that he lights wooden matches and lets the sulphur change the taste in the air. He knows he should give his father a full bath, at the very least a sponge bath. But he seems immobilized by the question at hand: *when?* When will he finally make the call and have his father taken away to an institution? Promises and pledges seem meaningless now, but he feels the weight of his father's hand on his shoulder still, the look in his eyes.

"Dad," he says. "We have big problems here. And a storm coming back in." He looks at his father, skin and bones, and wonders if the man can hear and think and understand anything.

"Can you understand me?"

There is nothing.

"I have to go again now. I have to go and talk to my chief. You remember Chief Gallagher. He may need some help, Dad. We all might."

Nolan sets the bowl of soup on the night table, leans down and brushes aside some grey hair, dry as broom bristles, and he kisses his father on the forehead.

Twenty-Eight

Madsen is in the middle of a circuitous argument on a cellphone with a bad connection when she hears someone entering the squad room. She turns, the phone cradled between ear and shoulder, and waves at McKelvey.

"I have to go," she says. "No. I have work to do. Yes, it is more important, actually. Anything is more important right now than replaying this same conversation over and over again. Okay. Yes. Goodbye."

She flips the phone shut and tosses it on the desk. She leans back in the chair and grabs her hair and pulls.

"God give me strength."

"You want me to come back in a little bit?"

She likes the older man's chivalry, though she would never admit the fact. She would also kill for a big bathtub, a bottle of good red wine, a week off from work … and her personal life magically figured out and back on track.

"No," she says. "You just caught me in the middle of acting out the cliché. You know, the one where the police officer is selfish, career-obsessed, emotionally closed up?"

"Ah, yes," McKelvey says, sitting down in Chief Gallagher's chair. "I know it well. At least you're not trying to have that conversation from a bar with a bunch of laughter in the background."

She smiles at the shared understanding. McKelvey is one of the last of his breed, she knows, the cops who didn't go to college or university, the tradesmen who earned their honorary degrees on the streets and in patrol cars. Despite the age gap, there is a mutual understanding of territory and glossary, and she feels somehow more at ease simply in his presence. They don't need to say anything. It's all there for them in the work, in this investigation, the details, getting it right. This is their relationship. They are married to this.

"I probably picked the absolute worst time to volunteer for an assignment in the middle of nowhere, I'll admit that much," she says, sitting up and gathering the notes and file folders on the desk. "He keeps accusing me of running anyway. Imagine that."

McKelvey gives her a little smile as though he knows of what she speaks, but that's all. And once again everything is communicated in that smile and those blue eyes, the whole truth of the world they know and share. The world that no spouse or child or parent can ever understand unless they, too, have carried the badge.

"Casey Hartman didn't get the meth from Carl Levesque," Madsen says, diving back into the work. "She got it from Scotty Cooper. Took a lot to pull that from her, I think she has a big crush on this Cooper kid. Guess he was the cat's ass in the high school, always had a little pot and some pills. Anyway, she did say that Levesque gave her a joint and tried to fool around. She was pretty grossed out by that. She figured she could score a few joints for her and her friends and be a hero."

"That confirms his story," McKelvey says. And he goes to say something else but he stops to search for the right words.

After a long pause, he continues. "In the interest of full disclosure, I should tell you that Carl Levesque got excited when I was interviewing him. He slipped and banged his mouth a little. Just so you know."

Madsen shakes her head, but she smiles inside. "I appreciate the courtesy. And for the record, I hope it hurt."

"He's a scumbag and he's likely committing fraud of one variety or another, but I don't think he's making and selling meth. There's something too lazy about him. He's looking for the get-rich-quick deal."

"Which brings us back to the starting point. I never got to interview Scott Cooper after Garson was murdered, and the Assistant Crown called to let us know his family has hired a lawyer from Toronto and he won't be offering anything up."

McKelvey leans back and taps a pen against his palm.

"You said you took a course on this meth problem down in the U.S. What sorts of ingredients besides cold medicine are required in the production?"

Madsen thinks back to the course put on by a squad of Iowa state detectives and a senior narcotics officer with the Drug Enforcement Administration. She marvelled at the slideshow of meth users, before-and-after shots depicting the apparent melting and deformation of once-attractive individuals. The festering red sores they picked at endlessly in their hallucinations of burrowing insects, the hollowed cheeks as the body shed healthy fat and vitamins quicker than any diet plan, but mostly she remembered the dead milky eyes devoid of hope, devoid even of pain. It took her by surprise, the grip of this seemingly new phenomenon, the insidious nature of its digging and carving at entire towns and villages, spreading town to town like an ancient plague.

"They can make it in industrial quantities, but mostly it's done in one-pound batches or smaller. Making the stuff is about the most dangerous occupation going. You need anhydrous ammonia, pseudoephedrine from the cold pills, lithium strips torn from a battery, a little bit of lantern fluid, and presto, you've got devil's dust."

"All of that is readily available and pretty much untraceable. What about the A-whatever ammonia?"

"Anhydrous ammonia. Farmers use it as fertilizer. You'd get it at the Co-op if there were any around here."

"There's a Co-op just north and a little ways out of town."

Madsen is already packing her case and pulling on her coat.

"I wonder how Nolan is making out with the Chief," McKelvey says.

As though on cue, the phone rings. The ancient sound of the clanging rotary startles Madsen and she fumbles with the receiver. She feels like a turtle in her parka and she strains to hear the caller. She hangs up and shakes her head.

"That was Nolan. Gallagher has bolted, he says. Clothes cleared out, vehicle gone."

"*Shit.* Half the highways are closed. He must be crazy or desperate."

"You put out a bulletin on Gallagher's truck and I'll head over to the Co-op, see if they stayed open in this weather."

McKelvey gives her a look and she knows that he wants her to ask him to come, probably even to drive in this weather. *Because she's a girl.*

"Why don't you and Nolan go over to the Station Hotel and rattle Mr. Celluci a little more," she offers.

McKelvey nods, but he looks like a little boy who has been spurned by an older brother. She has to laugh at these men, these adult-sized boys, and their ego and pride. It would be charming perhaps if it weren't so pathetic.

Twenty-Nine

Nolan swings by the station and picks up McKelvey. This is the life of sharing two cruisers among three cops. It reminds McKelvey of when Gavin first started to drive. How he hated to ask for the keys to the car because he knew his dad would run twenty questions on him — *Where? How long? With whom? Do I know that kid?*

It's snowing again, the downfall growing heavier. Nolan drives with both hands on the wheel, the wipers working steadily.

"You know Gallagher better than anyone," McKelvey says. "Are you worried?"

Nolan stares at the snow coming in at the windshield almost head on.

"I don't know what to think anymore. Everything I thought I knew has gone upside-down. The whole world. Gallagher is ... he's been like a second father to me, Charlie. He hired me when I left the armed forces and I didn't know what to do with the rest of my life, sent me down to police college. To think he's even remotely involved in killing Wade

Garson, let alone bringing meth into this town, well ..."

McKelvey understands what it is like to want so badly for someone you know or trust to not be involved in something as dark as this. He lost his way in life and on the job chasing down a rumour that Pierre Duguay was responsible for the killing of his boy. As the evidence began to mount and the connections became clear, his mind couldn't comprehend that a fellow cop, a narcotics officer on the take, could be responsible. The thin blue line unravelled that day and nearly choked McKelvey to death.

There is a notion that McKelvey has been playing with, this idea he wants Nolan to consider, so he says to him, "Given where Saint B is right now in terms of life support, do you think whoever is responsible might have introduced meth with a strategic intent?"

"You mean on purpose?"

"As a last straw. I don't know, I'm just throwing it out there. Like maybe Celluci and Gallagher started off with an idea that got out of hand. They never wanted anybody to get hurt. Just show the town how bad things are, and then maybe a stinky landfill with Detroit diapers doesn't look so bad."

"This is like a dream," Nolan says, "a nightmare. I don't know how to think like that, Charlie. To look at these people I know and hold them in suspicion. Maybe it's easy for you, from your days working in the city. I'm not cut out for this. I want to help people, not harass them."

"You're a good cop," McKelvey says. "A good cop stays open to the possibilities while maintaining some faith in the human race. Things got a little more black and white for me near the end of my job. I told you when you first asked me to help, Ed. I'm not the best example."

"I want my father to see me do something, *be* something," Nolan continues. "You know, make a difference somehow. He was always worried about where I would end up."

"I'm sure he's proud. From what I hear around town, people think a lot of you, Ed. It's early to be talking this way, but I'd say you're a natural for Chief."

Nolan shakes his head as though he can't go there, not this early, not with Chief Gallagher missing. McKelvey turns to the side window and watches the town. He is growing accustomed to the setting once again, how quickly the shock dissipates. The disorientation of those first few days, to step from the swirling vortex of Toronto to this, a child's train set village set in a fishbowl. But this place is no longer his home, and he misses the city. The stink of the air blowing at his face from subway grates, the taxis jumbled in a gaggle at Union Station, the always-third-place Blue Jays, the hot dog vendors every seven feet, the boats in the harbour.

"Mind stopping by my place, I need to make a quick call," McKelvey says.

"Use my cell if you want," Nolan offers. "I thought you had one, too."

McKelvey has not been able to find his cellphone since before he visited Carl Levesque. He pictures the red light flashing on the phone in some anonymous dark place.

"I'd rather use the land line. Old comforts."

While he can't read that far, McKelvey knows what the piece of white paper tacked to his front door says even as they pull into the driveway. He gets out of the cruiser and mounts the steps and rips the paper from the door, reading just enough of the typed message to understand that Levesque has delivered a directive based on his rights as the landlord of the dwelling. McKelvey tosses the balled paper in the sink and leans on the kitchen counter with the phone between his ear and shoulder. He listens to the soft refrains of cello and piano working in concert to ease any anxiety a caller such as himself might have. But the music has the opposite effect. His jaw clenches until his molars ache.

"Thank you for holding, may I help you?" a young woman's voice chimes.

"Dr. Shannon. I've been holding for Dr. Shannon."

"Ummmm ... sure. Let me just see here. Hold, please."

"No, wai —"

But the line fills once again with the piped-in muzak, flutes now competing with timpani. McKelvey hangs up the receiver and swears. How ironic that he waits weeks to return a call to this doctor, and now, when he finally has the drive to speak with the man, when he finally has the courage or the clear head or whatever it is that is pushing him forward, he gets a cello and piano duet.

"Shit show," he mutters.

He stares at the telephone hanging on the wall. If he can't make the connection with Dr. Shannon, perhaps it's time he tried to close another loop. He picks up the receiver and dials zero. The operator responds on the third ring.

"Operator. How can I help you?"

"Directory assistance."

"Go ahead please. For what name?"

McKelvey pictures the old codgers standing in the lobby of the Station Hotel that first morning, his welcome wagon. The one old-timer who spoke the most about McKelvey's father. The strike. The violence.

"I'd like a listing for a George Fergus in Ste. Bernadette, please."

*   *   *

The Station Hotel tavern is empty, save for the bartender using the downtime to sit with a coffee and sort through a pile of bills, and Tony Celluci throwing darts at the board. Nolan and McKelvey enter the room and Celluci turns to look at them, arm poised ready to release, and he nods at them and then looks back to deliver the dart. It's not a bull's eye, but its close. He regards his placement and shrugs.

"Boys," he says on his way over to meet them. "I assume I'm the reason for your visit during the middle of this snow day."

"We've got a few things to double-check," Nolan says. "Let's head up to your room, Tony."

"I wish you had called first. The place is a bit of a mess."

But of course the room is not a mess; it is as neat and tidy as Celluci himself, who is dressed in the midst of a storm in the middle of nowhere in black pants and what looks to be an expensive purple dress shirt that is likely tailored to fit his athletic frame. He sits on the edge of his bed and clasps his hands. Nolan and McKelvey both scan the room.

"Your friend the Chief has flown the coop," McKelvey says. "Any idea where he might be headed, or why he'd up and leave in the middle of all this excitement?"

Nolan moves to the dresser and starts picking up and examining various objects, a half-bottle of Canadian Club whisky, tiny paper cups stacked together, a gold watch. Celluci tries to keep an eye on Nolan while also paying attention to the man standing in front of him.

"You got me," he says.

"You ever see that gun he was so proud of?" McKelvey asks.

Celluci looks agitated as Nolan begins to open and close drawers.

"Sure, I did. We took it out and shot some bottles off a fence. Is that a crime around here?"

"You didn't mention that yesterday," McKelvey says. "Maybe you've thought about it and realized you need an excuse for that gunshot residue on your hands."

"Do you mind?" Celluci says, leaning to the side to address Nolan.

"And now that Gallagher's gone, he can't deny your story," McKelvey continues.

"It's the truth, what can I say? I think I'll talk to my lawyer before I answer any more questions."

Nolan shuts a drawer and opens another one, rummaging through clothes.

"Only the guilty lawyer up, Celluci," McKelvey says. "But that's fine. We can play your way. But tell me this. What does 'ashes to ashes and dust to dust' mean to you and Gallagher?"

Celluci's face betrays genuine confusion. "What are you talking about? Did Gallagher mention that?"

"Sure he did. Along with the trip and the tickets you bought him."

Nolan looks at McKelvey. The information about the trip is new, and he looks both hurt and worried. Celluci shakes his head slowly, as though he's just waking to some new reality.

"It's nothing," he says. "It's our inside joke about the landfill site, the incinerator making money for the town."

"Is this from your target shooting?" Nolan says. He turns to reveal a spent shell casing wedged between thumb and forefinger, a dresser drawer open wide.

"That's not mine," Celluci says, shaking his head. "You put that there, you son of a bitch. What kind of backwoods police bullshit are you guys trying to pull?"

"I imagine you'll want that lawyer now, Tony," McKelvey says.

*   *   *

Later that afternoon, as evening begins to fall in shades of purple, Madsen squints through a magnifying glass while using tweezers to hold the new casing to the bulb of a desk lamp in the squad room. She feels like an eighteenth-century detective, and she may as well be for all of the technology she has at her disposal. But it is amazing to her, for all of the advances made, how the basics of detection have remained the same. She sits back and looks across at McKelvey, who sits in the Chief's chair, and then over to Nolan, who sits on the edge of a desk with his arms crossed, watching and waiting. He has some white powder on the side of his face from a jelly doughnut.

"Same firing pin impression," she says, "just right of centre. And same manufacturer's markings. For all intents and purposes, this shell is of the same variety found at the murder scene and very likely was fired from the same weapon."

Nolan nods. "So Celluci killed Wade Garson. We've got the evidence."

Madsen watches McKelvey's face as the veteran cop begins to smile. She knows what he is thinking, how wonderful life would be, how easy their jobs would be, if things were that simple. But she also knows that this is the best they have.

"The man tested positive for GSR. A spent shell casing in his possession appears to match the casing found at the scene of Wade Garson's murder. People have been convicted on less than that," Madsen says. "We can file with the circuit Justice tonight and seek a warrant. We've got probable grounds."

"Celluci says he and good old boy Gallagher went out shooting at bottles," McKelvey says. "That would cancel out both the GSR and the spent casing. Maybe he kept one in his pocket. Just to be your devil's advocate here."

"Except he was at the truck stop when the crime was committed," says Nolan. "That's opportunity, right?"

McKelvey nods.

"Nolan's right," Madsen says. "When you add that to the mix, we'll have no trouble getting a warrant."

Thirty

The snowfall abates and the memorial service for Mark Watson is organized for the following morning. The town is quiet and still this evening, utterly devoid of human activity, a vision of its future perhaps, as the few remaining municipal workers set about to clear the streets and sidewalks. The task will take two days.

McKelvey has made contact with George Fergus, the old miner, and he now sits at the man's kitchen table with an untouched bottle of beer before him. Nolan is tending to his father and Madsen is catching up on some rest, having found the Co-op closed.

"The owner, a Gerry Kilrea, was caught in the storm picking up supplies down in Timmins," she had reported. "He'll be back later tonight. I'll catch him at the service for Mark Watson."

Now McKelvey fiddles with the label on the bottle, picking at it for purchase. How he used to spend hours in the bars and pubs after his shifts working to remove labels fully intact, as though this were some sort of accomplishment to be proud of. As though he would come home at midnight and wake Gavin to tell him the good news. *Daddy slid four labels fully intact from bottles of beer tonight, son ...*

"Your old man, he was the real deal," Fergus says.

The man's hair is thick and uncombed, the colour of bone. The wrinkles on his face are thick and deep as the rock he cut for decades. He must be eighty-five, McKelvey thinks, maybe even closer to ninety. The man's body has withered with time and gravity, but there remain the remnants of a once-powerful chest and shoulders, thick biceps.

"He didn't talk about work, except to bitch about management once and a while," McKelvey says. "He never talked about that year, that's for sure. Nobody ever did, not really. It's like everybody tried to pretend nothing had happened."

Fergus's face changes, as though a cloud has passed over the sun. He drinks from his bottle of Molson Export and McKelvey watches the man's Adam's apple undulate beneath a sheet of wrinkled and slack flesh. The old man sets the bottle down and wipes his mouth with the back of his hand, an action that reminds McKelvey immediately of his own father.

"You want to know about all of that," Fergus says. "Sleeping dogs, I'd say."

McKelvey turns the bottle in his hand, but he does not drink. He has lost the taste for the stuff, which seems an unfathomable miracle.

"I know all about sleeping dogs," McKelvey says. "Most of the men who were around at that time are dead or close to it. I just want to know the truth"

Fergus looks him in the eye. The old man's eyes are yellowed but otherwise sharp. "You so sure about that, kid?" he says.

McKelvey doesn't say anything.

"You think it's going to help you understand your old man, see him in a different light? Change your opinion of him one way or the other?"

"It might help explain a lot of things. What happened that year affected all of us. Everybody who lived in this town. Especially the kids who had fathers being taken down to the police station for questioning. We lived with the weight of that silence our entire lives."

Fergus pushes his empty bottle away and eases back in his chair. "The truth shall set you free. Is that it?"

"Duncan said I shouldn't believe everything I hear about my father."

"Maybe Duncan doesn't remember things too clearly."

"All I know is that my dad was questioned by the local cops more than a few times. And yet there's no record of a police report. I spent about two hours looking through the archives in the back room at the police station this week and there's no trace of the incident. It's like it never happened."

Fergus looks down at the beer bottle and turns it around a few times.

"I didn't sleep for about a year after all that shit went down," he says. "But then, you know, eventually you have to sleep again. Life goes on. You get as old as me, your mind gets good at mucking with the details, you know, changing things around to the way they ought to be."

McKelvey sits in silence. The room is warm, the closed-air heat that old people seem to love. The house is neat for an aged bachelor, and McKelvey sees his own future in this orderliness. But then he is reminded of the state of his health, the secret he carries within his cells, and the future becomes less clear, a stark image of a hospital bed, tubes and IVs.

"Did my father help kill that scab?"

Fergus blinks beneath untrimmed eyebrows.

"Know the father, know the son," McKelvey says. "I just want to know."

"Well," Fergus says, smiling now, "you're about as fucking stubborn as your old man, that's for sure."

* * *

McKelvey is back in the kitchen of his old home, one hand against the wall, the other hanging at his side as he stares at the telephone. He knows that he owes Caroline a call, an explanation, an updating of the state of the union where his health is concerned. It came to him in the middle of the night, this line of truth. *He would want to know if something was happening with her.* They were married for over thirty years, for God's sake. What kind of asshole keeps this stuff to himself? He no longer believes the lie he has tried to tell himself, that he wishes to protect her from a cold reality. The truth is, he is scared. Scared to speak the words out loud. *Charlie McKelvey is mortal …*

Caroline's phone rings four, five, six times. It clicks to the answering machine and he gets snagged on those first few words, inevitably sounding like a borderline moron.

"It's Charlie," he says, finally. "*It's just Charlie. I wanted to apologize for, you know … for being me, I guess. You don't deserve to be cut off like that. I got lost for a little while but I'm good now. I really am, Caroline. I feel good for the first time in years. I have some news for you, but it can wait until I get back to the city. And you're not going to believe this, but I'm working for the cops up here. I know what you're thinking. I just can't get away from it. I'll talk to you soon …*"

He hangs up and dials Peggy's home number. She's off tonight and answers on the third ring.

"Hey there," he says.

"Agent McKelvey."

"Special constable, actually."

There is silence between them, and he closes his eyes. He will practise with Peggy. He likes this woman. He trusts her.

"It's your dime," she says, playful.

"Are you going to the memorial tomorrow?" he asks.

"Of course." And again she waits.

"Charlie? Are you all right?"

He clears his throat. "Sure. I just wondered if you wanted to go with me. I could pick you up around ten thirty."

"I'd love to. I thought you might be busy with work. You know, watching the crowd for clues. Isn't that how they do it on TV?"

"Sometimes. Sometimes that works."

He thinks she might be on to something, actually. The memorial will provide an excellent opportunity to bring the entire community together. It will be interesting to see if Celluci shows, or Levesque. To watch the faces and reactions of those in attendance.

"If you were sick," he says, but stops. The words won't come; they don't even materialize within the ether of his thought process. There is empty space. *If you were sick, would you, would you ... What?*

"Do you want me to come over?" she asks.

Yes, he thinks.

"Charlie?"

"I'll pick you up tomorrow, Peggy. Okay?"

"Okay," she says. "Be good."

*   *   *

He dreams of his boy, Gavin. Standing there with his back to the light so that his features are burned away by shadow. But this *is* Gavin, there can be no mistake. The light is the sun or something even more powerful, it is a light that never falters. McKelvey stands there, he can feel his feet on the ground, but he looks down and can't see his legs.

"Why did you do drugs?"

The question has come from some place beyond his consciousness. It has been waiting there on the tip of his tongue for years, the letters forming words and the words forming a sentence.

"To feel better."

"You didn't feel good?"

"I didn't feel good *enough*."

"Your mother and I. We didn't love you?"

Gavin laughs. The sound fills McKelvey with love and hate and anger and sadness, longing and regret. He remembers now something he has long forgotten: the melody to a favourite song, the sound of his boy's laughter.

"Drugs made me feel better," Gavin says. "At first they fill a hole. But the more you take, the bigger the hole gets. It works against you. It's a trick. That's all. It's not very complicated."

"I wish there were no drugs, no addiction," McKelvey says, and his own voice sounds like that of a boy, overwhelmed by adult notions too obtuse to comprehend. "What are we supposed to learn from all of this?"

"Don't ask me," Gavin says, and laughs lightly. "I didn't live long enough to find out."

"What am I supposed to do?" McKelvey asks. And he feels the same old weight pressing on his chest now, this weight he has carried since that midnight phone call woke him and his wife from their ungrateful and sleepy lives.

"Where there is despair, hope. Where there is darkness, light."

McKelvey feels the grip on his chest releasing like a sigh.

"It is in pardoning that we are pardoned, and it is in dying that we are born to Eternal Life ..."

McKelvey steps forward to touch his boy, but Gavin recedes in synch with each step. McKelvey stops. Gavin glows white and then phosphorous, and McKelvey can feel the heat, like the warmth of the sun on his face.

Thirty-One

All three churches in Ste. Bernadette have lost their full-time ministers over the past decade, relying now on the gospel delivered according to the travel schedule of various circuit preachers. The ongoing criminal investigation against Scott Cooper has necessitated that Mark Watson's body remain in Toronto for further toxicology tests and autopsy. The family has chosen to proceed with a memorial service, and now what appears to be the entire community sits together in rows and stands along the walls in the Ste. Bernadette Community Centre. Everyone is here, and McKelvey can't help but think what a terrific time it is to be a house thief, to move from house to house like a ghost. He remembers working a case back in the Hold-Up Squad, this guy who read the newspapers and tracked the addresses of family members who would be attending funerals. He focused entirely on the rich families of Rosedale and Forest Hill. By the time he was caught, he was driving a BMW and supporting three girlfriends.

The community centre is normally the location of Lions Club meetings or, back when there were enough families around, this is where the Boy Scouts would convene on Wednesday evenings to learn about knots and morals. Today it has been decorated at the front with a podium and two large stands of flowers loaned by the funeral home. To one side there is a tripod holding a poster-size photo of Mark Watson. The young man has the shaggy hair of any teen, and he smiles only half-heartedly — for it is not cool to smile for class photos — and McKelvey marvels at the innocence in the boy's eyes, the lack of understanding of the dangers of the world. And perhaps this is the blessing of childhood, but he can't help but feel even the toughest among these children is completely unaware that they are participants in a new game with no replays, no pause, no second chances. Violins play through overhead speakers. The thought crosses his mind and he wonders if that is what purgatory is like, being on hold with Muzak piped in.

Peggy sits beside McKelvey, and she looks so different, as she always does, when she is out of uniform. Madsen is stationed at the entrance and Nolan sits beside the Watson family. McKelvey scans the crowd and spots Dr. Nichols, Laney from the arcade, Duncan and the old men from the lobby of the Station Hotel, the school principal, Gaylord the pharmacist, and even Celluci standing off to the side with his arms crossed as though there is nothing on TV so he might as well be here. He can't find Carl Levesque, though.

"You haven't seen Carl, have you?" he whispers to Peggy.

"Not yet," she says. "He's probably still doing his hair."

Peggy is dressed in a black pantsuit, her hair tied back, and she smells like a vanilla candle. McKelvey catches himself stealing looks at her. She gets more beautiful each time he sees her, and he hopes it's not just because he feels old and gets lonelier with each day. Mayor Danny Marko stands at the podium at the head of the room. The mayor appears disheveled, as though he hasn't slept in a week; his tie is knotted in a lump and his hair is messy. *He probably hasn't slept in days*, McKelvey thinks. The town has imploded. It can't be easy. Marko taps the microphone and clears his throat.

"Friends," he says, and then stops. He looks out among the faces, and the silence builds as though this is the last inning of a World Series game, the final batter at the plate crouching now in his stance, bat in hand, eyeing the pitcher. McKelvey supposes the crowd is thinking the same thing he is thinking: *What can this man say or do that will make any difference now?*

"Friends," he goes on, "something has happened to our town. Our mine is closing and times are tough. This is all true. But something even worse has happened. Our young people have no hope. And when our young people have lost hope in their own future, well, then we are all truly lost."

There are a few comments uttered, either people agreeing or blaming Marko himself for the entire state of affairs.

"This country was built in rural towns just like Saint B. A hundred years ago, everybody lived in towns like ours. The cities were these distant places that we read about or heard about from friends who travelled. The world has changed, and our rural way of life is disappearing."

"Tell us something we don't know," a man's voice heckles.

"We're here today to remember the life of one of our bright young lights," Marko says, and his voice changes a little. He is choking up. "Minister Harvey will lead us in that remembrance, but I wanted to come and talk to you about hope. And how the worst thing we can do for our young people is to take that away from them. When we stop believing in ourselves, when we stop believing in some sort of future for this town, well ..."

Again Marko stops and regards the crowd. He seems lost in his place, if he even has his words collected, and McKelvey feels the same empathy he always feels when a public speaker begins to stumble. He wants to jump up and create a diversion. But there is nothing to be done. The room is beginning to fidget, and there is a rustle of whispers.

"We must believe, friends, that even in the face of these problems ... even though this is our darkest day, the light will shine again on Saint B...."

"Save it for the election," a voice heckles.

"Sit down, Marko," another man's voice adds.

The mayor looks close to tears. His hands shake and he grips the sides of the podium. His face reddens and he swallows hard. Finally his town administrator, a silver-haired woman named Maria, has the courage to step in. She moves to her mayor's side and she gently places her hand at his elbow, leading him like a child or an old man to a seat in the front row.

The minister steps in and nods toward the mayor in a show of respect. Minister Harvey is a middle-aged man dressed in a simple dark suit, with his dark hair neatly cut and parted on the left. *Nondescript* is the word that comes to McKelvey's mind, the sort of man a witness would find difficult to describe.

"Let us pray," he begins, and all heads bow in unison. "God of all mystery, whose ways are beyond understanding" — the minister closes his eyes, his hands turned palm up — "lead us, who grieve at this untimely death ..."

And McKelvey closes his eyes now, too, for these very words bring back the service for his boy. He feels his chest tighten. He is too hot. The minister's words get drowned out by the thrum of his rising blood pressure, and he can hear someone sniffling — the grieving mother — and now it is full-blown tears, and he is back there again in those darkest of days, sitting useless beside Caroline when all she wanted was his hand in hers.

"I'm going to step out," he whispers to Peggy.

"Are you all right?"

He nods, and he stoops at the waist and excuses himself, in a hurry, moving like someone who might get the sick at any moment. He makes it to the back where Madsen stands like a sentry with her hands clasped in front of her, and he wipes his brow. His hair is matted from sweat.

"Are you okay, Charlie?" she says in a low voice.

"I need some air," he says, already unbuttoning his shirt at the collar. "I don't see Levesque in the room. I'm going to take a drive and see what he's doing while the rest of the world pays their respects."

The cold air outside feels like being reborn. He puts his hands on his knees and hauls air like a marathon runner who has just crossed the finish line. The day is crisp and not quite sunny or cloudy either. McKelvey has never been so anxious to get out of somewhere, as though the walls were literally falling in on him, and he wonders if his father ever felt that way down in the confined darkness of the mine. He straightens up and he thinks of his wife, where she is and what she's doing, and he thinks of the minister's words and wonders where Gavin is, too. For the first time in his life he wishes someone had told him about God, or made him memorize a few prayers, something he could use in a moment such as this.

He could use a cigarette, too. Or a pain pill. A cold draft beer pulled from the polished brass pipes down at Garrity's Pub. Maybe even all three combined for a *Triactor of Bliss*. Christ, he's given up everything. There is nothing left, as though he is a baby again, devoid of the awareness of vice. And then it hits him, he no longer feels the physical twist in his guts from those bastardly pills.

"Free," he hears himself say out loud.

* * *

McKelvey drives slowly out of the packed parking lot and down Main Street. He is struck by the loneliness of the empty streets, and again he wonders what will become of this place, and all of the places like it. There are small towns in every province, in every state, that have been forgotten by the cities, forgotten for a long time now. The places where the wheat is grown and cut for the food that gets served in restaurants on the Danforth in Toronto, bays where the crabs are caught and the mussels are raked, deep woods where the trees are cut and sliced into two-by-fours to build the cottages, where men and women descend thousands of feet below the earth to claw from its stubborn jaws the diamonds and gold we require for our shiny things, the nickel that makes our cellular phones work. More than a generation gap, or the expected turn toward nostalgia as one grows older, McKelvey senses a shift within the very fabric of society, of the stuff that makes us who and what we are, the strings that connect us across the expanse of the grid. When a place like Ste. Bernadette dies, it takes with it not only a part of history, but of our shared future as well. He passes the storefronts, more than half of them empty or boarded up, and he sees ghosts on every corner.

He passes the Station Hotel and then on down past the police station, and he turns off Main to wind through the residential area. He pauses in front of Chief Gallagher's house. The driveway is empty, the fresh snow untouched by either tires or feet. *Where have you got to, Gallagher?* He closes his eyes for a moment and plays through the steps, the possibilities here. *Gallagher gets in deep with Celluci for the landfill deal. Celluci needs access to Garson's property for the deal to work, and when Garson won't budge, Celluci intimidates or tries to kill Garson by blowing up his trailer. Gallagher argues with Celluci about his tactics. Gallagher takes off ... or Celluci has done something with Gallagher, with his body ...*

It explains perhaps one part, but it doesn't fit with the whole, McKelvey thinks. It doesn't solve the problem.

Garson isn't in the trailer when it blows, but he sees who has tried to kill him and he takes off on foot through the woods. Celluci tracks him to the truck stop and puts an end to any risk of Garson talking ...

It seems a long stretch that a man working for the city of Detroit — even a slick son of a bitch with a concealed-weapon permit like Celluci — would risk twenty years in prison over a plan that touches on the property of a modern-day hillbilly. The meth, that is the connection, the starting point from which all violence can be traced. *Travis Lacey hits Nolan; Scotty Cooper stabs Mark Watson; Wade Garson's trailer explodes; Garson is found shot to death; Gallagher goes missing; Celluci tests positive for GSR and is found in possession of a matching shell casing; the girl Casey Hartman has provided a statement indicating she got the foil of meth from Scott Cooper, not Levesque as she told her father, and Scott Cooper told Nolan that he got the foil from the arcade washroom ...*

Celluci — or someone with sufficient motivation — has introduced meth into the community for purposes beyond profit. The purpose of all this, that is where the answer lies. Who, why, and how. It occurs to McKelvey that the only good lead they have at this time is putting the Garson death on Celluci. It won't explain or stop the larger problem, though, and if they can't do that, they have failed the people of Saint B.

McKelvey rolls on, past the empty houses that once held the families whose fathers worked in the mine, and he drives by Carl Levesque's house. The black Caddy is gone, fresh tracks in the snow. He pauses there a moment and then turns around and comes back out onto Main, eyes scanning for sign of

Levesque's vehicle. He is turning off Main to come in behind the Station Hotel when he stops. Levesque's Cadillac is parked in the middle of the road, a black SUV turned across it at a forty-five degree angle. It looks like a police action, McKelvey thinks as he comes upon the scene. He sits in the cruiser thirty metres back, watching three men argue between the vehicles. This is not a simple traffic disagreement. McKelvey squints to make out who the other two men are. They are Natives, likely from the Big Water First Nation. He has never seen them before. The way the men are standing, the way Levesque is flapping his arms in some sort of hyper explanation, they appear like school kids in the midst of a shakedown for lunch money.

McKelvey honks and the sound yanks the men from their intense discussion, and they swivel their heads to look over. Levesque sees his opportunity immediately, as though a teacher has walked onto the schoolyard, and he slips from the grasp and walks hurriedly to his car. He pauses long enough to make a gun with his thumb and forefinger and he pretends to shoot McKelvey, and then he slides into his car, slams the door, and negotiates his big car around the angled SUV. McKelvey pulls to the side of the road and gets out. He walks slowly toward the two men, who make no effort to disperse.

"Good morning," McKelvey says.

The men each nod once. The older of the two is thickly built, dressed in a black wool overcoat that reaches to just below his knees, and his long hair is tied back in a thick ponytail. The younger man is thin and wiry, dressed in a leather bomber jacket. The younger man stares with eyes that barely contain their distrust, flitting between the cruiser and McKelvey. The two men could be related, likely are, McKelvey thinks.

"I couldn't help but notice you were having a discussion with Carl Levesque," McKelvey says. "Mind me asking what it was about?"

"We were talking about business," the older man says. "My name is Peter Whitehorse and this is David. We're from Big Water First Nation."

McKelvey recognizes the name. The man is Chief of the Big Water.

"McKelvey," he says, and removes the glove from his hand and holds it out. Whitehorse looks at the hand for a moment and then shakes. McKelvey offers his hand but the younger man won't take it.

"This is what we get for trusting the white man," David says. "Centuries of lies and betrayals and again we learn the hard way."

Whitehorse looks at David, simply looks at him, and the younger man takes a step back and leans against the front of the SUV. There is more to say, but he simmers in his anger.

"I am disgraced in front of my people," Whitehorse says.

David looks down at his feet and kicks at the snow. It obviously pains him to hear the older man speak this way.

"Levesque is a partner with you in a land deal for a casino, is that right?" McKelvey says. "I've heard about it around town, and from the mayor, Danny Marko."

"We gave the man our money and our good faith. Our lawyers conducted the title searches yesterday. His paperwork is all forged. Levesque doesn't have the rights to the land, just the dwellings. The town owns the land."

David can't help himself, and he lifts his head and says, "And Mayor Danny Marko doesn't want to sell the land to us, he wants to hold the property for the day when the power workers come to work on the transmission line. The payout for the line access will be double what they'd get from us."

"If you have the proof, Levesque can be charged with any number of crimes," McKelvey says. "Fraud, forgery, misrepresentation. I'd need copies of the paperwork he supplied to you, and the contract you both signed, a copy of the cheque you gave him."

Whitehorse nods, but his eyes search McKelvey, and McKelvey feels held there in his place. This man owns a power that is quiet and still, requiring of few words.

"I don't know you," Whitehorse says. "Why should I trust you?"

"I'm a man of my word. And wrong is wrong."

Again Whitehorse looks at McKelvey, and he blinks. The day is changing from a dull light to a strong sun, and now Whitehorse squints.

"You know," he says, "my uncle was killed here in the mine strike in the 1950s, and when nobody was charged with the killing, my family swore we would never set foot in this town again ..."

McKelvey feels his legs begin to buckle, and he consciously focuses on remaining upright. His mind swirls with the implications of the connection, the reach through years and generations. These two men, strangers, standing face to face on the side of the road. The secrets of their ancestors there in the air between them.

"But time passes and people forget," Whitehorse continues. "Or they don't forget, but they need something at the store that they don't have. So they ride back into town. And they feel a little sick, maybe, like they are betraying their family, like they are keeping a secret, but it gets easier the next time."

David has found his cigarettes in his jacket and he lights one. McKelvey finds his eyes drawn to the first curl of smoking dancing like a northern light as the strong smell of sulphur from a match reaches his nose and he breathes it in.

"We thought we could make a deal that would benefit both of our people," Whitehorse says. "But like my uncle before me, I trusted the wrong man."

"I'll help you get your money back and put Levesque away," McKelvey says.

"He should leave town before something bad happens to him," David says, and spits on the frozen ground.

Whitehorse regards the younger man and nods. He turns back to McKelvey.

"In there," Whitehorse says, and points to the Station Hotel tavern. "Tonight at seven. I'll bring my papers and we'll see what your word is worth."

"Uncle," David says. "Let me take care of this, please. This is between Big Water and Carl Levesque."

But Whitehorse simply turns and lays his hand on the younger man's shoulder and then gets into the passenger side of the SUV. David passes McKelvey on his way to the driver's side.

"You let my uncle down, you'll pay."

"I believe that," McKelvey says, and holds the icy stare.

David closes the door and backs the vehicle up so that he can use the entrance to the Station parking lot to turn around. McKelvey stands in the middle of the road, watching the vehicle drive away. He looks up at the sky. It its cloudless now, wiped clean.

Thirty-Two

Minister Harvey reads Psalm 23 and then invites Douglas Watson, the dead boy's uncle, to share a few words. The room grows quiet and still as the uncle collects himself at the podium. He begins with a story about Mark learning to use the potty, how proud and independent the boy was, and how he carried the thing around like it was a porta-potty. Madsen feels a lump forming in her throat, and she knows this is the precursor. She will begin to cry momentarily, silent tears that well and then flow. She is not a mother, but believes she understands something of loss, having tried for so many years. At first you listen to the doctors when they say everyone is made differently, everyone has a unique cycle, you just need to be patient. And then you explore the emerging technologies with a newfound sense of hope, and you spend a fortune on consultations and for experts to poke and prod. And then the hope turns against itself as you watch your friends and family members bring new life into their homes, and you stand by and you smile and pretend to be happy for them. The arguments lead to blame, and the blame leads to silence. And eventually, you run aground with the realization that this is it, this is your life as it is and always will be. There is no more to come.

"Mark collected things like it was his full-time job," the uncle says, smiling at his memories, enjoying the smile that feels so good against the pain and the tears of the last few days. "It was marbles and then it was bottle caps. It wouldn't have been so bad if he had kept them in a box or something. I still remember walking on those bottle caps in my sock feet."

Madsen tastes the salt of her tears, she wipes at her cheeks and takes a deep breath. That's it, all she will allow. She is a professional here, an outsider, and she has a job to finish. She composes herself as the service concludes with a prayer by Minister Harvey. She sees Nolan moving to cover Celluci as they had planned. She slips outside and watches the people talking at their cars, sharing their grief, and she hears them as they pass by sharing their own vision of what is happening to Saint B, and who is to blame. The rumours and accusations run the gamut. The truth is, everyone is scared.

Madsen's eyes stop on a middle-aged man fishing for keys at a white pickup truck with a sign that says CO-OP on the door. She cuts a straight line across the crunchy, snow-packed parking lot.

*   *   *

McKelvey opens the door to his former home and finds a legal-size envelope propped between the screen and front doors. He picks it up and reads it, believing it is yet another missive from Carl Levesque regarding some new extrapolation of the Landlord-Tenant Act. There is a note scrawled across the envelope in a beautiful hand script that you hardly ever see anymore.

Charlie McKelvey,
Everything you want to know is in here.
Do what you've got to do. I'm too old to care
about consequences.
George Fergus

McKelvey handles the package like a kid trying to squeeze clues from a wrapped Christmas present. It contains papers. The envelope is sealed. His heart palpitates, and he feels the sudden need to sit down. These spells seem to be increasing, as though the energy completely runs out of him all at once. He sees himself with a cane, or worse, a four-legged walker, shuffling through Toronto's parks one bench at a time, naming the pigeons.

He sets the envelope on the kitchen table and walks around it, looking at it, as though it could be the results of a medical test he has been anxiously awaiting. He wants to open it and he doesn't want to open it, wants to know and yet doesn't want to know. *Christ*, he thinks, *I just shook hands with the nephew of the man who was killed during the strike.* McKelvey wonders if his father would find this ironic. Then again, Grey McKelvey didn't believe in irony or fate or anything that he couldn't bend or shape with his hands, anything he couldn't see with his own eyes.

The phone rings and McKelvey jumps.

"Shirley Murdoch has been trying to reach you on the radio," Madsen says.

"I stopped in at home."

"I interviewed Gerry Kilrea, owner of the Co-op. I sat in his truck at the community centre after the memorial. He said his place was robbed back in early December."

"Let me guess," McKelvey says.

"That's right. Four gallons of anhydrous ammonia was among the missing inventory. Farmers use it as a nitrogen fertilizer, inject it into the ground. The thief took a couple of industrial-grade steel buckets, too, and a pair of leather work gloves. Nothing else."

"I'm assuming he filed a police report so he could make an insurance claim."

"This stuff is classified as 'Dangerous Goods.' And he was worried that if he made a claim the occupational health and safety folks would come down hard on him for not keeping it locked up the way he should have. Small town, he said he got too comfortable. But he did call the police to let them know this stuff was out there."

"Who responded?"

"Constable Pete Younger."

"Well, well …"

"Another interesting piece of information — I was asking Mr. Kilrea about what's been going on around town, the meth and the death of Wade Garson, whether he had any insights. He said Chief Gallagher was out one day trying to get Kilrea onside for this landfill site idea, and he had Celluci with him. He said Gallagher stopped at a barrel of fertilizer, tapped it and said, 'this is all you need to make your case, boys, or get rid of pesky varmints.' He said it was what the Oklahoma City bomber used in the back of that rental truck."

"The report on the explosion at Wade Garson's indicated the presence of a foreign accelerant," McKelvey says. "Too bad we didn't have a full forensics team up here. The fire marshal doubles as the town cobbler, I think."

"This is a mess, but there's something coming into focus here. I just spoke with Nolan and he spent some time with Mark Watson's family, since the Chief isn't around. Now he's tailing Celluci. He's ready to roll in as soon as I can get that paperwork sent in to the circuit Justice for an arrest warrant. I need to make some calls to my HQ. The weather's cleared, so they should be able to get off their asses and send us some help. I also need to finish a long conversation with my husband."

"I'll look at the shop for a copy of the report of the Co-op theft.... And the last I heard, this Younger kid had been upgraded to stable condition. Maybe I can get him on the phone at the hospital."

"Sounds like a plan. I'll relieve Nolan when I'm over there. He can run home and check in on his dad."

"Good luck."

"Good luck?"

"The phone call home."

"Prayers," she says. "Luck just ain't gonna cut it anymore."

McKelvey hangs up the phone. He stares at the envelope. Finally, he finds an old newspaper and places it on top.

Thirty-Three

Ed Nolan sits in the lobby of the Station Hotel with an endless cup of coffee supplied by the manager, Duncan, who is simply grateful for the company. He keeps telling Nolan that he'll leave him to his work, but then gets up from behind the front desk and talks about hockey or the service for Mark Watson or the guy from Detroit he knows Nolan is watching.

"Leafs lost again last night," Duncan says. "I still remember '67 like it was yesterday, boy. The Canadiens and the Leafs, Beliveau and Armstrong. God Almighty, that was when they played *hockey*. If I never see the Leafs win the Stanley Cup again, by God I saw it that night, Eddie."

Nolan nods. But he is not interested in hockey. He feels nothing when he watches it except for a sense of confusion. Where is the puck, and what are these obscure rules that result in the game stopping and starting every minute and a half? He has never spoken this truth, for he might as well tell everyone in Saint B that he's from another planet. He played hockey when he was a kid because his father made him.

Every kid in Saint B played hockey at least for a few years. But he didn't really play. He watched through the grill of the face mask as the other kids moved around the ice. He never understood the plays the coach smeared in grease pencil on the board, arrows and lines and circles. He has that same feeling now, dressed in his uniform and watching the other cops like Madsen and McKelvey make all the plays. He wants so much to shoot and score. So he sits in the lobby of the hotel and he nods and smiles as Duncan complains about Dr. Nichols's failure to diagnose his wife's bowel obstruction, and he waits for the call from Madsen that will allow him to climb the stairs, knock on the door, and arrest Tony Celluci for the murder of Wade Garson.

*   *   *

The little squad room is empty, and McKelvey pauses at the door as he flicks on the lights. If conditions were different, he thinks, if almost everything were different, this would be a great place to finish off your police career. He moves to the four filing cabinets against the wall and searches by date, by report type, marvelling at the variety of calls the force has taken and responded to, from missing cats to sightings of a naked man appearing every night at midnight outside the third-floor bedroom window of a local widow. As he did when he searched for a record of the strike death investigation, he comes up empty. There is no mention of the local Co-op in any police reports from the previous year.

Sitting in the Chief's chair, he calls the Sudbury General Hospital and gets patched through to Constable Younger's room. The young man is groggy and dry-throated. McKelvey asks about his condition and brings the man up to speed on the turn of events, the basics of where they sit with the investigation, which seems like a whole lot of roads leading nowhere.

McKelvey asks him about the theft at the Co-op. "Some dangerous materials were stolen. A base ingredient in the manufacture of meth. You responded to the call by the owner, Gerry Kilrea, correct?"

Background sounds of the hospital fill the line.

"I remember that, sure. It was early December. I turned the report over to Nolan. I thought it was probably a bunch of kids who didn't even know what they stole. Once Mr. Kilrea told us how caustic that stuff is, I worried about the kids burning themselves more than anything."

"Nothing ever came of the report?"

"Figured Nolan and the Chief poked around on it, I guess."

McKelvey makes a few notes.

"What do you know about Tony Celluci and your Chief?"

"Celluci? I know he's a good shot for one thing. Took him and Gallagher out to the woods near Wade Garson's place to target shoot about two days before the trailer blew. I think Celluci wanted to intimidate Garson. We set up bottles on some barrels and they shot about a dozen rounds a piece, I'd say. They were getting real chummy together, always talking about landfills like it was exciting stuff."

McKelvey makes more notes and circles a few words for emphasis. The target shooting story has now been corroborated. Things have just grown more rather than less complicated.

"Tell me about the explosion and the fire," McKelvey says.

And Younger repeats, almost verbatim to his original statement, how he was on patrol out on the highway at the edge of town and saw flames shoot above the treeline just before eleven. He responded to the scene and attempted to gain entry to the trailer, unsure whether Garson or anyone else was inside. The trailer exploded. The trucker passing by placed a call to 911 at that time.

"It was like everything got right quiet for a split second, like something was taking a deep breath, and then the whole world ripped apart. I was blown back into the yard. I was out for a little while and then Nolan was leaning down and blowing air into my mouth. Next thing I knew I was waking up in the hospital. Wrapped up like a mummy. Guess I got burned up pretty good. I haven't seen myself yet ..."

They talk for a little while, Younger asking about where his Chief has gotten to and what they are doing to find him, and McKelvey hears in the young man's voice the confusion and anger that every cop feels when he has been injured and removed from the field. Younger wants to be in Ste. Bernadette right now. He feels useless in the hospital bed. McKelvey understands the notion, and knows also where it can lead a man. Younger's voice has grown tired and he yawns.

"You'll need to talk to somebody about all of this," McKelvey says.

McKelvey can almost hear the man rolling his eyes. He is too young, too strong, and too invincible to need help with his feelings about what has happened to his town, to his own police department.

"Tell Nolan thanks for me," he says. "Doctor said he saved my life."

"I'll tell him, Pete," McKelvey says.

Thirty-Four

N olan answers his cellphone and tells McKelvey that by some miracle he is still awake. Celluci has not left his room for the past five hours. In that time, he says, he has received an update on the health and social status of most of Saint B's population, courtesy of Duncan, who could likely be classified as a civilian informant.

"You remember the break-in at the Co-op," McKelvey says, throwing it out there. "Younger said you requested the report he wrote and that he assumed you and the Chief had followed up on it."

There is silence.

"I looked here at the shop and can't find a record of the report," McKelvey adds.

Nolan sighs. "I fucked up," he says. "With my paperwork. I got behind and I started taking it home to sort through. But with my dad and everything. Charlie, there's no excuse. We're a small town and you get lazy. I'm behind on all of that stuff."

"Did you discuss the theft with your Chief?" McKelvey asks. "These were highly dangerous chemicals. There must be a procedure for informing the community."

"There were no real leads to follow," Nolan says. "We figured it was a poor farmer needing some materials for his land or a bunch of drunk kids. We dropped the ball, I guess. Will this go on my record?"

"You have a copy of the police report at your house?"

"I'll take a look tonight."

There is a long pause. And then Nolan sighs again and says, "Are you disappointed in me, Charlie?"

"Don't worry about me, Ed. Find that report."

*   *   *

Madsen is just walking into the lobby of the Station Hotel when her cellphone rings.

"Madsen."

"You somewhere you can talk right now?"

It's McKelvey.

She looks over at Nolan sitting on the bench that runs beneath the stairwell. The young cop is closing his cellphone and slipping it in his pocket. He looks over at her and nods.

"Go ahead," she says.

"A report on the Co-op theft was filed by Pete Younger. There's no trace of it at the station. Younger said Nolan asked for the report but he never filed it. Nolan says now that he got sloppy with paperwork because he's been preoccupied with his father."

She looks over at Nolan. The young man who still wears the toque rolled on top of his head to hide the damage done by Travis Lacey's shovel.

"What are you thinking?" she says, and moves through the lobby to the hallway leading to the tavern side.

"It's plausible," McKelvey says. "I mean, we all get sloppy from time to time. But on this, I'm just not sure he isn't protecting someone."

"His chief," Madsen says in almost a whisper.

"Maybe. Is there anything in this kid's profile or background that would suggest this is anything besides bad timing for shoddy paperwork?"

"I can have the geeks at headquarters run a few checks."

"I've got another update, too. I'm meeting the chief of Big Water First Nation at seven. He's got a package of documents that should prove Carl Levesque committed fraud with his land deal. We should ask Nolan to head over to Levesque's place and camp out there after you relieve him. That way we know where both of them are."

"Long day for him."

"Welcome to the life of police stakeouts."

"It's interesting," she says, this thought just occurring to her. "A person of interest is watching a person of interest."

"And who says small towns are boring, eh?"

Thirty-Five

The Coffee Time is empty and McKelvey is glad. Peggy's back is facing the door as she fills the machines with water, but she turns when the door opens. She smiles, and McKelvey smiles back. He smells burnt coffee and icing sugar.

"Special auxiliary agent McKelvey," she says. "Did I get that right?"

"You forgot *senior*. Senior special auxiliary agent."

"Coffee?" she asks, but she's already filling a mug.

He takes one of the swivel seats at the counter.

"Thanks. The other night when I called. It was …"

She sets her forearms across the counter and leans in. There is such a quiet peace that runs through this woman, it is something he wants to better understand. He has wondered if it's something he could himself learn to own. *Can he head back to the city and face what he must face with peace and grace?*

"You don't have to say anything," she says. "I figured there was something on your mind, that's all."

"There was," he says. "There is."

He turns the hot mug by the handle. Steam rises from the black brew. "I need to be back in the city. I ran away, I guess. From my responsibilities. I feel like a teenager saying that. But it's true. I should be in Toronto right now taking care of some health issues. And I'm not. I'm sitting here in a coffee shop five hundred miles away."

Peggy tilts her head a little, regarding him.

"You have the bluest eyes I've ever seen, Charlie." And she smiles that smile. "But they're sad most of the time. There's so much going on up there. And I know something happened to you, something that changed everything. I used to have the same look in my eyes."

"If you got all that from my eyes, you should read my palm."

"And I know how you hit and run and deflect, like you did just now."

"Old habits," he says, and shrugs.

"We can change," she tells him. "We can know a new freedom from our past."

He takes a drink of the coffee. "I'm turning sixty," he says. "I feel like a hundred and eleven."

"We're never too old to believe in God."

He recoils at the word, and his face changes. "This is not going to turn into a sermon about being born again, is it?"

Peggy laughs. She shakes her head, as though she both understands and expects the reaction. "It's not like that, Charlie. It's not about religion and church or any man-made concepts of fear and punishment. I'm talking about *spirit*. And power. Knowing that you don't have to do anything alone. You've got that power inside you, Charlie. We all do. You know as well as I do that you can look back across your life and see things that happened that can't be explained as coincidence. People coming into your life at exactly the right moment. It's amazing how everything changes when we release the grip a little bit.

The things we thought were most important in life slip to the bottom of the list. Sometimes they even fall right off."

"I just, what, sit back and wait for the transformation?"

She nods her chin at him. "Already happening," she says.

He lifts his head and smiles at her. He sits there and his mind again recalls the lines from the poem or the prayer that she gave him. And he understands now, he sees the connection from there to here. He is unsure how to walk that distance, but he feels a new confidence or comfort simply in the knowledge that he, too, might just make it yet.

"That's quite a cup of coffee you pour," he says.

*   *   *

The envelope seems to stare at McKelvey, even from beneath the old newspaper which he has placed on top. It is as though the package gives off a signal or a current, something he can feel inside the very centre of his body, pulsating or stabbing. It makes his heart race and his stomach clench in anticipation. He paces in the kitchen and then picks up the envelope and holds it and turns it in his hand. He reads the handwritten inscription for the hundredth time. *The truth the truth the truth the truth …*

This thing that happened, this event that hung over the town like a storm cloud for a generation. And almost nobody who was around back then is around today to sit and look the truth in the eye. Nobody will be held responsible, there will be no charges laid, of that he is almost certain. But the truth is there. The truth about his father. He thinks of Peggy, and he thinks of the lines from that prayer: *It is in pardoning that we are pardoned. And it is in dying that we are born to eternal life …*

He gets a butter knife from the drawer and opens the envelope. His heart presses against his ribs. He pulls the papers free and sees immediately that this is an old police report. The top page features a faded inked stamp of the Saint B police mark, the date — July 15, 1954 — and then a handwritten statement across the following three pages. He flips through to the last page and squints to read the signatures. It is signed by George Fergus and initialled by the investigating officer, R. Douglas.

The room closes in and he has to sit down at the kitchen table. He takes a moment to catch his breath. He feels like a boy again, watching his father unseen from around the corner. And he reads:

> My name is George Fergus and I'm a steward with the union. I'm giving this statement to make clear what happened the day Clifford Whitehorse was killed. We pulled a wildcat on account of the management taking away shift premiums for working doubles or if you worked the midnight shifts for more than two weeks in a row. It was that and other things too, more than I can list here. Safety was of no concern for the company, and the equipment was always breaking down.
>
> The men voted in favour to walk off and we did. The company had no right to bring scab workers onto the site. Different things got talked about. Actions we could take. I authorized the boys to make a little bomb just to damage one of the company trucks they parked to block the yard. It was a bad time and we had no choices left but to think of our families not eating and getting into debt because of these scab workers, and to send a message to the company that we were serious.

Duncan Stewart, Nick Jalonen, Grey McKelvey, and myself took the lead on that operation. It was Grey McKelvey who was the only one of us could make the thing because of his army experience and I had to convince him to do this. I take responsibility for telling him what I did, which was a guarantee that nobody would get hurt. We were to put the little bomb in the truck at night and let her go off. I'm the one who went and moved the box over to that shed. I had seen the Indian scab working in there the day before. I'm not giving up my job to any man, but I'll be damned if I'll give up my job to an Indian. I moved that bomb to the shed and put it under some rags in the corner.

Duncan got wind of this and he told Grey and then there was a fight between all of us that night and some punches thrown. Grey went down there to the yard and he climbed the fence to try and get in that shed and get the bomb out. That's why the security guard told you in his affidavit that he caught Grey McKelvey by the fence that night. He was climbing the fence to get in, not out. Duncan said Grey tried to tell the security guards about the shed and the bomb but they wouldn't listen. They beat him with their sticks and chased him off ...

There is more, but McKelvey has read enough. He sits back and exhales. He imagines George Fergus provided this statement with the intention of clearing the air once and for all, perhaps even to take responsibility and face the consequences. Given the times, the racial and labour tensions, McKelvey can easily imagine a mayor, the company president, or even a police chief pulling this report and burying its secret — the fact the company's own security guards were negligent in failing to prevent the replacement worker's death.

McKelvey sits at the table for a long time. He sees his father standing right there, the fridge door open, counting bottles of beer, the laces of his workboots untied. He wants to go over and hug the man's leg from the floor, the way he did when he was so little, to look straight up at this towering man. And he can't imagine how his father lived with this for the rest of his days, his role in the death of a man, his valiant but futile attempts to stop it. And in the end was it for the better of the whole community, for all of the families of all of the workers, that these few men lived and died with their secret?

It is not McKelvey's place to forgive his father, but he understands and sees things in a new way, with the clarity of truth. His father was a good man, a hard-working man, a man who made a mistake that cost a man his life.

He tucks the envelope under his arm and he heads back out into the night and to the Station Hotel. There are four vehicles in the back parking lot, one of them a black SUV he recognizes. He removes the mic from the holder and presses the talk button.

"McKelvey to Nolan."

The radio snaps some static, a faint sound like popcorn popping.

"Nolan here." His voice comes across the radio. He sounds tired, dozy.

"What's your 10-20?" McKelvey asks.

"Sitting half a block down from Carl's place," Nolan says. And then he yawns. "He came home about an hour ago with a case of beer. No movement since."

"Ten-four," McKelvey says, feeling himself slide easily back into the life of patrol cars and speaking in codes, the constant action relayed across the radio. "It'll be a long night, kid. But we can't risk Levesque slipping out of town."

"Are we any closer to that warrant for Celluci? I know Madsen's keeping an eye on him, but he's the real flight risk. Carl's too lazy to bother running, and he thinks he's too smart for us anyway."

"You just sit tight, Ed," McKelvey says. "Madsen is working on the papers. We're close."

"I'm starving," the younger cop says.

McKelvey smiles as his mind floods with memories of his first stakeouts. Sitting in unmarked cars across from pool halls or taverns, outside banks, these endless hours with nothing to do but stay awake and talk to the asshole sitting beside you. Doughnuts, coffees, cheeseburgers, and sometimes, in the middle of the night, a pull from a mickey of rye, something to warm the bones. Within those moments McKelvey had felt fully alive, connected to something bigger than himself. And he feels it again now.

"I'll roll by with something after I meet with the chief from Big Water."

"I'd kill for a stale doughnut."

*   *   *

Whitehorse sits alone at a table with a glass of what looks like ginger ale, a file folder to the side. His hands are clasped and McKelvey thinks for a moment the man could be meditating. The tables around him are empty, and three men sit in a row at the bar, older men nursing draft beers and talking about the way things were.

The bartender nods as McKelvey walks across the room.

"Pint?" The bartender is holding a clean glass, hopeful.

McKelvey shakes his head and the bartender gives him a dirty look. Business is down, business is slow, and this is not a community drop-in centre.

"Good evening," McKelvey says, and pulls up a chair. He sets his envelope on the table.

"My nephew didn't want me to come," Whitehorse says. "His counsel was to the effect that we can and will deal ourselves with any trespass against the people of Big Water."

"I understand," says McKelvey. And he does. God, how he does. He wishes he could tell this man the lengths to which he himself has gone in order to feel the grip and the squeeze of vengeance within his own grasp, to believe with a fervent righteousness that you are vindicated to any extent.

"David is like a horse that is still more wild than tame. I'm older and I've learned to listen to my head as much as my heart. I am accountable to my people for trusting this man Levesque. And I will face whatever consequences I must face. But you and the law you represent must hold him accountable."

Whitehorse gathers the file folder and hands it to McKelvey.

"There are falsified deeds," Whitehorse says, "a copy of the cheque we issued, and signed copies of the contractual agreement we drew up and had witnessed."

McKelvey flips through the pages. He understands the world of misrepresentation and misappropriation having worked the Fraud Squad for six years before making the Hold-Up Squad. It is a world of forgery and lies, paperwork and bafflement. So many of the fraud artists escape punishment due to the embarrassment of their victims. So many companies turn the other cheek rather than admit to shareholders and the public that they were duped from the inside.

"This is good for a warrant," McKelvey says.

Whitehorse takes a drink and the ice cubes rattle.

"I have something for you," McKelvey says, offering the envelope. And he feels as though he is watching himself, watching the scene from a distance. He sees the face of his father, the face of George Fergus, old men with silver hair and memories that can't be trusted.

"What's this?" Whitehorse asks, holding the envelope as though he is not yet certain he will accept it.

"The strike," McKelvey says. "The day your uncle died."

"He didn't die," Whitehorse says gravely, "he was killed. We recognize the difference."

McKelvey nods. "I believe there's information in there that will shed some light."

The men look into each other's eyes for a long moment. The history of their respective ancestors passes between them. There is nothing more to be said. McKelvey stands and extends a hand. Whitehorse looks at him for a moment and then stands as well. Their hands clasp and they shake.

Thirty-Six

The water stopped just as Madsen lathered her hair with shampoo for the first time in three days. She stood there in the shower, groping blindly to part the old stained curtain in search of a towel. There was a moment there where she thought she might cry. This dump, this town, this shower with its brown water, and the fact her husband has not answered his phone in eighteen hours. But she stopped herself, and she stood there for a moment to collect herself. *What is the solution*, she asked herself. *Get the soap out of your eyes.* And so she took a towel, wiped the soap from her face, and dried her hair the best she could. She finds a silver lining in the fact she had her hair cut shorter not two weeks ago.

Now Madsen is dressed and sitting at the desk, her laptop illuminating the room in light blue as she puts together the notes from her two most recent calls. She pauses every few minutes to listen to the room next door, where Celluci has been holed up all day, and she hears sounds of the floor or the bed, someone walking in circles, and she pictures Celluci pacing as he tries to contact his lawyer down in Detroit. She re-reads the last notation and realizes she is hesitating in sharing the information with McKelvey. She is not sure why exactly, except to say it has something to do with the way Nolan looks at McKelvey. She tries McKelvey at home first, and he answers on the second ring.

"I didn't wake you up, did I?" She looks at her watch. It's midnight.

"Just stepped from the shower," he says.

"With hot water and everything? Sounds luxurious."

"You can borrow it if you want. We're like that in small towns. We share everything. And then we bitch about how people take advantage of our kind nature."

"I may need to take you up on that. I'm turning into a hobo. Listen, I got a call from Shirley Murdoch about an hour ago that a farmer out on a concession road south of town found a 1997 Jimmy abandoned by some trees on the side of the road."

"Gallagher's?"

"Confirmed by his plates. The vehicle was unlocked, no signs of foul play."

"He ditched the vehicle and had someone pick him up, or …."

"Something has happened to him."

They are both quiet for a moment, playing through the possibilities.

"Any intel on Nolan?" McKelvey asks.

"He was given a discharge from the armed forces three years ago. It was an administrative discharge for medical reasons. A little digging on the coding indicates it was a health issue of the mental variety."

"Could be anything — stress, anxiety, depression …"

"We tracked his ex-wife down in Edmonton. He was married for eighteen months while he was stationed out there with the third battalion of the PPCLI. This woman, Jennifer Martin, she's remarried now and has a little boy, and she was reluctant to relive the past. But her first words to the investigator who called were 'did Eddie hurt somebody?'"

"Ed Nolan," McKelvey says, as though uttering the name out loud will somehow provide a new clarity that he requires. "I don't see it. But then, I can't say I know the man intimately. From the work we've done together, I saw more reluctance and hesitation where violence or temper was concerned, that's for sure. He has a good nature."

"Maybe he controls it, I don't know," Madsen says. "Or maybe now he's on medication and he's doing well. I'm just reading the report. I think it gives us pause to review some of the facts in a new light. Consider the theft report from the Co-op that was never filed. He was at the truck stop pretty fast, even if he left as soon as you called him. He was the last one with the Chief when they went up to look at Wade Garson's place. He had access to the Chief's gun. He was in Celluci's room when you guys found the spent shell casing."

"Constable Younger said he was there the day Gallagher and Celluci did some target shooting with the Chief's prized pistol, which confirms Celluci's story and accounts for the GSR." There's something different in McKelvey's voice now, as though he is coming to accept a new reality.

"What did you get on Levesque?" Madsen asks.

"Enough. More than enough. What are you thinking?"

"I'll radio Nolan and let him know we're finishing the paperwork on both Celluci and Levesque. He needs to sit tight for a few more hours. You head over to Nolan's place and see if you can talk to his father, learn anything we don't already know."

"We'll need to stay off the radio. I lost my cellphone, so I'll make the call from Nolan's place."

Madsen smiles to herself, but does not bother telling McKelvey that she watched him staring at his cellphone one afternoon, the flashing light indicating waiting messages, and then she watched him bury it in the bottom of a drawer in the squad room.

Thirty-Seven

The house is in darkness. McKelvey knocks three or four times, but there is no response. He understands Nolan's father is infirm and likely asleep at this hour. Still, he doesn't want to frighten an old man, so he uses the weight of his body against the door and the screwdriver he has brought from the glove compartment to create just enough space where the lock's bolt finds a home within the door frame. It is within this imperceptible space that burglars have been conducting their profession for long centuries. A sharp push with the shoulder, a hand turning the doorknob, and he's inside.

McKelvey stands inside Nolan's house. There is choking heat, a closed-air staleness that makes him unzip his coat and rub at his neck. He speaks quietly, but there is no response.

"Mr. Nolan? It's Eddie's partner. I'm just coming to check on you."

McKelvey finds the small flashlight in his coat pocket and casts a beam of light across the living room, which is pristine and appears untouched since Nolan's mother passed away, a sofa and two chairs with the protective plastic still in place, a coffee table with bric-a-brac. He shines the light down the hallway and walks. He passes what must be Nolan's bedroom. The beam of light catches posters on the walls, hockey players and girls in swimsuits, the bedroom of a teenager. He moves on. The next door is closed, and he turns the knob quietly and steps inside.

He can't breathe, the air is so closed and rank. He moves the back of his left hand to cover his mouth and nose and he inhales the smell of leather from the winter gloves.

The light shines down on the old man, who sleeps the sleep of the sick.

He reaches out and touches the man's shoulder and it is as solid as petrified wood. McKelvey leans down and sees in the dim light the face of death, the flesh turning to leather, eye sockets closed and sunken ...

"Fuck. Jesus."

His voice sounds like it comes from someone else. McKelvey stumbles back and stops himself from gagging. He stops long enough to collect himself and then goes in again and pulls the sheet back. The body is clearly in active decay, the third of five stages of body decomposition. The cadaver has already moved through the bloat stage during which the insects feast, and now what remains of Mr. Nolan is simply turning to dust.

McKelvey steps back out of the room and closes the door. His mind reels. *Nolan*. The Chief. Garson. The kids, Travis Lacey, Scott Cooper, Mark Watson. He wants to believe there is no connection to Eddie Nolan. But as he reaches the door leading to what must be the basement, he already knows what he will find.

The basement is unfinished, little more than a cold storage area, and the wooden stairs are steep. McKelvey ducks his head and takes the stairs carefully, feeling with his toe first for purchase. He wishes he had a sidearm, a club, a knife, something, anything. At the bottom he steps onto the hard concrete floor and shines the light from left to right. He holds the light on a workbench that runs along the far wall.

Four large industrial-grade steel basins are stacked. He moves closer and sees on the floor the container of ammonia. His heart beats so heavily he can feel it in his throat. He picks up a small bowl that contains traces of powder residue and he smells. It is bitter and sharp, the chemical scent of crushed pills. There are books, too, all about meth in the U.S., a book on chemistry, magazine articles, finally what appears to be a recipe is printed in neat block letters and tacked to the wall behind the work bench.

"Jesus Christ, Nolan," McKelvey says. "What did you do?"

He moves the light around the space, the concrete floor and walls, cobwebs glued in the corners of the rafters like thick cotton candy. He notices the washing machine and dryer have been moved recently, long black scratch marks on the floor. He sets the flashlight in his armpit, grabs hold of the washing machine, and pulls it forward. He can already see the outline, the denim, a coat.

He leans over the appliance and looks down on Chief Gallagher's body, hands bound with handcuffs behind his back.

I have to get out of here, is the only thought that runs through McKelvey's mind.

And then he stops. Holds his breath. He hears footsteps above him. He turns off the light and his world is made black.

The footsteps stop, as though the walker can sense McKelvey listening.

He waits for sounds from upstairs, for the door to the basement to slam shut and seal him down here. It is within this quick contemplation that he understands finally that he has been ungrateful for the span of time he has been provided, for the close calls. And there is only one response to the long unanswered question about where Charlie McKelvey stands on the issue: he chooses life, has always chosen life whether he knows it or not.

A flashlight beam fills the stairwell, and McKelvey's eyes dart around the basement in search of a suitable implement. There is an old garden hoe propped against the wall beside the workbench. He calculates the steps required to close the distance and put his hands on the hoe.

"Charlie?" a whispered voice comes from the top of the stairs.

McKelvey exhales a long breath.

"*Madsen*," he says. "You scared the shit out of me."

* * *

Madsen has found a string that employs a series of bare bulbs to illuminate the basement. They have moved the washer and dryer to better access Chief Gallagher's body.

"No signs of obvious trauma," she says, leaning down to the body. She uses a pen from her coat pocket to move the Chief's shirt and jacket collar out of the way. "Correction, bruising is consistent with ligature strangulation. Luckily, it's chilly down here. He's just starting to turn. Based on his colouring, I'd say the time of death is consistent with his disappearance."

She stands and shakes her head.

"You found his father?" she asks. "How long has he been expired?"

"A long time. Months. I'm not a psychologist," McKelvey says, "but I'd say it's a good guess Nolan's father died right around the time Ed started brewing this stuff. For whatever reason."

"I told Duncan at the front desk to call my cell if Celluci left, but that seems a moot point now," Madsen says, and glances at her watch. "It's quarter after one. We need to scour this place, take some photos, and get all of this evidence tagged. The provincial forensics team will be here tomorrow by eight or nine and can take it from there."

"This team you keep talking about, they're really coming?"

"I got the word from the very top…. The message has been received."

"What are you thinking about Levesque and Nolan? Given the situation, do we let Levesque ride until the reinforcements arrive? Hope he's slow to catch on to what we've got on him?"

"I'm thinking," she says, "that with just the two of us, we need to bring all the rabbits together or we risk one slipping through the snare."

"Go on."

"We let Nolan know we're taking down Levesque at first light. And we take him down at the same time. Two birds, one stone."

"Sounds like a good plan."

"I learned it from you. I was listening, you know, all those years ago."

Thirty-Eight

By the time they have made their notes and a list of all visible evidence for the forensics team, it is closing in on five o'clock. McKelvey finds a piece of blank paper in a notebook on the workbench and writes on it POLICE SCENE — DO NOT ENTER in capital letters. He tacks this to the front door on their way out.

"Who needs caution tape," Madsen says.

McKelvey suggests she ride with him in the cruiser rather than take separate vehicles. He looks over at the loaner the mayor provided her in the absence of an extra cruiser, and he tries to imagine fitting inside the thing. He starts the truck and they sit there in the laneway of Nolan's home for a while. Finally, Madsen turns to him.

"What is it?"

"I know I don't have to remind you how quickly these types of things can go bad," he says. "I just want to make sure we're on the same page here for the takedown. You cover me taking down Levesque, and then we both take Nolan."

She nods and moves her coat so that her sidearm is visible and accessible.

"You're the only one with a gun," he says. "You and Nolan."

"I score well on my range tests every year, but I've never had to fire at anyone," she says, as though the thought has just occurred to her. "Maybe you should take it."

McKelvey shakes his head.

"I'm not worried about Levesque," he says. "He'll just make a lot of noise. But Nolan, I don't know what to expect. He has a gun. He's killed two men."

"So we move quickly," she says. "The element of surprise."

"Let's hope so," he says, and shifts the cruiser into reverse.

*　*　*

McKelvey's headlights illuminate Nolan's cruiser parked a block up the road from Levesque's house where his Cadillac sits in the driveway. He shuts the engine off and they sit there for a last moment in silence, each of them getting ready for this in their own way. McKelvey opens the door and steps into a world coloured with the in-between purple of last light and first light. Madsen walks on the right side while McKelvey approaches the driver's side of Nolan's cruiser. They can make out the shape of a man's head reclined in the seat. Nolan has fallen asleep during his one and only stakeout.

McKelvey uses the flashlight to tap gently on the glass. Nolan springs to attention, dazed and sleepy-eyed. He fumbles with the electric window to lower it.

"Charlie," he says. "I just closed my eyes. I swear."

"We're taking Levesque down," McKelvey tells him.

"And what about Celluci?" Nolan asks, having noticed Madsen at the other side of the cruiser. "Who's watching Celluci?"

"It's okay, Ed, we've got him down at the station," says Madsen.

"I'm going to go and get Levesque up, bring him down here and set him in the back of your cruiser," McKelvey says. "I need you two to cover me."

Nolan nods, then opens the door and stretches his legs. They have fallen asleep and he stamps his feet on the ground. Madsen remains on the other side of the cruiser by the passenger door. She has already put an ungloved hand on the butt of her service Glock. Nolan looks over at her and nods.

They watch as McKelvey crosses the street and climbs the front stairs. He bangs on the door loudly with his flashlight. Lights come on inside and they can hear Levesque swearing. The front door swings open, painting a swath of yellow light across McKelvey and the front yard. The dark night is beginning to release its grip, and the sky glows with a faint golden pink.

"You dirty son of a bitch," Levesque yells, "after I gave you a goddamned roof over your head. This is the thanks I get from you people!"

McKelvey tugs at the man, but Levesque says he has to go and get pants on. He reappears in a moment, zipping the fly, a fleece shirt open to reveal his hairy belly. McKelvey puts a hand on Levesque's elbow and guides him down the lane toward Nolan and Madsen.

Nolan prepares to receive Levesque into his custody. He readies a set of handcuffs and opens the back door to his cruiser. Madsen takes slow steps to come around the front of the vehicle, hand on her weapon.

"You stupid bastards are going to be sued to bankruptcy. Take the word of a bunch of Indians over me?"

McKelvey slaps him in the back of the head and Levesque recoils like a child who has been hit by a parent. Madsen is a few feet behind and to the left of Nolan. McKelvey nods to her, and she pulls her weapon discreetly, keeps it at her side. McKelvey shoves Levesque into the cruiser and slams the door. Levesque tries to right himself, for he has tumbled into the vehicle head first.

"Charlie," Nolan says, "the cuffs."

Nolan holds the handcuffs aloft and searches McKelvey's face.

Madsen raises her weapon and points it at Nolan.

"Ed Nolan," she says, "you're under arrest for murder."

Nolan turns, the cuffs still hanging by a finger, and he blinks at Madsen. He turns back to McKelvey.

"Charlie?"

"Put your hands on the roof," McKelvey orders, "and spread your feet."

Madsen keeps her weapon trained and moves slowly around the front of the cruiser so that now she is beside Nolan. McKelvey takes slow steps toward Nolan, takes the cuffs from his grip, and guides the younger man's hands to the roof of the cruiser.

"I just want to help, Charlie. My father, I couldn't do anything. I couldn't do anything to help him. I just watched him lay there. I couldn't do anything to help anybody. I kept reading these stories about small towns. I wanted to see if I could save my own town."

"What about Wade Garson?" McKelvey asks, reaching carefully to remove Nolan's gun from his holster. He ejects the clip and throws the weapon over to Madsen. "You killed him, not Tony Celluci."

"He was a cancer in this town for years. His whole family was. I thought he'd get the message and take off after I blew up his trailer. I thought that would be the end of it, two problems solved. But he called you. And then you called me. I had to clean it up. Things just kept getting out of control."

Inside the cruiser, Carl Levesque is horror-stricken. He sits, watching and listening. The front window is still open a few inches from when Nolan lowered it, and he can hear the whole conversation.

"You got to Wade first," McKelvey says. "And used your Chief's gun."

Nolan nods. McKelvey brings down one arm and then the other behind Nolan's back, working slowly and methodically. He slips the cuffs on and locks them tight.

"I thought it would be hard, more than I could do," Nolan says, and McKelvey turns him around to face him. "But everything was so easy. Wade's eyes when he saw me. He *knew*. He knew what was happening. He had such clarity in that final moment. Everything was the way you imagine it to be."

"All of these kids, Ed," McKelvey says, and he is both angry and lost. "What about the damned kids? You ruined their lives. Scott Cooper is facing murder charges and his friend Mark Watson is dead. You were there for the memorial. You comforted his parents, for God's sake."

"Nobody is blameless, Charlie. The kids around here had a choice to make and they made the wrong one. I put the packs of meth in the washroom at the arcade, just where I'd caught Wade Garson putting his pot before. I left it there and I walked away. They should have reported it to me and I would have confiscated the drugs. It could have been so different for this town, for the people in this town, if the right choices had been made."

Nolan nods toward the back seat and he says, "Carl Levesque is a predator, you said that yourself. These young girls he preys on. And he's a cheat and a liar. He deserves what he gets."

"Levesque will face a judge," Madsen says, "and he'll do serious time for forging property deeds. But that's up to the judge, not me or you."

Levesque is there, listening. "I'm not going back to jail," he shouts. He grabs the door handle and yanks it hard, but the auto locks are employed and he can't open it. He leans back like a big pendulum and throws all his weight at the door. He does this three or four times, banging the door.

"I need to go check on my dad."

"Your father's dead, Nolan," Madsen says quietly.

But Nolan simply stares. "My dad needs his soup at nine o'clock."

"The OPP has a team on the road," Madsen says.

"I'm sorry," Nolan says. "I thought about what you said, Charlie. You know, about being chief. I think I'd like that. I could be a good chief."

Madsen lowers her weapon now that Nolan is cuffed, and she shoves his sidearm into the waistband of her pants. McKelvey hears the hammer cock from inside the back of the cruiser, turns to Levesque, turns too late, catching the slug square in the centre of his upper body — the critical mass at which he'd trained a lifetime to aim his own line of fire — glass from the back window exploding to dust. Another two shots follow, quick as an echo, and Levesque topples over sideways across the seat, a black .38 in his hand. He doesn't move. Madsen steps to the vehicle and holds her weapon trained on Levesque until she can reach in through the shattered window and take the .38. She tosses it into the snow on the other side of the cruiser.

The slug seems to have cut McKelvey in half, splintered inside his chest cavity. He falls back with the force of a hard shove, lands on his ass, and now he rolls to the side, winded. He tries to set himself right by planting his hand to the cold ground, but the earth wavers and rolls. There is no pain. There is no feeling, not yet, simply a pressure that won't allow his lungs to fully inflate, as if he can't quite catch his breath.

He is rolled to his back by unseen hands. The sky above is splitting open in gold and crimson. Two hands push into the meat of his body just beneath his collarbone, and he looks down for the first time and sees the blood, his blood, pumping through Madsen's naked fingers like oil sprung from a leaky crank case, and steam rises from the wound as the warmth meets the cold air. The blood begins to fill his mouth so fast that he can hardly swallow it. He is drowning in this taste of deep rusted iron, the taste of his life.

He tries to slow his breathing, all of those mandatory first-aid sessions coming back as they said it would: *slow the breathing, slow the flow of blood, do not succumb to shock.* He turns his head to look toward Nolan, who is now slumped cross-legged on the ground, hands behind his back, face white and terrified.

"Goddamned rookie mistake," McKelvey says, pulling the words breathlessly. "Levesque told me he had a gun the other day. He warned me ..."

He feels the weight of the world pressing down on his chest, his ribs bending to the breaking point. But there is no pain. Not like when he was shot by Duguay in his own home. He thinks of this in the longest moment, a moment that spans his lifetime from boyhood to that very instant in the darkened hallway, and he thinks: I survived *that* to come to *this*.

He can't hear. The world is muffled, under water. Madsen is yelling into her cellphone. *Are they out of range?*

Everything is waiting for us.... The things we do in the moment, in the action, the line and the drive. What we get lost in, these small details, these tiny moments that we believe to be so incomparably important ...

Madsen is kneeling beside McKelvey now. She has pulled her long blue scarf free and she balls it against the wound, pressing down.

"Charlie, they're coming," she says. "Hang on ..."

The words play through McKelvey's mind.

Hang on.

How he's been hanging on his whole life, fingers curled around those monkey bars, swinging against the wind. The stubbornness his father always pointed out in him, the apple not falling far from the tree.

He sees all of the medical brochures, the pictures of grey-haired men playing with grandchildren, smiling through the slow carving out of their bodies, the cancer eating them in increments. *A Survivor's Checklist.*

But you didn't get me, he thinks. *You didn't get me …*

McKelvey closes his eyes. He sees Pierre Duguay pulling the gun, he sees Detective Leyden stretched on the catwalk of the old factory, he sees his son set out on that cold steel bed in the morgue, his father climbing a fence at a mining yard … the bodies, the lives lost to all of this human fumbling.

"One two three and up."

Feels himself lifted and carried, and his hearing rushes on like a TV set, the heavy *thump-thump* of the air ambulance rotors cutting through air. He hears a young paramedic talking into his headset, and then the paramedic leans down to McKelvey's ear and shouts that they'll be landing at the hospital in about seventeen minutes — ETA.

Seventeen minutes.

Sixteen minutes.

Fifteen minutes.

McKelvey opens his eyes but it hurts too much, the early sunlight shreds like shards of glass. He closes his eyes tight, knowing it won't be fast enough, not by a long shot. He is leaving; he is in many ways already gone.

Against the blackness of his closed eyes he sees projections of his boy with the perpetual cowlick. And he holds the final and brutal inequality of burying that precious child before his time, this notion he wants so very much to bring before the feet of God, lay it at His feet and say *what for, and why?*

And Caroline. She is young — they both are — before loss and disappointment came uninvited into their lives, all of the dark confusion that drove a wedge between them. This woman who loved him more than he ever loved himself, she is here, right here, her fingers moving the sweaty hair from his forehead …

"Was I good?" he asks. But they can't hear him.

The rhythmic *thud-thud-thud* of the long rotors reverberates through his body like a voice whispering words he can't understand as he sails through the air somewhere between heaven and earth. And for once in his life, Charlie McKelvey figures he is exactly where he is supposed to be.

Acknowledgements

I owe thanks to my editor, Allison Hirst, and the dedicated team at Dundurn; Emma Dolan for the great cover art; Allister Thompson and Sylvia McConnell for early support; Tracy Forrest for surviving early drafts; Abby Forrest; Tim Wynne-Jones; Katherine Hobbs; Dave MacDonald; Ariane Sabourin; Ulrike Kucera; Lejla Latifovic; Eryn Kirkwood; the Anatomical Pathology crew at The Ottawa Hospital; John Churchill; Stephanie Smith; Vicki Delany and Barbara Fradkin for patronage; Scene of The Crime; Bloody Words; Capital Crime Writers; Crime Writers of Canada; Margaret Cannon; Linda Wiken; Don Graves; Derryn Collier; and the motley gang at BTN.

Also by C.B. Forrest

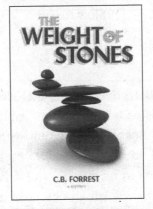

The Weight of Stones
9781894917780
$15.95

Detective Charlie McKelvey's life has been stuck on pause since the murder of his runaway son. As his wife focuses on healing, McKelvey is burdened with guilt for kicking the teen out of the family home — and his inability to solve the case. Obsessed with the stalled murder investigation, McKelvey's behaviour becomes increasingly unhinged.

Slow Recoil
9781926607061
$16.95

Retired Toronto detective Charlie McKelvey's tedious life is
torn wide open when a friend, Tom Fielding, enlists his help
locating a recent Bosnian immigrant who has disappeared.
When a woman's body turns up in Fielding's apartment — and
Fielding is nowhere to be found — McKelvey finds himself a
prime suspect in an increasingly obscure murder investigation.

Available at your favourite bookseller.

What did you think of this book?
Visit www.dundurn.com
for reviews, videos, updates, and more!